DEATH *of a* DOUBLE DIPPER

A STORMY DAY NOVEL

BOOK #5

ANGELA PEPPER

CHAPTER 1

The dispatcher on the phone tried to talk me out of opening the bathroom door.

"Well, I'm here already," I said bravely.

I pulled a fresh handkerchief from my purse and used it to delicately turn the door handle. My overactive imagination helpfully played horror movie music in my mind—the kind with screaming violins.

I nudged the door open with my toe and quickly took a few steps back. If someone had been trapped in the room and wanted to escape, they could do it right past me rather than through me.

Nobody ran out.

The only sound was water dripping.

I steadied myself and looked inside.

There was a man lying in the tub, staring lifelessly back at me.

Michael Sweet.

Someone had stabbed him.

Someone had stabbed him a *whole bunch* of times.

Who could have done this?

Off the top of my head, I could think of a few people.

Oh, Michael, I thought with sadness. *You had to keep pushing, didn't you? Now look what you made someone do, you bully jerk.*

His lifeless body didn't offer any thoughts. For someone who always had to get in the last word in a fight, it was strange to be near Michael and not hear him.

But here we were. Just me and another dead body. Time was ticking.

There were a few things I wanted to do before the authorities showed up, including getting an estimated time of death. I turned away from the horror in the tub and opened the vanity over the sink in search of a thermometer.

CHAPTER 2
SATURDAY

(2 DAYS BEFORE MURDER)

"Stormy, you've slept in long enough. I've already eaten breakfast, so you'll have to eat yours on the way. Would you *please* tear yourself away from the arms of your lover and get your butt out here?"

I opened my eyes and stared at the closed door of my bedroom.

Groggily, I called out, "Jessica, why don't you come in and join us?"

The door opened. My best friend and roommate, the blue-eyed and red-haired Jessica Kelly, smiled as she shook her head at me. "Look at you two, tangled up in each other's arms. It's almost revolting."

I blinked innocently. "How can you say that about a love as pure as ours?" I snuggled up closer to my sleeping companion, a sleek gray cat named Jeffrey Blue. "Ours is a true love that transcends space and time. I think we were cuddle buddies in a previous lifetime."

Jessica fixed one of her looping red braids, tucking it up into her elaborate hairstyle. "No wonder Logan gets jealous of you two."

I rolled my head to the side to give Jeffrey a kiss on his shiny gray nose. The air in the room was dry, though. I accidentally gave him a static electricity shock on the nose. He jumped up on all four paws and gave me an indignant look before stomping over me on his way off the bed.

He padded over to Jessica with his tail held high, then wove a figure eight around her pale ankles. She was already dressed for our Saturday plans, wearing a pretty flowered sundress that made her look even more like the sweet-as-a-peach small town girl she was. She'd been living with me for nearly eight months—since February—and my big-city cynicism hadn't rubbed off on her yet.

My cat continued his dance around her bare ankles. He was fully grown now, a year old, and while he retained his kitten-like vigor, his lovely green eyes were different now—more focused. Maybe my cynicism was rubbing off on him? The poor cat heard all the worst stories from my private investigation business. Last night, my furry friend had consoled me with his calm, detached listening style. I'd come home late with my faith in humanity being tested yet again. Sometimes I didn't know who was more pathetic—the guy who lied about a disability claim to scam his employer for more money, or me, the thirty-three-year-old woman who recorded video of the man from her banged-up car and then scurried out with a bathroom scale to weigh his bags of garbage.

Ah, the glamorous life of the private investigator.

On the plus side, handling bags of other people's garbage did transfer plenty of interesting scents onto my clothing for Jeffrey to inspect when I returned home in the wee hours of the morning.

Jeffrey let out a sweet meow, still rubbing Jessica's legs.

"Now I'm your favorite person," Jessica teased as she looked down into his eyes. "Cat, if we knew each other in a previous lifetime, I bet I was a sucker in that one, too."

She was feeling sorry for herself again. "Jessica, you're not a sucker. You have a good heart." I pushed my covers aside and rolled out of bed.

"That's exactly what makes me a sucker," she said, her lower lip trembling. "I'm so busy trying to see the good in people that I don't notice them taking everything."

I raised my eyebrows. "Anything you want to talk about?"

"Not really." She wrinkled her nose. "Why does it smell like garbage in your room?"

I feigned ignorance. "Garbage?"

She narrowed her eyes at me. "And the bathroom scale is missing. You were out weighing garbage again weren't you? Was it to catch insurance scammers?"

"It wasn't for recreation."

She chuckled and waved the air under her nose. "You shouldn't bring your work home with you."

I grabbed the jeans and sweater from the floor next to my bed and tossed them into the hamper. "Most of the stink is contained now." I sniffed my hands and arms. "Give me ten minutes to have a quick shower, and we can be on our way to that open house."

"Five minutes," she countered. "You're always bragging about how low maintenance your short pixie haircut is, so let's put it to the test." She crossed her arms and in a more serious tone added, "I want to get there before the start of the open house. Poor Samantha is losing her marbles over this one. Don't tell anyone, but she hasn't had so much as a low-ball offer."

"Since when do you care? Weren't you the one who threw a hissy fit over how Samantha staged that little house with undersized furniture to trick people?"

"I still don't approve of her tactics, but the poor girl is doing the best she can, raising two kids while running a real estate business. It turns out Michael Sweet isn't exactly the world's best husband. Surprise, surprise."

"Who knew," I said dryly. We'd gone to high school in Misty Falls with Samantha's husband, and I'd never been a fan.

A blood-curdling howl came from the vicinity of the kitchen.

Jessica shook her head. "Sounds like His Royal Fluffiness is either being murdered or has noticed his kibble bowl is less than 90% full."

I made a horrified expression. "How *could* you," I said breathlessly.

Jessica rolled her eyes and left to fill Jeffrey's bowl. She called back over her shoulder, "Five minutes or I leave without you! And don't forget to use soap, Stinky McStinkerpants."

* * *

It was the last weekend of September, and the weather that Saturday was almost too good to be true. We'd had a cold snap and frost two weeks earlier, but the seasons had changed their minds. Now we were enjoying a hazy, smoky sort of heat in our little slice of Oregon—a true Indian summer. The monotone grayness of a Pacific Northwest winter would be upon us soon, but not yet. I'd worn my strappy summer sandals to give them one last fling before the snow returned.

Jessica and I stood on the sidewalk admiring the work our real estate agent friend, Samantha Sweet, had put into that Saturday's open house.

Since we'd last seen the hundred-year-old home, the porch, gingerbread trim, and even the front door had been painted. The home now had a lime-green door that made the raspberry hue on the wood siding look fresh and vibrant.

"Good colors," Jessica said. "It's a good thing I don't have any money, or I'd be in danger of buying this place."

Keeping my voice low, I said, "These heritage houses are a money pit for maintenance. Notice how Samantha has added those boxwood bushes along the front. It's probably to disguise a crumbling foundation."

"I'd never buy without a full inspection," Jessica said.

"Even if it is stable, even the cutest paint job can't make the house any bigger on the inside."

Jessica laughed and punched me on the arm. Hard. As usual. "You don't have to talk me out of buying it. I'm broke, remember?" She looked up and down the sidewalk. "Where's Samantha?"

I looked around. Thanks to Jessica rushing me, we'd arrived a full thirty minutes before the open house was to begin. Samantha's car was parked on the street in front of the house, but there was no sign of the realtor.

"Looks like the house is unlocked." I pointed to the freshly painted lime-green house door, which was open a crack.

"She must be inside."

We walked up the steps of the house and across the porch. The paint was not fully cured, and I could feel it threatening to stick to the bottoms of my shoes. If I knew Samantha, she'd been on her hands and knees the night before, finishing the painting herself. For a real estate agent, she really went above and beyond for her clients.

Jessica knocked on the doorframe as she entered. "Samantha? I'm here with Stormy. We're here to talk up the place for you!"

I chimed in, "And eat cupcakes!"

There was no response.

Jessica entered the house hesitantly. "She's probably putting out signs and balloons on the main cross streets."

I made a straight line for the home's kitchen, following the scent of cupcakes. "Samantha would want us to make ourselves at home."

Jessica followed me into the kitchen and watched me attack a pink cupcake.

"Easy, killer," she said.

"This one was asking for it," I said around a mouthful.

She swished her lips from side to side. "You really have changed, Stormy."

I swallowed down half a cupcake and gave her a questioning look. "What's that supposed to mean?"

"When you moved back to Misty Falls a year ago, I'd have to twist your arm to get you to eat a cupcake. And you'd freak out if anyone tried to eat in your car."

I shrugged. "So?"

"I was just in your car, and I found wrappers." She paused, as though preparing to accuse me of a horrific crime. "Wrappers from gas station hot dogs."

"Are you saying I've let myself go?" I crammed the rest of the cupcake in my mouth. "Just because I regularly wake up smelling like garbage doesn't mean I'm not a classy"—crumbs of cake and icing sprayed out of my mouth—"sophisticated woman."

She stared at me. "Gas station hot dogs," she repeated.

I used a napkin to wipe my mouth daintily. "It's the weird hours. Surveillance can be boring, and when I get bored, I eat."

She looked at my midsection pointedly. "You're lucky you've always had a good metabolism, but it's going to catch up with you one of these days."

"Everything in moderation." I waved my hand past the cupcakes and over to the platter of vegetables. I chose a handful of baby carrots and swirled one through the dip, followed by another. "I think this is hummus," I said around my mouthful.

Jessica's bright blue eyes widened. "Double Dipper," she gasped. "I saw what you did. You double dipped your carrot. Now your spit's all mixed into the hummus."

"I'm not a double dipper. I took *three* baby carrots and dipped them separately. You can't even double dip a baby carrot. It's too small."

She made a tsk-tsk sound. "Dirty Double Dipper."

We stared at each other in silence. I couldn't tell if she was teasing me or if she genuinely believed I was a filthy Double Dipper who'd completely let herself go.

In the silence, the old house squeaked. I knew instantly the sound was coming from upstairs.

We weren't alone.

My heart pounded, and the skin on the back of my neck prickled.

With another creak of the home's old wood, I was transported back in time, to the first day of January that year. I'd entered the too-quiet house of a fortune-teller, expecting nothing more than an afternoon's harmless entertainment. Instead, I'd found the poor woman upstairs in a pool of blood. And the killer who'd shot her might have still been there in the house, hiding in a gap between rooms, watching me make the grisly discovery.

My mind made a horrible leap. I pictured Samantha Sweet lying upstairs in a pool of blood, her pretty blond hair turning red and her bright green eyes staring vacantly at the ceiling.

Jessica furrowed her brow and asked, "Did you hear that? Like someone's upstairs?" She turned to go up the stairs. "Samantha?"

I ran after her and passed Jessica halfway up the creaking stairs.

I had to lead the way. If something had happened to Samantha, I would protect Jessica. Thanks to me, my best friend had already been exposed to too many horrible things that year. She'd seen Logan get stabbed in the stomach, and then she'd climbed a tree while hallucinating after an accidental poisoning. Plus there was our adventure getting snowed in at the Flying Squirrel Lodge, trapped with a zombie-like victim and his killer, whom she'd inadvertently flirted with. Poor Jessica.

Recent events hadn't been good for her nerves. She was sensitive. She hadn't grown up the way I had, hearing stories from my father the cop.

Upstairs, I held up my arm to block her from passing me. She stayed behind, albeit with an impatient sigh.

One of the bedroom doors was closed. As I lifted my knuckles to knock on the door, I heard voices inside.

A man was saying, "Mikey doesn't deserve a fine woman like you."

A female responded with a flirtatious laugh.

I yanked my hand back and used it to cover my mouth. I turned to Jessica, who was doing the exact same thing, her blue eyes wide with surprise.

Samantha's husband was named Michael Sweet. Back when Jessica and I went to high school with him, he'd been known as Mikey. Whoever was in this room, he wasn't wrong. Mikey was a bully, and he didn't deserve a woman as fine as Samantha. But he was the man she'd married, and the two had kids together. From the outside, their marriage was picture perfect—the sort of attractive family you see in the sample picture for photo frames. At the gift shop I owned, Glorious Gifts, I had a whole assortment of families who resembled the Sweets.

Behind the closed door, Samantha said something softly. I couldn't make out her words through the door. Unfortunately, getting my private investigator's license didn't magically give me superhuman hearing.

The man in the room said, "How about next Monday? I've got the whole day off. No responsibilities. Let me take you out for lunch. I've got a few things to discuss with you."

"Not about Michael, I hope. Honestly, I don't want to know what he's been up to."

"So, you've heard the rumors?"

She paused before replying, "I'm not a fool. Plus I have an excellent sense of smell."

"You've smelled other women on him?"

"I... I don't know what it is. Maybe it's just paranoia."

"How could a man do that to you?" His voice got low and husky. "Those green eyes. Those beautiful lips. Kissing you must feel like falling into heaven."

She didn't say anything.

There was the sound of furniture creaking.

I turned to Jessica, who was silently mouthing what looked like *holy crap.*

We had to do something. We certainly couldn't stand outside the door and listen to some guy kissing our married friend.

Before I could interrupt, someone at the front of the house stomped noisily across the porch and rang the doorbell.

DING DONG!

At the sound of the loud chimes, Jessica made a startled noise beside me. By the look on her face, you would have thought she'd been busted kissing a married person.

Downstairs, a woman called out in a singsong voice, "Hello? Are we too early? We're here for the open house!" There was the sound of shoes on the hardwood floors. "Larry, take off your shoes," she instructed someone. Larry grumbled in response, and she hissed, "She's going to know we're lookie-loos if you don't take off your shoes." He grumbled some more.

Jessica and I had barely taken a few steps back from the bedroom door when it swung open.

Samantha Sweet met our eyes and made a strangled noise even squeakier than the one Jessica had made.

"You two," she wheezed. "I didn't hear you come in." Her hands fluttered up around the fringe of her blond hair and then down the front of her crisp white blazer.

Behind her stood a man who was very clearly not her husband. He was using the back of his hand to rub his lower lip.

"Stormy Day," the man said, grinning right at me. "I was just talking about you. What's that saying? Speak of the devil, and she appears?"

CHAPTER 3

"If it isn't the industrious Mr. Colt Canuso," I replied to the handsome, broad-shouldered, black-haired man.

Colt grinned and adjusted the strings of his bolo tie. He was sporting his usual look, a dark gray suit with a bolo tie, and western-style boots with pointed toes. As I looked down at his footwear, he shifted his feet so the toes pointed directly at me.

"That's my name," he said. "Don't wear it out." His deep voice squeaked up at the end, reminding me of the younger, skinnier version of Colt Canuso I'd known in high school. He'd been shy and reserved as a junior, but by the time we graduated, he was the class clown who'd do anything to make girls laugh. He and I hadn't stayed in touch after graduation, but I'd been seeing him around town in the last year since I'd come back to Misty Falls. He'd even helped me with a case during the summer, supplying me with eye-in-the-sky surveillance video from the casino his family owned, out on Canuso Lake. Who needs a warrant when you've got old friends?

I was glad to see his friendly face that day despite my concerns about how close his face had been to my married friend's face.

The room we'd caught him in was a child's bedroom with a narrow bed. The bed had been neatly made, but the duvet was rumpled with two butt imprints, right next to each other.

I lifted my chin and fixed Colt Canuso with a businesslike stare. "And what brings you here today, to *Mrs.* Sweet's open house?" I put a strong emphasis on the word *Mrs.*, for all the good it would do. By the two butt imprints on the bed plus the guilty look on Samantha's face, the horses had left the stables already.

"Same as you, I imagine." He flashed me a luminous grin. He'd always had big, naturally straight teeth. They'd been too big for his face when he was a skinny kid, but he'd grown into them perfectly.

I blinked at him and licked some icing from the corner of my mouth. "Oh? Same as me? You came to taste Samantha's sweet little cupcakes?"

Beside me, Jessica made a horrified squeak.

Colt's lips twitched as his smile broadened. A dimple appeared in one bronze cheek. "Stormy, I never realized you were so funny."

"I'm no class clown, but some people find my directness amusing."

His dimple deepened. "I am, indeed, amused by your directness."

Samantha Sweet hadn't said anything. She was looking down at her white blazer, flicking away imaginary spots of lint.

Jessica cleared her throat.

The four of us surveyed each other in uncomfortable silence. The doorbell sounded again. Jessica broke away to go downstairs and greet the visitors who were muttering to each other in the entryway. Larry was still grumbling about having to take off his shoes.

Samantha Sweet finally looked up at me, her lower lip trembling and her sparkling emerald-green eyes filling with water.

Not again, I thought. *Please don't cry on me, Sam.*

I gave the real estate agent what I hoped was a friendly, supportive look.

Samantha took in a sharp gasp of air. She darted out of the bedroom in a bright flash of blond hair and white blazer, heading for the stairs.

The first couple who'd come in were still bickering over the removal of shoes. And even more people were arriving and ringing the doorbell.

Over the din, I heard a shriek behind me. I twisted around in time to see Samantha's arms flail into the air as she stumbled down the stairs. Jessica, who was partway down the stairs, calling out a greeting to the open house visitors, wheeled around in the nick of time and caught Samantha in her arms.

Colt and I dashed to the top of the stairs to make sure everyone was okay.

Jessica's elaborate hairstyle had come partly undone, and her cheeks were pink, but she'd caught Samantha. Jessica was the hero of the day.

"I'm okay," Samantha huffed and puffed. "This stupid cheap shoe tried to kill me." She leaned over and pulled off her shoe to show everyone the snapped heel that had caused her fall.

Jessica quickly took off her own shoes and handed them to Samantha. The blond real estate agent thanked her, donned the borrowed shoes, and continued on her way to greet the visitors with a cheerful ring to her voice. That was Samantha Sweet. She wasn't the most confident person or even the brightest penny in the jar, but she was a hard worker, and she did everything wholeheartedly. I'd never gotten a text message from Samantha that didn't contain enough exclamation points to warm up my mood a few degrees.

As Samantha got to work greeting the visitors, Jessica followed behind, barefoot, stuffing Samantha's broken shoes into her purse.

Colt and I still stood at the top of the stairs. As I turned to him, he followed Samantha with his gaze and quipped, "Samantha keeps saying this house will be the death of her, but I didn't believe her until today."

"Was it really the house, or the shoe?"

He turned his dark brown eyes toward me and quirked an eyebrow. "You should launch a private investigation into that suspicious accident," he said. "Someone looking to sabotage this open house must have loosened the heel on *Mrs.* Sweet's shoe." He also put a strong emphasis on the word *Mrs.*

I snorted. Ever since word had gotten around Misty Falls about me being a licensed private investigator, people had been making lame jokes about me looking into not-so-suspicious events.

"She's lucky Jessica was there," I said. "Back when we were in the cheerleader squad, Jessica was the one person you could count on to never, ever drop a girl."

Colt leaned toward me and tipped his head forward. A section of raven-black hair crossed his raised eyebrow. "I try to live my life with no regrets, but I do regret never trying out for the cheerleader team."

I tilted my chin up. "Colt Canuso, you would have been a great cheerleader, except for one thing. You were so scrawny back then. No hips at all. Even the smallest skirt would have fallen right off you."

He chuckled. "I'm not so scrawny anymore, but you're as mean as ever."

"Mean?" My jaw dropped. "I was *never* mean to you in school."

"You were downright cruel. You wouldn't let me buy you a root beer."

I rolled my eyes. "Colt, you never offered. You'd buy yourself a root beer and try to get girls to share your drink, with all your spitty backwash."

"Backwash?" He pretended to be horrified. "I'm a careful sipper. I never backwash."

He hadn't made a move down the stairs yet. We were alone on the upper floor, listening to Samantha giving the early bird open house visitors a tour of the downstairs. She expertly listed off the home's unique features: original stained-glass windows, pocket doors, wood wainscoting. Her pitch was almost good enough to take my mind off what I'd witnessed in the small bedroom. Almost.

I cleared my throat. "Speaking of other people's spit, how long have you been conducting business with Samantha? You two seemed to be having a very friendly meeting in here."

Colt didn't blink. "Stormy, you know I'm a big flirt. That's just how I am. I'm generous with my compliments and attention." His brown eyes remained fixed on mine, unwavering. A little too fixed. Liars always overcompensated with too much eye contact.

"You weren't trying to taste Samantha's sweet little cupcakes?"

He looked me steadily in the eye and swore, "There's nothing inappropriate going on."

I grabbed his hand and held it tenderly.

He blinked three times in a row. He hadn't been expecting physical contact.

I brought his hand up to my mouth and whispered, "It's good to know you're still available."

He kept on blinking rapidly. "Aren't you dating the lawyer with the beard? The one who dresses like a hipster urban lumberjack?"

I batted my eyelashes. "He hasn't put a ring on my finger," I said breathily. "And I see you've taken off your wedding band, which must mean you're up for grabs again."

Now *his* jaw dropped. While Colt was distracted, I looked down at his hand. Colt was left-handed, so I'd grabbed his left hand, which was where the lipstick he'd rubbed off his mouth had transferred. With my free hand, I grabbed a cloth handkerchief from my pocket. I used the crisp white cotton to quickly scrub the top of his hand.

Then I dropped his hand, took a step back, and held up the white handkerchief as though performing a magic trick. A telltale pink mark stained the center of the square.

"Ta-da," I said. "Samantha's lipstick, from her mouth to yours, and then onto your hand, and now on my hankie. Which confirms you lied to me."

Colt frowned. He straightened up, and a dark look flashed across his face. A monstrous look. That of a person caught up in their own lies. And then, just as quickly, he hung his head in shame, gazing down on the floor.

Without looking up, Colt said. "I take it back." He shuffled his feet so the toes of his western-style boots pointed away from me. "You're not as mean as you were in high school. You're meaner."

I put my hands on my hips. "She's got little kids," I hissed. "I know Mikey was a jerk to you back in the day, but we're all adults now. Let it go."

He glanced up, his dark brown eyes darker than ever. "Michael Sweet wasn't just a jerk," he spat out tersely. "He was a bully. He made my life a living hell."

"I remember," I said softly. "He called you Tonto, and he used to make all those insensitive jokes." I shook my head. "We grew up in different times. That racial bullying wouldn't cut it today."

"You'd be surprised," he said, moving his head stiffly. "Things are not as progressive as some folks would like to believe. Not even here in Oregon." He tilted his head to the side. "It's a small town, and no matter what I do with my life, some people will always dislike me for the family I was born into."

I broke eye contact, looking down at the handkerchief. I tucked it in my pocket and deliberately softened my posture. "Colt, I'm sorry," I said. "I shouldn't have invaded your privacy like this." I remembered a phrase I'd read a number of times in my investigation training manuals. "A person has a reasonable right to privacy." I gave him a sheepish grin. "I don't know what got into me."

"You're a force of nature, Stormy." He took a step back and rolled his shoulders forward, slouching the way he had as a scrawny teen. "And I'm sorry I called you mean. That wasn't fair. You're not mean. You're..." He gave me a blank look. "Well, you're just Stormy."

"Thanks," I said dryly. It wasn't the first time someone had used my name to describe me. It always stung, no matter how many times I made the same self-deprecating cracks about myself.

Colt glanced over at the stairs. Samantha's voice was getting louder as she herded the lookie-loo couple and more visitors toward the access for the upper floor.

He said without looking at me, "For the record, I'm glad you're here. You always did know how to talk sense into me. I still remember that day in the cafeteria, and I owe you one."

That day in the cafeteria? A memory started to surface, albeit slowly. I felt the emotions first. The fire inside me. The desire for justice. The details of who did what to whom and who started it were jumbled.

"And another thing," he said, his luminous grin gradually coming back. "That kiss I stole from Samantha was the first one ever. I swear."

I met his gaze. "First and last?"

He nodded once. "First and last. I've got a new crush now." He looked me up and down. "Technically, it's an old crush, but it's back with a vengeance."

I said nothing. He knew very well that I was dating "the lawyer with the beard," also known as Logan Sanderson. My boyfriend really did dress like a hipster urban lumberjack, with his smart suits and his neatly trimmed beard. Despite a few minor quibbles, I was quite happy to be dating Logan. It didn't hurt that he lived under my roof, renting the other side of my duplex. A girl couldn't ask for more convenience than that. Our situation was comfortable. Convenient and comfortable.

Colt Canuso turned toward the stairs and started down. "See you around, Stormy Day. Let's share a root beer real soon."

CHAPTER 4

Colt Canuso left immediately, without saying goodbye to Samantha.

Jessica and I both stuck around for the open house. We did the duties we'd promised to perform for Samantha—pretending to be interested in the house, saying positive things whenever prospective buyers were within earshot.

I played up the positive investment angles of the house, since anyone who knew of me and my history in venture capital would know I was good with money. And I wasn't lying. The surrounding neighborhood had been increasing in value lately, as more and more young families turned away from new homes on the outskirts of town in favor of fixing up older homes in walkable neighborhoods near amenities. In fact, the more I listed off the home's potential, the more I wondered if it might make a good addition to my own portfolio. If only I could get past the strange upstairs bathroom with its awkward sidesaddle toilet.

Jessica wasn't nearly as positive. She struggled to talk up the house while staying true to her beliefs. She wanted to help our friend, who'd been struggling for months to make a sale, but Jessica was a terrible shill due to her unflinching honesty. I heard her tell one couple the house was "perfect for embracing minimalism," due to its lack of closets. The couple, in their early twenties and expecting a baby any minute, hadn't noticed the lack of storage space until Jessica mentioned it. The young woman's eyes bugged out as she glanced around, noting the size of the bedroom. It held a single bed because there wasn't room for anything bigger.

The husband said, "But it's in our budget."

She replied, "I'd rather live with your mother than live without closets."

His eyes bugged out to match hers. "That bad, huh?"

She grabbed the features sheet from his hand and discarded it on a dresser.

As they exited, I overheard the man telling his wife, "We really dodged a bullet, thanks to the chatty redhead."

Samantha must have overheard this as well, as she called us over for a private meeting in the walled-off kitchen and politely dismissed us from our shill duties.

Jessica stuck out her lower lip. "But we're barely twenty minutes into the open house."

"You've done more than enough," Samantha said through a tight smile.

Jessica turned her pout in my direction. "But what else are we supposed to do for Roomies' Day Out? We can't go home without doing something fun."

"Movie matinee? Shopping?"

She scrunched her lightly freckled face. "Until my next payday, I can afford a non-fancy coffee and a leisurely stroll in the dog park. But only if you buy my coffee."

"I'll buy you a coffee, silly. In fact, I think I've got a—"

Jessica cut me off with a raised hand. "No, Stormy. Don't you dare tell me you have a two-for-one coupon for coffee. I won't be your charity case. I'm on to your little tricks."

"Tricks? Me?" I shrugged and tried to look innocent.

Samantha interjected, "If you're looking for something free to do, I have the perfect thing." She opened her brown leather briefcase, pulled out a newspaper, and handed it to Jessica. "They're doing an open casting call at the casino."

Jessica asked, "Is that what you and Colt were talking about?"

Samantha's cheeks flushed pink. "Sure, along with other things. He's really excited about it. They're casting actors for the new *House of Hallows* series on HBO."

"That's still happening?" I shook my head in amazement. I had fallen behind on my entertainment news. The last I'd heard, the epic fantasy series had seemed as good as canceled following the death of its creator. Samantha and Jessica, who were both fans of the books, quickly caught me up. According to them, a young woman named Piper Chen had taken over the writing of the series. Rumor was, she was being aided by the ghost of author George Morrison. Either that or she was a prodigy. Regardless of the implausible paranormal details, all the *House of Hallows* franchise plans were moving ahead.

Samantha excitedly told us how the Sweets' eldest child, Sophie, was trying out for the role of Kinley, the precocious young dragon master in training.

"Sophie's been practicing all of Kinley's lines for weeks," Samantha said. She glanced over her shoulder at the new group who'd entered the open house and gave them a friendly wave.

Jessica frowned and gave Samantha a sidelong look. "You don't let Sophie read the books, do you? They're not exactly family friendly."

I chuckled at her understatement. "But the royal family in the series sure is friendly. Maybe the *wrong kind* of friendly."

Jessica pretended to gag.

Samantha pushed us toward the door. "Michael tore out the chapters with Kinley and made the girls a mini booklet. Sophie and her best friend Q have been rehearsing like professionals. Q is so confident. She says she'll get the role of Kinley for sure, but has graciously offered Sophie the role of stunt double."

"Aww," Jessica said. "Kids are so cute. With all their naive hopes and dreams." She looked down at the newspaper. "Why are they doing a casting call all the way up here in Misty Falls?"

"Publicity, I guess," Samantha said with a shrug. "They're doing a whole national talent search. Plus, you know, there's the whole neutral accent thing for child actors."

I did know what she meant. A number of child actors had come from our area, because their natural accent was close to what some call General

American, the neutral style favored by news anchors.

"Sounds like it might be crowded," Jessica said.

"The casino's huge," Samantha said. "You'll have fun. You might even bump into Michael."

I asked, "How is Michael?"

Her face reddened. "You know Michael," she said vaguely, herding us toward the front door. "Busy, busy."

As I stared at her, fascinated by the depth of her blushing, I noticed something was wrong with one of her eyes. Her left eye was swollen, puffier than the right, and she seemed to have the telltale purple of a bruise peeking through underneath yellow-tinted concealer.

"Is that a black eye?" I leaned in to look closely.

She turned away. "It's nothing. I wasn't paying attention, and he bumped me with his head."

"Who bumped you?"

"Michael." One of the visitors asked another person where the agent on duty was. Samantha jerked her chin up and called out, "I'll be there in a minute!"

I wanted to ask more questions about her black eye, but the woman was practically shoving us out the freshly painted door. I could take a hint. She didn't want me staring at her, trying to figure out if her husband had hit her on purpose or what she and Colt Canuso had been up to in the bedroom. And she sure didn't want Jessica talking about the lack of closet space and scaring away buyers.

We both wished her luck with the house, complimented her on the work she'd done sprucing up the porch, and walked over to my car.

Jessica was still barefoot due to loaning her shoes to Samantha. I popped the trunk of my car and sorted through my EDC—Everyday Carry Kit. Before becoming a private investigator, I hadn't given much thought to the assortment of items I kept in my purse and car. Now that I was a professional, though, I'd stepped up my game. The newest addition to my EDC was a can of Crisco. Shortening is useful for so much more than creamy frosting. It's a great source of emergency calories, a lotion for chapped skin, and with the addition of a simple twist of paper, can be burned like a candle for several hours, serving as a source of light and heat.

I unzipped my clothing bag and offered Jessica her choice of two types of footwear.

"Gee, I don't know," she said flatly. "Tough choice."

"Let me guess. You want the sandals?" I snorted and tossed the army surplus combat boots back into the bag. "You're such a girly girl, Jess."

"You are getting to be so weird," she said with a laugh as she pulled on the sandals.

She opened her purse, took out Samantha's broken shoes, and looked back at the open house. "Do you think Sam wants these back?"

I glanced at the shoes. "You could put them in the mailbox, but she's right about them being cheap. The soles may be red, but those are not Christian Louboutins. They're probably not worth fixing."

"Are you a shoe expert now?"

I smiled. "At Fairchild Capital we did a few rounds of funding for a company that was designing a new kind of stiletto heel. The heels are slim and exposed metal, like actual stiletto knives."

Jessica grinned. "If I ever see your ex Christopher again, I'm going to hit him up for free samples. Or volunteer as a shoe tester." She tossed the broken shoes into my trunk. "I'll keep them at the house in case Samantha wants them back for sentimental reasons."

I closed the trunk and dusted off my hands. My car was dirty, which shouldn't have been surprising, since I couldn't remember the last time I washed it.

"Jessica, are you sure you want to go to a crowded casting call at a casino?"

"If we go home now, I'll just bake things and eat them."

"Doesn't sound so bad to me."

"Let's go to the casino," she said with a swing of her arm. "Come on, it'll be fun."

"Nothing fun has ever started with the phrase *come on, it'll be fun.*"

Jessica made a puzzled face and then an ah-ha face. "That explains why my mother said it all the time before family road trips with my brothers."

CHAPTER 5

While we drove away from town and toward the casino, I told Jessica about the lipstick-stained handkerchief and my exchange with Colt Canuso.

Jessica's first question was, "Are you going to tell Logan?"

"Tell him what? This has got nothing to do with Logan."

"Colt was kissing Samantha, but told you it was over, because he's got his eyes on you now. I may be unlucky in the love department, but that doesn't sound like nothing to me."

"Nothing happened," I said with an exasperated sigh. "You know how Colt is."

"Exactly. He comes on pretty strong, and when he looks at you, those eyes are like tractor beams. It can make your knees weak."

"No kidding." I cleared my throat. "I mean, I can imagine. But those big brown eyes have no effect on me." I swallowed. "None whatsoever."

She snorted. "The flirting was mutual. I saw you looking up at him while you twirled your hair. And you really don't have much hair to twirl, so it took some serious effort on your part."

"I've never twirled my hair in my life!"

"Hah!" She held her hand out toward me, directly over the center console of the car. "We'll discuss your hair twirling another time. Show me the smoking gun, please. By which I mean the stained handkerchief."

"I was thinking we could dig into your love life. What happened on your date with Mitch, the fireman?"

"His name is Mitch. It's not Mitch the Fireman. You make him sound like a character in a children's book."

He actually looked like a character in a children's book. He was tall and enormous, like an oak tree, or Vin Diesel, or a cross between an oak tree and Vin Diesel.

I bit my tongue on describing him back to her and asked, "How did it go?"

"Not great. I don't want to talk about it." She wriggled her fingers. "The handkerchief, please?"

"Is he still calling you chipmunk? Or was it squirrel?"

"I don't want to talk about it," she said tersely.

Jessica was easygoing as a roommate, but she did have rigid boundaries about a few things. Talking about her dating life was one of those things.

She had a deep fear about guys calling her "weird" or making sweeping generalizations about redheads. She got along with Logan easily and had plenty of male friends, but they were all firmly in the friend camp. As soon as someone crossed over into being a potential boyfriend, her behavior changed. She became the thing she feared the most—weird. I'd seen it myself, and I couldn't explain it, except as a self-protective behavior. By never letting a man in close, she'd never have to worry about being rejected. It would be simple to blame her father, a con man who'd abandoned her family, for her condition, but I sensed there was more to it.

Or maybe not.

Occam's razor states that the simpler explanation is often the true one. Her father was unreliable, so she perhaps feared all other men would abandon her as well.

"Don't make me dig into your pocket myself," she threatened.

I gripped the steering wheel with one hand while I pulled the white square of cotton from my pocket and handed it to Jessica. The handkerchief was part of my personal everyday carry. I always kept one freshly laundered cotton square in my pocket as well as another two in my purse, along with paper towels, zipper-seal bags, self-defense spray, and a whole array of goodies, including items for stabbing or crushing.

Jessica examined the lipstick evidence on the white cotton. "Good job swabbing Colt's luscious lips. That was a really clever trick. I don't know why I'm surprised. You were always the smart one."

"Growing up with a cop for a dad means you pick things up by osmosis."

"Sure, but you've been learning so much more lately. If you don't watch out, you're going to be famous some day." She waved one hand at my windshield as though gesturing to a brightly lit marquee containing my name. "Stormy Day," she intoned. "The world's sneakiest private eye."

I chortled. "I'm sure you meant that as a compliment, but forgive me if I'm not flattered by praise for being sneaky, or devious, or crafty." I gave her an exaggerated stern look. "Word choice, Jessica. Word choice matters."

"Okay, I won't call you sneaky. But I truly do admire the way you get the truth out of people. I tried to talk to Samantha a couple times during the open house, but she wouldn't admit to anything going on with Colt. If it wasn't for this hard evidence," she waved the pink-stained handkerchief, "I'd probably convince myself that my eyes were lying, and I hadn't seen anything inappropriate in that tiny bedroom."

"You mentioned something this morning about Samantha going through a rough time. Is it just the house that won't sell, or is she having problems with Mikey?"

She hesitated before answering. "They've got some money problems, but who doesn't?"

I didn't have money problems, but I kept that to myself. I'd been thinking about the bruise on her eye.

"Mikey always was a bully," I said. "Do they fight over money? Or how to raise the kids?"

"Not too much. Sophie's going to need braces, but they're in agreement. The kid's teeth are super crooked. I didn't want to say anything in front of Samantha, but there's no way her daughter has a chance of getting cast in a TV show. She's a cute kid, but with those teeth, she won't get an acting role in anything, except maybe a before-and-after commercial for braces."

"Poor thing. It's too bad she didn't inherit her father's teeth. Mikey always had a great smile. That's probably why the teachers let him get away with murder." The more I thought about Michael Sweet in high school, the more my old memories came back. At that moment, a song that had been popular fifteen years ago started playing on my car's radio. As the chorus played, more old emotions returned in a flood.

In my mind's eye, I could see Mikey Sweet's perfect angelic smile as he stuck his foot out and tripped the unpopular kids in the cafeteria. I could also see his outraged expression when I "accidentally" dumped a tray of fries and gravy all over him. And then again the next week. And the next, due to Mikey Sweet being a slow learner. By the time he finally smartened up, I had started to wonder if Mikey actually *enjoyed* me dumping food on him.

It had been fifteen years since those cafeteria lessons. Had he learned how to be a better person, or had he simply switched to abusing people someplace I couldn't see him?

"This song reminds me of that spring dance," Jessica said. She leaned over and turned up the volume on the radio. "Remember how Quinn got all the cheerleaders to wear the same outfit?" She laughed. "I thought I looked exactly like Britney Spears."

"I thought you were going for Christina Aguilera?"

She giggled. "My hair was so straight, it looked like a red sheet of plastic."

"At least your hair would go straight," I replied with a groan. "My curls just sizzled and fried in the flat-iron. I spent a fortune on lotions and oils that didn't do anything. Hey, do you remember putting a raw egg and olive oil in my hair as a conditioner? Did that really happen, or am I mixing up home beauty treatments and Caesar salad recipes?"

"Was there anchovy paste?"

"I sure hope not. The fishy smell would have clashed with that sweet body spray we all used to bathe in."

"I remember an incident involving your hair, and mayonnaise. I bet I have the photos to prove it."

"You'd better not. As soon as we get home, I'm going to find all those photos, and the negatives, and make a bonfire."

She flipped down the passenger-side sun visor and looked at herself in the small mirror. "Thankfully my eyebrows eventually grew back from those little comma shapes that were all the rage."

"You had *perfect* eyebrows. You looked like a redheaded Gwen Stefani, especially with the rhinestones glued onto your forehead."

"Thanks." She flipped the visor up with a snap. "And you were a true friend, the way you stood by me through my tanning salon phase. I was such a sucker, the way I believed the girl at the counter. She swore my freckles would disappear once I built up enough of a base tan. She probably worked on commission. I hope she's as wrinkled as a raisin now." She shook her head. "Thank goodness I switched to bronzer."

"Sorry, but your self-tanning lotion phase wasn't much of an improvement. You were so orange, people kept asking me if you were sick. You looked like a Cheeto."

She snorted. "Oh, yeah? Remember your chunky blond highlights? You looked like a zebra."

"My zebra hair went perfectly with the eye shadow with sparkles so sharp they made my eyelids bleed." I stared at the road ahead. "Guys are so lucky. The worst high school fashion crime they can commit is growing a wispy mustache."

"Remember when Mikey Sweet came back from spring break in senior year with a goatee? He was so proud."

"Yup." I shifted uneasily in the driver's seat. "And when our history teacher teased him about it, Mikey got up and punched the guy in the face. I can't believe he didn't get expelled."

"He was such a psycho," Jessica said.

The song on the radio finished, and the DJ started talking about the *House of Hallows* casting call at the casino. The local rock station would be broadcasting live from the event that day. It was also the Casino's grand re-opening following extensive renovations. We listened for a few minutes, until the annoying jingle for the furniture store came on and I switched it off.

After a few minutes, Jessica asked, "Do you think people ever change their nature?"

"We're all capable of change. Is there some way you want to change?"

"I dunno."

"Something's bothering you," I said. "Are you sure you're up to this casino thing? It's going to be crowded and noisy. You always get wiped out by too much stimulation."

"I want to go," she said. "I just keep thinking about Samantha. She's so much like me. I wonder if she lets Mikey boss her around."

"You think he's still the same bully he was in high school?"

"Yeah."

I stole a glance over at my best friend. "Has he ever hit her?"

She answered quickly, "Of course not."

"I saw the bruise on her eye. And she said it was from Michael."

After a pause, she said, "I've never heard about him being abusive, physically. But then again, Samantha knows I tell you everything. If I ever did find out Michael hit her, I'd tell you, and then you'd tell your father, and then Mr. Day would jump into action. Michael would find himself dangling upside down from a suspension bridge over a creek, like what happened to that other guy."

"Allegedly," I said, clearing my throat. "You're referring to the rumored incident when my father *allegedly* dangled an abusive man over a canyon by his boots."

Jessica snorted. "Sure. Allegedly. They must have gone up there for the after-hours bungee jumping."

"No comment." I turned my head away from the road to give Jessica a quick eyebrow waggle. Could I help it if I was proud of my dad? He drove me nuts, and his texting skills hadn't improved at all over the last year, but I loved him fiercely and admired him for the good he'd done in our community.

* * *

We arrived at the Canuso Casino, where I let out a low whistle of surprise at the quantity of vehicles on the premises. It was amazing Samantha had gotten any visitors to her open house, since it appeared the whole town of Misty Falls had driven out to the lakefront casino.

Since the main parking lot was completely full, we followed the hand-lettered signs to overflow parking. We eventually squeezed into a spot in the parking lot for the lake's campsites.

As we got out of my car and stretched from the drive, Jessica squinted at me in the autumn sunshine.

"Stormy, is it true you made Samantha cry?"

"I didn't *make* her cry. I said some things, and she cried, but I didn't *make* her cry."

"Hmm."

"It's been ages since we had one of those incidents," I said. "Last winter, I simply pointed out some fundamental problems with the business investment opportunities she presented me with. Sometimes the truth hurts. But I never tried to tear her down. If anything, I've done my best to build her up. I've given her a number of pep talks."

"That explains it." Jessica made a face, wrinkling her nose. "No offense, but your pep talks could use more *pep*."

"What's that supposed to mean?"

"Just that it's hard for other people to keep up with you and your high level of standards." She reached into the car and grabbed her floppy, wide-brimmed hat.

"My standards aren't that high," I retorted. "And I think the fragrant aroma of garbage currently coming off my clothes hamper will attest to that."

"True. You're not exactly a perfectionist, or a neat freak. And your diet lately leaves a lot to be desired. When I say high standards, I mean something else. It's hard to put into words, but I can see why men like Colt always chase after you. You're like a wild horse."

"Thanks, I think."

She donned her floppy hat, glanced up at the clear blue sky, and then sneezed three times from the bright light. She muttered, "Why do I always do that to myself?"

Her question was rhetorical, but I answered anyway. "People are paradoxical," I said. "We want what we can't have, and we do things we know are bad for us. And then we lie about it."

She reached into the car again, grabbed the wrapper from my recent gas station hot dog, and playfully flung it over the roof of the vehicle at me. "Tell me about it, Miss I Never Eat Gas Station Hot Dogs."

I picked up the wrapper, folded it roughly into a paper airplane shape and sailed it back at her. "That's not mine," I lied. "My dad borrowed my car last week while the Torino was at the garage. It must be his."

She caught the wrapper, unfolded it, and examined the interior while she rubbed her chin thoughtfully. "There's a smudge of mustard in here, but the real evidence is the *lack of evidence*. No ketchup or green relish. Being a close friend of the Day family, I happen to know that Mr. Finnegan Day would never eat a hot dog without every kind of condiment."

She had me. "No comment," I said.

She pursed her lips in my direction before walking over to the parking lot's bear-resistant garbage bins to dispose of the hot dog wrapper.

I opened the trunk of the car, grabbed two bottles of water, and cracked the lid off one as I looked down the long access road at the distant casino. I'd never seen the place so busy. People must have come from miles around to audition for a few roles.

The DJ on the radio had been talking about the odds of a local kid landing the role of Kinley. Paradoxically, the more he talked about it, the more I actually wanted to win the role for myself. And I was twenty-some years too old for the part.

Funny how we always want what we can't have.

CHAPTER 6

The casino had finished their costly expansion since my last visit in the summer. It was no longer just a simple casino with an attached boutique hotel. It had been officially renamed the Canuso Lake Casino and Resort, with a sign boasting about its new conference and spa facilities.

Between the upgraded Canuso facilities and the Flying Squirrel Lodge up in the nearby mountains, our little corner of Oregon was becoming quite the tourist attraction.

As we entered the crowd of people milling around in the entry atrium, Jessica took my elbow and murmured, "The whole town must be here."

"Plus a whole lot of the surrounding area." I scanned the crowd. "Times like these, I wish I was taller," I commented.

Jessica saw me scanning and asked, "Are you looking for someone in particular? Maybe Colt Canuso? He probably came right back here after he left Samantha's open house. This is a huge event for the casino, and I'm sure he'll be around to keep an eye on everything."

"I've seen enough of Colt Canuso for today," I said with a snort. "The man I'd like to have a few words with is Michael Sweet."

"No!" She made a face like she'd just eaten a lemon. "You and Mikey don't mix."

"We're both adults now. We can have a simple chat about current events."

"You'd better not breathe a word about Colt kissing Samantha. Give me that handkerchief."

She moved with surprising speed, grabbed the handkerchief from my pocket, and stuffed it into her bra.

"You've lost your mind," I said. "I just wanted to talk to Mikey and see if I get a guilty vibe from him. I could drop some hints that if I ever see a bruise on his wife, he might find himself dangling over a canyon."

"Let it go," she said, still making the lemon-pucker face. "This isn't one of your detective cases. I get that you're bored of weighing people's garbage, but you can't go stirring up trouble for no good reason."

"Stirring up trouble?" I was genuinely surprised at my best friend's vehemence. She was usually more supportive of my wacky schemes.

"Don't you have some sort of ethics code? We don't even know if Samantha willingly kissed Colt back. He might have *stolen* that kiss."

I gave her a dirty look. "I'm not a monster, Jess. I'm not going to tell Michael Sweet his wife has been smooching other guys all over town. I just want to chat with him for a few minutes and get a feel for whether or not he's changed since high school. I've barely seen the guy since I moved back to town. Maybe he's become a totally decent person."

"And if he hasn't? Then what?" She looked down and adjusted the handkerchief she'd stuffed in her bra. "This isn't one of your cases. It's none of your business." Softly, she added, "Plus you might make everything worse for Samantha if you start asking questions."

I stared into her serene blue eyes. In addition to being an excellent baker and cheerful roommate, Jessica did have some sensibilities where I was lacking. Sure, she was the first one to jump into freezing cold water at the annual Polar Bear Dip, but when it came to personal boundaries, she knew when to be cautious.

Jessica made a good point. If Samantha was having problems with Michael, the best thing we could do was be patient and listen to her. Unfortunately, one side effect of becoming a private investigator was that I'd forgotten how to be patient and let things unfold in their own time. Or maybe it wasn't the PI thing. Maybe I'd always been pushing people into motion, poking at problems to move conflicts toward their conclusion. Was this the indescribable character trait people were alluding to when they said I suited the name of Stormy?

"You're right," I said begrudgingly. "The Sweets' marriage is not my business now. But I swear, if anything happens, I'm going to *make it* my business."

She gave me a patient smile. "Your heart's in the right place."

"It's not my heart that Mikey needs to worry about." I glanced around the crowded atrium.

The local news crew was interviewing people on an elevated platform. Daphne, the clueless weather girl, was handing a microphone to a dark-haired young woman in a sparkling dress. It was Della

Koenig, the town's wealthiest widow and an aspiring pop singer. I quickly turned my back to the platform before Della could catch my eye. She'd hired me for a few small investigative jobs over the last two months, and I was in danger of becoming someone she considered a friend. People's tongues already wagged about me now, just being a private investigator, but if I started hanging out with Della the Diva Widow, all those tongues would be moving at light speed. We'd need to get a tongue specialist set up in Misty Falls to reattach all the tongues that went flying off people's faces.

The scent of baked goods hit my nostrils. Bagels? Panini sandwiches? I sniffed the air.

Jessica must have smelled the delicious aroma at the same time. "Soft pretzels," she said. "I see a sign over there. Eee! Free samples!"

"Sold," I said, moving in the direction of the heavenly scent. "Let's go line up for a soft pretzel. If we just *happen to* bump into either Colt or Michael, I'll try to be normal. I'll even make"—I pretended to gag—"small talk. About the weather and stuff."

"Good," she said. "Do you want your hankie back?"

I eyed her chest. "It's yours now. Do you want another hankie for the other side, to even them out?"

She rolled her eyes as she grabbed my elbow to steer me through the crowd and into the line for the free soft pretzels.

We found a gap in the crowd and took our places.

Behind me, an indignant male voice called out, "Hey, lady! No budding in the line."

Hey lady? I knew that voice. A chill ran up my spine.

He called out again. "Hey, lady, the line starts behind me."

I knew that voice. Hearing it brought me back to a day of tragedy. It was last November, not long after I'd returned to Misty Falls to help my retired cop father following his hip replacement surgery. On that crisp winter day, I'd met my sweet little cat, Jeffrey Blue, as well as my future tenant and boyfriend, Logan Sanderson. But I'd also discovered the frozen body of my father's neighbor. And I'd had my first encounter with Chip the Mailman.

I turned around slowly. "Hello, Chip," I said through gritted teeth.

It was Chip, all right—the mail carrier whose regular route included Warbler Street, where I'd grown up and where my father still lived. Chip the Mailman was in his early thirties, like me, but bigger and taller—average height for a man. Despite his job that had him walking around most of the day, he sported a build that could be kindly described as "big-boned." He had a round face, pale with splotches of red on his cheeks, and fair hair that was straight and fine, like a baby's. In many ways, he resembled an extra-large toddler, albeit one who was constantly sweating.

The air conditioning inside the casino was working well, and the space was almost uncomfortably cool, even with the large crowd. Chip wore shorts and sandals, yet he was sweating, drips of moisture beading on his wide forehead. I'd seen him sweating outside in the middle of winter, which was one reason I'd initially suspected him of killing my father's neighbor and hiding the body in a snowman. Chip and I had encountered each other a few times since last November, but we'd never gotten over our first, suspicious impressions of each other.

"It's you," he sputtered, his pale blue eyes widening. He looked so much like a surprised baby, I expected him to squeal and clap.

"In the flesh," I said, still through gritted teeth.

"Miss Day," he said. "Sunny's sister. Finnegan's daughter. The private eye."

I raised my eyebrows. Did he still not know my name? If so, he'd be the only one in town.

"Chip, if you're looking for another thing to call me, I'm also your second-cousin's boss and the owner of Glorious Gifts."

He shook his gaze off me and looked down at a pint-sized blond girl who was tugging his hand. "Daddy, is that her? Is that Stormy Day?"

Daddy? Chip the Mailman had a daughter?

She let go of her father's wrist and clapped her hands together. "It's really you," she said excitedly.

Since it was the most enthusiastic greeting I'd gotten from anyone who wasn't my cat, I knelt down to be eye level with the kid.

"That's me," I said, offering my hand.

The girl had a round, friendly face and perfect teeth. She looked like a miniature professional newscaster as she shook my hand.

"You're famous," she gushed. "Your name is on the wall at the coffee place."

"You must mean the House of Bean," I said. "I don't know if I'd call myself famous, but it's true they named a drink after me. It's a latte with vanilla, cinnamon, and a dash of the same chili pepper powder they put in the Mexican hot cocoa."

She gave me a dazzling, angelic smile. "I know." She seemed to be about eight years old, or possibly a precocious seven-year-old.

Chip leaned over and asked the girl, "Q, Mom doesn't let you order coffee, does she?"

"I can get a small one," she said defiantly.

Chip shook his head. "Sweetie, coffee's bad for kids. It'll stunt your growth."

She used both her pointer fingers to jab him in the round stomach. "Dad! You drink coffee all the time, and you have this big belly!"

He rubbed his stomach and frowned. "It's true. I'm addicted to their Teenie Weenie Beanie Steamer."

Still kneeling, I tilted my head up and looked from Chip to his daughter and back again. This was a side of the mail carrier I hadn't seen before, and it did a lot to soften my impression of him. How could I have been so shortsighted? But *of course* Chip the Mailman had a life away from his delivery route. The big-boned man didn't just appear by magic to deliver mail to my father's neighborhood and then puff away to another dimension once the mail bag was empty.

Jessica joined me in kneeling before the precocious child. She said, "Q, it's not nice to comment about people's tummies. Not even if they're family."

I asked the girl, "Your name is Q?" I made the connection to the conversation we'd had with Samantha Sweet at the open house. Her daughter, Sophie, was best friends with a girl named Q. I hadn't known it was Chip the Mailman's daughter.

The blond girl nodded. "Q is short for Quinby. Q-U-I-N-B-Y. Some people call me Queen Bee, but it gets confusing, because that's my mom, too. You can call me Q."

"Quinby," I said, nodding. "And you know Jessica?"

Jessica answered, "I used to babysit Q when I lived in the apartment, which was near her house."

The little angel-faced girl said, in a very mature voice, "Jessica used to babysit me, but now we're just friends."

She reminded me of someone. I smiled and told her, "Jessica and I went to school with a girl named Quinn. She was a real queen bee."

"I know," the girl said. "That's my mom. She was the head cheerleader when she was in high school. We have the trophies on our fireplace. One day, I'm going to be a cheerleader, too. But first I'm going to be an actress."

I looked up at Chip in yet another whole new light. "You're married to Quinn Baudelaire?"

He gave me a big grin. He had gaps between all of his undersized teeth, which didn't take away his giant-baby appearance.

"Actually, I'm married to Quinn *McCabe*," he said proudly. "She changed her last name when we got married."

Quinby said, "That's spelled M-little-C-big-C-A-B-E. There are two Cs."

Jessica and I both stood up again. I looked from my friend to the mail carrier and back again.

My inner voice was screaming *Quinn the Perfect Queen Bee married a chubby mailman! Oh my God!*

Stupidly, I said to Jessica, "So, Quinn still lives here in Misty Falls?"

"I told you that," Jessica said. "You were invited to her birthday party, in the summer, but you were too busy to come with me. Remember?"

"Right," I said hesitantly. How was it I could clearly remember the sting on my butt from Quinn slapping me when I wavered in the pyramid fifteen years ago, yet I couldn't recall what month her birthday party had been? It had to be shock over seeing who she married. "That was back in..." The date didn't come to mind.

Jessica caught on and covered for me. "Stormy, you couldn't make it because you had a business appointment with Countess Octavia of Krengerborg."

"Ah, yes. The Countess," I said with the snooty tone we used for talking about the woman.

Quinn and Chip's daughter, Q, couldn't have looked more interested if she'd tried. She whispered, "You know the Countess, too?"

"We famous types stick together," I joked.

Chip said, "You should invite us along some time. I'd love to meet Countess Octavia when she's in town."

"Sure," I said. "And I do hope to catch up with Quinn very soon." I smiled at the round-cheeked mail carrier and his precocious daughter, who'd very luckily gotten her mother's good looks. "And her adorable family, of course."

"Of course." Chip wrinkled his nose and lifted his upper lip in a baby chipmunk expression.

He gave me a long stare before saying, "I know what you're thinking, Miss Day. How could someone as hot as Quinn end up marrying a chunky guy like me? Trust me, I've heard all the jokes. Our friends say we're like those sitcom couples, where they pair the comedian guy with a hot wife. Like Kevin James and a supermodel."

"For the record, I happen to like Kevin James," I said.

"Sure, but you wouldn't marry him."

I tried to look nonchalant. "Who knows? He hasn't asked."

Beside me, Jessica chuckled softly.

Chip didn't laugh. He stared at me with a look no less accusatory than the one he'd given me back when we'd first met.

I quickly reviewed everything I'd just said to Chip. I hadn't made any comment about his physical attractiveness. But I *had* been thinking about it. Quinn was a nine or a ten in high school—long legs, blond hair, button nose, flawless skin, big blue eyes, and the kind of perfect hourglass figure that all the guys ogled and all the girls longed to have. Even if she'd let herself go these last fifteen years, surely she was still a seven.

Chip the Mailman, however, exuded all the sex appeal of an organic turnip. How much better shape could he have been in when he'd snagged Quinn as his wife?

As he stared me down, I tried to picture them as a couple, but I couldn't. In high school, Quinn had dated athletic guys, some good ones but mostly jerks. She'd taken Michael Sweet to the senior prom, despite my protests.

"Quinn used to date jerks," I said to Chip. "If you're good to her, that's all that matters."

"I am," he said. "I'm her devoted subject, and she's my queen."

"I'm happy for you both," I said, and I meant it. I looked down at the girl they called Q. "Just the one kid or are there more cuties?"

Chip pulled a handkerchief from his pocket and mopped his sweaty forehead. His cotton square was the red-and-white kind, not like the plain white ones I carried.

"We've only been blessed with one little firecracker so far," Chip said. He lifted his upper lip in the chipmunk expression again. "I run hot. That's why I always wear shorts on my delivery route, even in the snow. The doctors say there's nothing wrong with me. That's just how some people are. But body heat's bad for the little swimmers."

"I've heard that," I said, nodding sagely. "Not about you specifically, but about"—I looked down at the kid to make sure she wasn't listening too closely to our discussion of her parents' baby-making issues—"the little swimmers."

The crowd around us shifted. The scent of hot bread wafted through. A space opened up, and we found ourselves at the counter being asked what heat level of mustard we wanted with our soft pretzels.

I was thankful to have the conversation changing away from talk of Chip's body heat and its side effects.

We placed our orders, and Chip graciously bought us a round of refreshments.

We thanked Chip, and before we parted ways, I made a vague promise that I'd be seeing him again soon.

"Not if I see you first," he quipped, and then he held his stomach with both hands and laughed silently. "See? I'm funny, just like Kevin James."

Jessica and I exchanged a look.

I started to step away and excuse myself, but young Quinby grabbed my hand and looked up at me with her big blue eyes.

"Stormy Day, I'm going to be famous, just like you," she said. "I'm going to get my own drink named after me."

"How are you going to do that? You need to get *super* famous to get your own beverage."

"I know."

"Do you want me to put in a good word for you with Chad? He's the manager at House of Bean. We're pretty tight."

Jessica snickered as she took a big bite of her soft pretzel. Chad and I weren't tight, but he had stopped rolling his eyes at the other baristas whenever I came in and refused to order their version of a vanilla latte by its full name: Teenie Weenie Beanie Steamer.

Quinby covered her mouth with both hands and smothered a laugh. Then she flung her arms in the air and dramatically whisper-yelled, "I know a secret!"

Jessica and I made the appropriate *ooh* faces.

Chip made a fatherly growl. "That's enough, Junior Queen Bee."

Jessica asked the girl sweetly, "What will they put in this drink they name after you? Lots of honey? Honey from the queen bee's hive?"

"No." She gave us an adorable you-grownups-are-always-so-stupid look. "Warm mead with cinnamon. Like what Kinley drinks after sword fighting, in the books."

Chip clamped his hand over his daughter's mouth and gave us a nervous laugh. "That's enough making new friends for today." He began herding her away. "See you around. Miss Day, I hope you can make it to the next party. It's our annual hootenanny."

"I wouldn't miss it for the world," I said. "It's high time I caught up with Quinn Baudelaire. I mean, Quinn McCabe." I smiled at the little girl. "And the future most-famous-person of Misty Falls."

"It really is a hootenanny," she said brightly. "With a live band and everything!"

"Will there be straw bales for sitting on?"

"Duh!" She shook her head at me adorably before taking another bite of her pretzel and walking away with her father.

I turned to Jessica and said, "Duh! Of course there are straw bales. It wouldn't be a hootenanny otherwise."

Jessica took a bite of her pretzel. "Quinn wants us to wear our old cheerleader uniforms to the hootenanny."

"You'll have to kill me first," I said.

"The party's in three weeks. We can do lots of jogging before then."

"But we always jog a route that leads us to the bakery. It sort of defeats the purpose."

She murmured that I had a good point about the fatal flaw in our exercise plan.

I turned and looked in the direction I'd seen the McCabes walk away. "That is not the man I expected Quinn Baudelaire to marry."

"Who'd you picture her with?" She giggled. "Quick. Say the first name that pops into your head."

"Voldemort," I said.

She doubled over with laughter. "The wizard villain from Harry Potter? But we hadn't even heard of him when we were in high school."

I shrugged. "You told me to say the first name that popped into my head."

Her expression sobered. "It's actually a good match," she said.

CHAPTER 7

Three hours later, after Jessica and I had partaken in many free food samples, played some games, toured the renovated areas of the resort, and even gotten two-for-one manicures at the beauty spa, we headed for the exit, exhausted and smiling.

Roomies' Day Out had been a marvelous success, we both agreed as we admired our new nails. Jessica had gotten her fingernails painted pink, to match the flowers in her sundress, whereas I'd opted for the no-polish men's manicure with just a cuticle trim and nail-buffing.

My decision to not get any polish was met with cheeky comments by Jessica, who thought I might be embracing the role of "macho film noir old-timey detective" a little too hard. Her jokes stung enough for me to allow the bubbly girl at the makeup counter to give me a quick makeover. I just had to prove I could still be a girly girl if I wanted.

Now I had *smoky eyes*. Or as my father would have called it, *raccoon eyes*.

Each time I caught sight of myself in a reflective surface, I looked over my shoulder to see who was following me.

We were on our way out of the casino when we bumped into Samantha Sweet.

"Wow," she exclaimed as she took in my raccoon eyes. "Stormy, are you..." She struggled to find the right words. "Oh, it's makeup!"

I squinted at the dark mark next to her eye. How ironic that the woman with an actual bruised eye had been upset by my fake ones.

I turned to Jessica and said, "I told you my coloring doesn't suit dark eye shadow."

"You need more color on your lips to balance it out," Jessica said.

"It looks nice," Samantha lied, wincing. She looked around at the crowd with tired, half-lidded eyes. "No wonder my open house was slower than molasses in January. The whole town is here."

Jessica asked, "How did the rest of the open house go? Did you get an offer?"

"No," Samantha said tiredly. "Have you seen Michael and Sophie around?"

"We didn't see your family, but we did bump into Sophie's friend Q. She's really something."

Samantha raised her eyebrows. "Q is full of... confidence."

We were being jostled by the crowd, so we moved away from the door and toward what seemed to be an open area in the atrium. It turned out to be a gurgling water feature, a pint-sized replica of the waterfall Misty Falls was named for. The sound of the water crashing over the rocks created a powerful white noise that canceled out the din of the people around us.

"Ooh, misty," Jessica said, waving her hands through the air over the base of the water feature, which was surrounded by a rock wall with not-so-subtle signs reading DO NOT SIT, STAND, OR PLAY ON ROCK WALL.

The three of us breathed in deeply, commenting on how pleasant the misty air was around the fountain.

"It's like a misty oasis," Jessica said.

Samantha stuck her tongue out like a thirsty lizard.

I handed Samantha an unopened bottle of water from my purse. She thanked me and drank it while giving me an appreciative look.

A few minutes later, she had rejuvenated thanks to the hydration. Her emerald-green eyes were glowing again.

"The power of water," she said, smiling.

"Sorry your open house didn't go well," I said. "The home does show nicely. Maybe an offer is just around the corner."

Samantha pulled a tube of lipstick from her purse and applied it using a compact mirror. Jessica and I exchanged a look. The pink lipstick was, without a doubt, the same shade I'd wiped off Colt Canuso's mouth earlier that day. Was she here at the casino to meet her husband, or was she hoping to see Colt again?

Samantha put her lipstick and compact away. "Actually, girls, I did get a proposition today, but it wasn't the sort of offer I was looking for."

"Oh?" I tried to keep my face neutral. If she was going to tell us what happened with Colt, I didn't want to overreact.

"And what an offer it was," she said, laughing. "A ninety-five-year-old gentleman offered to give me a ride on his electric scooter."

I said, "Sounds like you had quite the eventful day."

Samantha's emerald-green eyes darted around nervously, and she reached up to fix her hair but succeeded only in making the blond fringe at the front stick straight up.

"The guy on the scooter wasn't even the weirdest part of the day," Samantha said.

"Oh?" *Here comes the confession about kissing Colt.* I leaned in expectantly.

She fluffed her hair again, sending more blond fringe straight up. "At the end, when I was closing up, I walked into the kitchen and found a guy in there. By himself. Just standing there."

"Creepy," Jessica said.

Samantha nodded. "And he was clutching an enormous knife."

Jessica gasped and covered her mouth. "What did you do?"

"I screamed," Samantha said matter-of-factly. "As one does when they encounter a man in the kitchen with a big knife. But then he screamed, too. And he immediately dropped the knife. Then I started apologizing to him for scaring him! Can you believe it?"

Jessica slowly lowered her hand from her mouth. "Was this the ninety-year-old with the scooter?"

"No, just a regular guy, about our age. I didn't know him. He said he just moved to Misty Falls."

I asked, "What was he doing with the knife?"

"Cutting a cupcake in half," she said. "It turned out he only wanted to have half a cupcake. Isn't that bizarre?"

I shook my head. "Those mini cupcakes are already pretty small. That is suspicious. You should put in a report with the police. I can ask around for you. Dimples is always at my father's house."

"No need," Samantha said. "The guy seemed harmless enough. We chatted for a few minutes. He said he was on a low-carb diet and it was making him crazy for sugar. But on the plus side, he said he might come back to take a second look at the house."

"Make sure you bring Michael with you," I said. "You shouldn't be alone with this guy. It could be dangerous."

Jessica said, "Next open house, we're staying for the whole thing. I'll be quiet, I swear."

"I'm not an idiot," Samantha said with some irritation. "We do have security. We always get people to sign in and out of the visitor's book."

I shook my head. "A book? Someone could kill you and then rip the page out of the visitor's book."

Her emerald-green eyes widened. "Really?" She swallowed. "I guess you're the expert on these things."

"Better safe than sorry," I said. "A logbook is not security."

Jessica cried out in alarm.

Someone in the crowd had bumped into her, nearly sending Jessica tripping over the rock wall into the fountain. I caught her by the arm and hauled her back to safety.

"Speaking of safety," Jessica said with a laugh. "Maybe we should move this party out of here to the relative safety of home."

"We were just heading out," I said to Samantha. "Can we help you here with anything? Are you looking for someone?" *Like, say, Colt Canuso?*

"Michael wasn't at home, or answering his phone," she said. "I thought he might still be here with Sophie and the McCabes. They all came down here as a group to have the girls audition for that acting role."

I said, "Speaking of the McCabes, did you know that Chip is my father's mailman?"

"Mail carrier," she corrected. "That's the preferred term. Not that Chip cares. Chip marches to the beat of his own drum."

"His daughter seemed confident about getting a starring role in *House of Hallows*. She reminds me a lot of her mother, Quinn, as a teenager. A chip off the ol' block." The word *chip* rang a bell. I couldn't help myself. "You could say she's a chip off the ol' Chip."

Jessica gave my bad pun a pity chuckle.

Samantha gave me a blank stare. "I wouldn't know," she said. "I didn't grow up here like all of you did. I've only known Quinn the last five years, since our girls met in school and became inseparable. Those two are like sisters."

"Like us," Jessica said, looping her arm around my back.

"You're better than a sister," I joked. "I actually get along with you."

The three of us chatted for a few minutes about little girls and sisterhood before the sound of an angry altercation distracted us.

"Oh, no," Samantha said. "Does that sound like my husband to you?"

Jessica leaned from side to side, trying to peer through the crowd in the atrium. "You mean the guy yelling? I can't tell. Just sounds like an angry man to me."

The three of us cocked our heads and listened.

Over the noise of the crowd, I heard a male voice yell, "You dummies spent a fortune to class this place up, but it's just lipstick on a pig! You can't polish a turd!" And then he followed up with a few racial slurs for good measure. The casino and lake were on reservation land, and he had a few opinions about that.

Samantha's eyes widened and her skin paled, like it was covered in a fresh snowfall.

"Oh, dear," she said, and then she used a few stronger words.

Jessica gave me a grim look. "That does sound an awful lot like good ol' Mikey Sweet."

"He must be drinking," Samantha said. "He gets belligerent after a few drinks." She made a high-pitched, keening noise. "I told him not to drink today!"

I jumped up onto the rock ledge surrounding the water feature to get a better view over the crowd. "I see him," I said. "He's by the pretzel stand."

And there was Michael Sweet, red-faced and belligerent, being held by two of the casino's security guards. I couldn't hear what he was saying at the moment, but based on what I'd already heard, it was probably for the best that his speech wasn't being broadcast clearly.

Samantha was frozen in horror. Their real estate business was based on their reputation and trustworthiness in the town. Michael yelling and making a scene in front of the whole town was bad news on many levels.

I reached down for Samantha's hand to pull her up onto the stone ledge with me, but she wouldn't budge. She put her hands around her mouth and called out, "Michael! Where's Sophie?"

I'd forgotten about their daughter. I scanned the crowd near Michael and the guards, looking for a small blond girl. I spotted a dozen kids who could have been Sophie. The place was packed with children who'd come for the open auditions. The kids couldn't go into the gambling areas of the casino, but there were plenty of little girls here in the atrium, where the free food samples were.

Samantha screamed again for her husband and daughter.

Michael swiveled his head and glanced in my direction. There was about fifty feet between us. He looked at me and then through me. As Samantha screamed his name again, he yanked away from the two security guards. The crowd reflexively pulled away, giving them room. I watched helplessly from my elevated position on the rock wall as Michael wound up his fist and punched one of the guards in the face.

A shockwave of gasps went through the crowd. The few people who'd been minding their own business were now paying attention.

A hand tugged on mine. It was Jessica, wanting to join me up on the rock wall. I took her hand and pulled her up to stand beside me.

Samantha had left our side. I saw the back of her head as she wove through the crowd toward her husband, who was still yelling while fighting with the uniformed men.

The crowd moved as though choreographed, stepping back to give Michael and the two security guards space to fight.

Here we go again, I thought. This was a familiar scene, indeed, right down to me observing the fight with a raised view. Jessica and I had climbed up on cafeteria chairs back in high school. History was repeating itself. Once again, Mikey Sweet was goading other guys into fights and taking on anyone who stood up to him. *Once a bully, always a bully*, I thought grimly.

Michael and the two security guards circled each other within the makeshift boxing ring.

Suddenly, a new person entered the fight zone.

Colt Canuso.

He shrugged off his suit jacket and tossed it at a woman wearing a casino uniform. He entered the ring, fists raised. Now it was three against one. Michael was a big guy, but even he couldn't take on three grown men. And Colt had muscled up since high school. He was no longer a slouching, scrawny teen who could be pushed over by a strong breeze.

The crowd got quiet—so quiet, I could hear a small child, unaware of what was happening, demanding more ice cream, and the parent shushing them.

In the center of the ring, Colt pointed an angry finger at Michael.

"Mikey, this is not your domain," Colt said coolly. "This is Canuso territory. Our land, our rules."

Michael straightened up and ran one hand over his fair hair defiantly. "Isn't it enough that you and your family don't pay your fair share of taxes?" Michael rolled up his sleeves and raised his fists. "You need to stay out of my business."

Colt cracked his knuckles. "You stay out of my business, and I'll stay out of yours. I'll make it easy for you. Michael Sweet, you are hereby banned from entering these premises. For life."

Michael puffed his chest out. "I go where I want. I'm a free man."

Colt shook his head and backed away slowly. "We're done here." He pointed his finger at Mikey again. "If you ever show up here again, on my turf, it'll be the *last thing* you ever do."

A shocked murmur rumbled through the crowd. That was a threat, for sure.

As Colt backed away, he nodded to the incoming wave of reinforcements dressed in black security uniforms.

Michael hurled another racial slur at him, but Colt didn't take the bait.

Colt said to the new wave of security, "Show Mr. Sweet to the exit, please. Make sure he gets all the way to his vehicle safely. We wouldn't want him to trip and mess up that pretty face."

Colt started to put on his jacket and then seemed to think better of it. He lay the jacket neatly over his left forearm then whipped around and sucker punched Michael Sweet in the stomach.

The whole crowd collectively gasped.

Jessica made a strangled sound next to me on the rock wall.

Back in school, Colt had never hit Michael back. Not once, despite all the times he'd been picked on. But today, after years of simmering rage, he had. And what a punch it had been.

Outwardly, I was calm as can be, but on the inside, I had to cheer. It may have taken fifteen years for the karma to come around, but Mikey Sweet truly did deserve at least one punch in the guts. There was a poetic beauty in that it had come courtesy of Colt Canuso, who'd grown into such a powerful, self-assured man.

People started talking, murmuring to each other. Kids started pestering their parents for more ice cream and mini donuts.

Over the fray, I heard Samantha again. She was yelling for her daughter. "Sophie! Michael, where's Sophie?"

Michael was still reeling from the gut punch. His head swiveled around, looking for his wife or his daughter or both. Two security guards had him by the arms. He tore away from them and rushed forward, into the crowd of people. He wasn't being careful about where he was going. Elbows flailed as people bumped into each other and got knocked over.

The crowd's noise got louder. People were getting out of the way now, trying to get their little kids to safety, but they didn't know what was happening or where to go. The atrium was even more packed than it had been minutes earlier. A brawl always draws spectators. As panic levels rose, more people went sprawling. I watched helplessly as the crowd turned into a stampede.

Panic turned to terror. People screamed. The stampede changed direction, and before I could formulate an escape plan for myself and Jessica, a group of people started tipping over toward me, like a chain of dominoes.

Arms, heads, and bodies struck me from the waist down. I couldn't keep my feet under me, and I had nowhere to go except... straight into the splashing fountain.

I reached out to steady myself, but all I caught with my hands were the red braids of Jessica's hair. I tried to let go, but my fingers curled in reflex.

I tried to warn her, but another body from the crowd hit me hard enough to knock the words from my lips.

Over we both went, straight into the misty, rushing water beneath the replica waterfall.

CHAPTER 8

After the security guards fished us out of the water feature, they took us to a staff area for a towel-off and a talking-to.

The casino's head of security, a jowly man with dyed black hair, gave us a stern lecture about not standing on ledges that were clearly marked with signs reading DO NOT SIT, STAND, OR PLAY ON ROCK WALL.

We asked about the Sweet family and were assured that everything was under control.

I asked, "Did Samantha find Sophie in the crowd?"

"She's just a little girl," Jessica said. "I hope she didn't see her father getting beat up."

The jowly man snorted. "Nobody got beat up."

"I know what I saw," I said evenly. "Michael Sweet better have made it to his vehicle without further incident."

The man lifted his jowly chin defiantly. "He strikes me as the clumsy type."

I shook my head. "This may be private property, but the laws regarding assault are still applicable here."

The man raised his gray-specked eyebrows. "Oh, really?"

I explained, "Fourth degree assault is a Class A misdemeanor, carrying up to one year in jail and a fine up to six grand. But if one were to commit this offense in front of a child, it could be elevated to a Class C felony. And Class C felonies can carry up to five years in prison and much higher fines." I gave him my steeliest look, which took serious effort with fountain water dripping down my face. "And the atrium was filled with families and seven-year-old girls."

"Then it's a good thing nobody assaulted anyone," the man said. "I'll make sure everyone with the last name of Sweet makes it safely off the property."

"Good," I said. I could feel my cheeks flushing. I'd just rattled off some facts about misdemeanors, but if the casino was on Native American land, the laws and fines might be quite different. I was certainly no expert on Tribal Council law. But I had learned, from spending time with my lawyer boyfriend, that if you talk fast and spout off a bunch of numbers, people take you more seriously. Even if you're wrong. And even if you're sopping wet and dripping fountain water on the carpet.

The head of security checked his phone screen. "Everyone's been accounted for," he said. "Safe and sound."

"I'd like to see Colt now, please."

"Sure. Let me arrange a meeting." He grinned. "Do you two young ladies promise to stay out of the fountain?"

Jessica said, "It was an accident, honestly."

I added, "There should be a guardrail around the base of the fountain."

He stared at us.

"We promise to stay out of the fountain," I said.

"We do," Jessica agreed.

That seemed to satisfy him. He called over two security guards and gave them instructions, presumably to take us to see Colt Canuso.

We followed the guards down a hallway.

"Your meeting is right through here," the smaller security guard said.

He opened the door and shoved us through.

It wasn't a corridor leading to Colt's office. We'd been kicked out through a side door, into the bright autumn sunshine. The crisp breeze made me shiver in my wet clothes.

Jessica and I exchanged a look.

She muttered, "So much for saying goodbye to Colt."

"We can still make a dignified exit," I said, and started walking along the side of the building.

Our wet shoes made squip-squip sounds with every step. So much for a dignified exit.

Over the squip-squip sounds, I heard the security guards chuckling over how much fun it was going to be reviewing the video footage of us "frolicking like water nymphs." They went on to say some things that were less delicate, concerning the sheerness of our outfits when wet.

I stopped my squip-squip walking and wheeled around to face them.

"You two chuckleheads had better watch your mouths," I said fiercely. "My associate and I are old friends of your boss's, and I don't think he'd appreciate that sort of talk."

Jessica grabbed my elbow and whispered, "Stormy, your smoky eye shadow is dripping down your cheeks."

"So?"

"You look exactly like a scary clown who's just escaped a carnival of nightmares."

"That's perfect," I hissed back.

At the doorway, standing in the bright sunshine and casting perfect cinematic shadows against the stucco wall of the new building, the two guards continued laughing at us.

I lifted my chin defiantly. "Gentlemen, I believe the words you're looking for are *I'm sorry*."

The bigger and more mountain-shaped of the two uniformed men made a scoffing sound. "You two ladies don't know the boss," he said. "You're nobody."

"We're old friends of Colt Canuso's. The three of us go way back."

The bigger guy waved one wide mitt dismissively. "You and every other lady in this town. Especially the broke ones." He chuckled, his big voice a deep rumble. "Especially the *crazy*, broke ones."

Now he had my interest, but for a different reason.

I changed tack, the apology forgotten. "Exactly how many crazy, broke girls? Is Colt dating anyone in particular? Maybe a blonde?"

The two men exchanged a confused look.

Mountain-Shaped Guy lifted his chin at me and demanded, "What's it to you, lady?"

This wasn't my first day on the job. I already had the cash in my hand. I stepped forward and casually presented him with my offering like a professional.

The big guy handed half the cash to the other guard, and they both tucked the bills away. Their postures softened.

"No blondes," the large man said. "Colt's not dating anyone, even though he could have his pick."

"But you said he's friends with all the crazy, broke girls."

"Just friends," he replied. "Colt's all talk, like a dog who barks a lot but doesn't do nothin'. If you ask me, he's still not over Susan." He added in a softer tone, "That's his wife who died a few years back."

I nodded. I knew about Susan. Jessica and I had gone to school with her as well, though she was two years younger than us. The Mountain-Shaped Guy's words rung true. The last time I'd seen Colt before today, he'd been wearing his wedding band. The ring had not, however, been there today.

The other security guard piped in, "I always try to get him to open up and talk to someone about his pain. Grieving doesn't have to be something you go through alone. But Colt's one of those tough guys who doesn't know how to talk about his feelings. I don't know what to do. If he doesn't get it off his shoulders, I'm worried he might crack some day."

I sniffed. "Some day? You mean like just now, when he punched an unarmed man in the stomach?"

The big guy puffed out his chest and fixed me with a serious glare. "You didn't see anything like that. You couldn't have seen nothin' while you were swimming in the water feature.”

The other guy said, “Today wasn't the first time Colt lost his temp—”

The big guy elbowed his buddy to shut up. And then he gave me a stone-faced look I recognized. The interview, such as it was, had ended.

I thanked them and started walking away. I'd gotten what I wanted to know.

Under her breath, Jessica asked me, “Now you're bribing people?”

“Would you prefer it if I'd challenged them to a two-on-two kung fu battle?”

“Oh, Stormy.”

It was a long, soggy walk back to the car with our shoes going squip-squip the whole way.

My heart felt heavy for Colt. I wondered if he had many friends to talk to about his feelings. I did worry, like the smaller security guard, that his pain might cause him to lash out or find trouble.

CHAPTER 9

My boyfriend, Logan Sanderson, hummed to himself as he scraped the carbon off the barbecue racks. We were in the backyard, enjoying what might be the last Sunday barbecue of the year.

I sipped a beer from a can and checked my phone for messages from my roommate.

"No veggie burger," I told Logan. "Jessica's having dinner with her mom."

"What?" He hadn't heard me over the sound of his scraping. I started to repeat what I'd just told him, but he impatiently started scraping the racks again before I could answer.

I yelled, "No veggie burger!"

He paused long enough to say, "Does she want it well done? I never know how long to cook these stupid mushroom-oat-bran-quinoa things." And then he tossed one of Jessica's veggie burgers onto the grill with a sizzle.

I got up from my patio chair and went to hug him from behind. He pushed me away. "Hot grill!"

I took a step back and bit my tongue. Logan had been working long hours, and today had felt like the first time I'd seen him in years. But with that treatment, I was feeling like a stranger in his life. I wanted to yank the spatula out of his hand and paddle his butt with it for not listening to me, but you know what they say. Violence is not the answer to relationship problems.

"Jessica's not coming home for dinner," I said.

He gave me an indignant look. "Why didn't you tell me? Now this lemongrass-tofu burger is going to waste."

"I'll eat it," I said. "And it's a lentil-cashew burger."

"It smells like wet cardboard," he said. "If you eat this, who'll eat your steak? Will your father eat two of them?"

"Dad's not coming tonight," I said. "Which you would know if you actually listened to me."

"Oh?" He returned his attention to the grill, turning his back to me, but there was no mistaking the fight in his voice. I could imagine the facial expression that went with it.

The urge to hit him with the spatula returned. I retreated back to the picnic table and my beer.

Logan glanced back over his shoulder at me, eyebrow raised. "That's it? You're not going to talk to me?"

"I'm letting you grill in peace."

After a few minutes, he asked, "Is it just the two of us tonight? What are the neighbors up to?"

"Dean and Eve? Beats me."

Dean and Eve Lubbesmeyer had just moved into the house next door in August. They'd arrived on the day of the town's annual Forest Folk Run, a charity event that people walked or ran while wearing costumes ranging from furry Forest Folk monster suits to zombies. The zombie look had been increasing in popularity lately. Dean and Eve had been driving their moving truck, which was packed full of all their earthly possessions, when a volunteer stopped their vehicle to let a group of zombies cross the street. Dean and Eve had looked at each other in horror, doubting their decision to move to Misty Falls. Did people in the town normally dress in tattered clothes and walk at a shuffling pace? Wave after wave of zombies surrounded the moving truck, all moaning and groaning. A few muscular troublemakers came up with the fun idea to shake the moving truck, so they did. And the squeaking of the truck only spurred the zombies on. Now, the Lubbesmeyers didn't have a Forest Folk Run where they came from, and they'd never seen zombies outside of Halloween, so what were they to think? Confusion turned to panic. After a few terrifying minutes of having their truck rocked by zombies, Dean leaned on the horn. The zombies all jumped back. That was when Eve noticed the blood and falling-off body parts were just makeup and monster effects. The whole spectacle was all in good fun. They rolled down their windows and congratulated the zombies for giving them a good scare. After the zombie horde cleared away and let them continue on their way, Dean and Eve laughed the rest of the way to their new home.

Other than their colorful entry to the town, I didn't know much about Dean and Eve Lubbesmeyer, except that they were empty nesters whose kids had all left for college, and they'd been flirting with the idea of early retirement when they discovered that the factory that made their favorite potato chips was for sale. They visited Misty Falls in the spring of that year on a zombie-free day, toured the factory, and soon became the new owners of Aunt Jo's Crispy Spuds. The first time I met Dean and Eve, we bonded over our shared love of the chip company's logo featuring Aunt Jo, with her curls freshly set from the hairdresser, and her good pearls worn proudly around her neck.

"We should see if Dean and Eve want these other steaks," Logan said. "We can't let them go to waste."

Suddenly, a face appeared over the fence separating my backyard from the Lubbesmeyers'. It was Eve, with her spiky, pale purple hair. She must have climbed a ladder to peer over at us with comically good timing.

Logan laughed. "Speak of the devil!"

She asked, "Did I hear somebody talking about steaks going to waste? That's a crime where we come from. Punishable by public shaming in the local newspaper."

Logan replied, "Were you doing some gardening just now?"

"No," she said with a straight face. "I always kneel on this side of the fence and listen in when you two lovebirds are back here. Between your law practice and the private investigation business, it's my best way to get all the local gossip. Then I go down to Ruby's Treasure Trove and sell the intel to Ruby piece by piece."

Logan laughed again. I couldn't help but notice he found Eve's antics far more amusing than my own. I sipped my beer and watched him chat with Eve. She called for her husband to come outside, they negotiated with Logan on side dishes, then they disappeared into their house to rustle up a salad. Logan finished grilling the three steaks and lone veggie burger without saying a word to me.

I got the sense I'd done something to upset him, but I couldn't think of what.

I recalled what one of the security guards had said about Colt, about how he was the kind of guy who bottled up his feelings. Was Logan bottling something? I watched his careful movements as he set the platter of grilled food on the picnic table. He barely even glanced up at me. He could have been alone right now, for all the interaction he was giving me.

Jeffrey appeared in my lap as if by magic. I was petting his head before I even realized he was there.

"You're like smoke," I told him. "You waft in on a breeze, don't you?"

He looked at the steaks and licked his lips. "Just one little piece," I said, reaching for the platter.

"Don't," Logan said. "Steaks need to rest after grilling, or the juices will leak out."

I looked down at Jeffrey. "Sorry. You heard the grill man. Stop trying to ruin dinner."

Logan sighed. "Now you're making me the bad guy."

"He doesn't speak English," I said. "He's a cat." I tilted my head. "What's gotten into you?"

Logan didn't get a chance to answer—not that he looked like he wanted to.

"Knock, knock," said Dean Lubbesmeyer as he entered the backyard from the back of the house. Grinning, he said, "We should cut a hole in our fence to make it easier to get over here for the free food!"

Eve said, "Or dig a tunnel underneath!"

Logan looked right at me. "You'll have to discuss it with the land owner herself. I have no stake in this property."

Eve and Dean looked at each other for a moment before bursting into laughter. That was the great thing about the two of them—they took everything as a big joke, whether it was or not. Given Logan's cranky mood, I was happy to have them there.

Later, when Dean cut a piece of his steak into tiny cubes and "accidentally" dropped them on the concrete patio pavers, Jeffrey was even more happy to have the Lubbesmeyers there.

"These are great steak knives," Dean commented. "*Laguiole*. If you ever need them sharpened, let me know. You have to sharpen each serration separately."

"Thanks for the offer," I said.

"Oops. Dropped another piece," Dean said.

Jeffrey pounced on the chunk of steak. He was well beyond trying to appear cool and practically begged like a hound dog.

"Butter fingers," Eve said with a tsk-tsk.

As the sun set and the air turned chilly enough for us to bring out blankets to drape over ourselves, Dean and Eve regaled us with tales from the potato chip factory. In the short time since they'd taken over as owners, they'd cycled through a number of shift supervisors and support staff. Even their management team had been fighting with each other like unsupervised children.

"Some people can't handle change," Logan said. "They're acting out because they're afraid."

Eve batted her lashes. "Afraid of little ol' me?"

Dean patted his wife on the shoulder. "You and your army of robots," he said.

I leaned in. "Robots?" Now he had my attention.

Dean explained, "The old owners still had staff hand-picking out the chips with brown spots. We brought in a machine that scans every chip visually, sends the imaging to a computer, which then controls these nifty little hot-air jets that remove the flawed chips. The burned ones, and the green ones that contain trace amounts of solanine."

Eve grinned. "It's an incredible piece of equipment. Very expensive, but it will pay for itself in saved labor."

"What do you do with the flawed chips?" My mouth watered at all the discussion of potato chips. My cashew-lentil burger hadn't exactly filled me up.

"We're debating leaving a few in," Dean said. "One or two per bag gives it that authentic artisanal quality people enjoy."

"Plus it gives you a target for Last Chip Standing," I said. They appeared to be perplexed by this, so I explained, "When you're eating chips, you always have that one you think you won't eat at all, but then the perfect ones are all gone, and you think, oh what the heck. You eat the grisly brown one. But then you have a burned taste in your mouth, so you have to get something else to snack on."

Dean and Eve stared at me in stunned silence then burst out laughing again. Eve declared me to be the Funniest Person in Misty Falls.

I said to Logan, "Did you hear that? I should write down all my many thoughts and adventures and get a big TV series on HBO."

"Leave me out of it," he said moodily.

Eve said, "Speaking of HBO, did you see that crowd at the casino yesterday? You'd think they were giving away buckets of money to everyone with a cute kid. I tell you, someone's going to be coming into a few bucks real soon."

Dean patted his wife on the shoulder. "My wife isn't materialistic. She just loves money, and she's a whiz with it."

Eve smiled. "I do love money. But not in a materialistic way."

Dean gazed lovingly at his youthful-acting, purple-haired, fifty-something wife. "And I love seeing you scheming about money, babe."

"I love that you love my scheming."

They leaned in and touched their noses in a sweet gesture that was almost too sweet.

My heart buoyed as I witnessed the Lubbesmeyers' everlasting love. I looked across the table at Logan.

He was reading the ingredients on the bottle of barbecue sauce.

CHAPTER 10

Sunday night, I crawled into bed feeling like a bag of junk with no handle. The cashew-lentil burger sat low and heavy in my stomach, plus I hadn't smoothed things out with Logan. I didn't get a chance. He'd excused himself for bed at the same time the neighbors went home.

I tossed and turned so much that even Jeffrey abandoned me.

Once I did get to sleep, my dreams were as vivid as reality.

I found myself at Samantha's open house, alone in the tiny upstairs bedroom with Colt Canuso. He took me by the hand and gazed at me with his sensitive, soulful, dark-brown eyes. He told me, "You're too good for Logan. He doesn't appreciate what he's got."

And then we kissed.

We kissed so vividly that when I woke up at five o'clock in the morning in a panic sweat, I had to say to myself, out loud, "It was just a dream."

I couldn't get back to sleep. I lay in the dark and listened to the garbage trucks moving up and down the street. And I suddenly remembered I'd forgotten to put out the trash the night before. Should I pull on my housecoat now, and run out? Was that the sound of the garbage truck moving toward my house or away?

I drifted in and out of consciousness, imagining myself running around in Pam's old housecoat.

Running away from her while she fired my father's gun at me.

More bad dreams and panic sweating.

The garbage trucks were getting closer, and they were full of dead bodies and secrets. Everyone was angry at me, disappointed in me.

I woke up with a dry mouth.

Jeffrey came padding into the bedroom and gave me a chatty meow from the doorway. *If you're up already, how about we make it Kitty Play Time?* He slipped underneath my bed, swatted something around on the wood floor, and then hopped up next to me with a mouse-shaped toy in his mouth. Even in the darkness, I knew the toy had gotten covered in dust bunnies under my bed. I didn't want him to ingest the fluff, so I flicked on the bedside lamp and picked the mouse clean while Jeffrey tried to wrestle it from my hands. By the time I was done cleaning his mouse, I was fully awake.

I climbed out of bed and flicked on the overhead light, since the sun wasn't up yet. By the time I'd picked out some clothes to wear to work at the store, Jeffrey had finished swatting the stuffed catnip toy around the bed. He curled up on my pillow, clutching his mouse in his front paws and licking it with his noisy, raspy tongue.

"Busy day planned?"

He kept licking the mouse, making the tiny bell on its nose tinkle.

"Me, too," I said. "It's Monday, so I'll be putting in the store's orders. I'll get an early start on things."

He gave me a dopey look.

"You're high on catnip," I said.

More dopey blinking.

I carefully pinched his mouse toy by the tail and gave it a few tugs. His eyes widened and he twitched his head from side to side as he extended his claws into the stuffed toy. I curled up next to him and immediately fell asleep again.

I awoke when my alarm clock went off. I was partly dressed and lying sideways on the bed, with one arm underneath myself and numb. I'd left the lights on, and the room was strangely bright, like a warehouse grocery store.

So much for getting an early start on my day.

I was brushing my teeth when the vivid dreams about Colt came back to me.

By the time I got to Glorious Gifts, I was still thinking about the love triangle between Samantha Sweet, Michael Sweet, and Colt Canuso.

I meant to get started right away on the store's restock orders but didn't.

The manager of my gift shop, Brianna Chang, arrived for her shift. She walked into the office at the back of the store and caught me stalking Colt Canuso via his social media accounts.

"Busted," Brianna said.

I wheeled my computer chair around and gave her a guilty look.

Brianna looked a bit less than her usual perky self that Monday morning. Had she also been plagued by weird dreams and demanding pets?

Unlike my own fuzzy hair that day, Brianna's hair looked nice. She always wore her thick, dark-brown, pin-straight hair combed forward to hide her ears, which she was self-conscious about sticking out. Her round, makeup-free face looked different that morning. She had a tiny pimple along the edge of her jaw, and her big brown eyes weren't as bright as usual. Her outfit was one of her Librarian Chic looks —pencil skirt, white blouse with rounded collar, and a lightweight red cardigan. The cardigan had one button fastened, but it was a mismatch, paired with the wrong hole.

She leaned over my shoulder to look at my computer screen, which was showing the photos on Colt's personal social media account.

She made a tsk-tsk sound. "That sure doesn't look like the candles order."

I gave my employee a sheepish one-shoulder shrug.

"Sorry, boss." I snapped my fingers. "Oh, wait. You're not *my* boss." I pointed at myself slowly and then at her. "I think maybe I'm *your* boss. Could it be? Could someone as smart and sophisticated as myself actually pay someone else to boss her around about candle orders?"

"We need those candles," Brianna said tersely. "Her Royal Highness put in a special order for three dozen of the lavender ones."

"The Countess?"

"No, the Queen of England," Brianna snapped. "She shops here regularly. With all her corgis and everything. You haven't noticed?"

"Your sarcasm is bordering on actual nastiness today, Brianna. Did Evil Chad make your mocha decaf for some wicked reason?"

"I wish." She wrinkled her nose. "I didn't stop at the coffee shop. Before I left home, I had an herbal cleansing tea that's supposed to get rid of my toxins."

I snorted. "Without your toxins, what would be left?"

She blinked at me with a faux-murderous expression.

"Go," I said, waving her away. "Go get yourself a full-caff mocha, and pick me up a you-know-what."

"What about my cleanse? I have a pimple. From toxins." She pointed to her chin and the teeny tiny bump.

"Brianna, everyone knows you don't have to drink herbal cleansing tea until you have three pimples." The key to lying is to make it broad yet also specific.

She bought it. "Oh. Cool."

Brianna left me to my cyberstalking, which I picked up right where I'd left off.

I read the newest post on the casino's website. After the public altercation between Michael Sweet and casino staff on Saturday, the casino's publicist had issued a statement of apology for an unspecified event. *We regret any negative impact this unfortunate event may have had for families attending the festivities*, it read, and so forth.

Michael and Samantha Sweet had posted their own vague regrets as well. Their real estate office had issued a statement of apology that didn't quite apologize so much as spread the blame over a wide range of factors including hot weather, a crowd-induced panic attack, and even the side-effects of medication for a lingering ear infection. I rolled my eyes. Their publicist was certainly creative.

On the positive side, nobody had been seriously injured during the ruckus. Jessica had talked to Samantha over the weekend and gotten more details. Young Sophie had been happily occupied with her best friend Q, chaperoned by both Chip and Quinn McCabe. During the "regrettable incident," the four of them had been in another part of the resort, getting butterflies painted on all of their faces.

What I couldn't figure out from the social media posts, though, was the exact cause of the argument between Colt and Michael.

A few anonymous commenters had cited an incident that day at the casino, between Michael and an employee who was a niece of his. According to internet user Rainbow733, Colt had witnessed Michael playing fast and loose with the rules at the Roulette table where his niece was the dealer. He'd issued a warning through his staff, and when Michael had turned belligerent, the staff had started escorting him out. Michael had been on his way out when the kerfuffle in the atrium happened.

I'd heard Michael yell at Colt, "Isn't it enough that you and your family don't pay your fair share of taxes? You need to stay out of my business." That didn't sound to me like a man telling off his niece's boss. But then again, Michael had never been one for words when he could use his fists.

The front door chimed. A minute later, Brianna appeared in the back office holding both the coffee she needed to deal with me plus the one I needed to deal with her.

We still had ten minutes of quiet before we opened for business. We slurped our caffeinated beverages in easy silence, as was our Monday morning ritual.

Most other weekdays, Brianna opened the store on her own. On Mondays, I came in early to deal with paperwork and put in restock orders. If I got straight to work without delay, I could be done by three o'clock. And I should have started already, not reading gossip on the internet. Our candle order truly was overdue.

I would get to it immediately... right after I finished looking at the last five years' of Colt's posts and photos. As research.

"Hey, I know that guy," Brianna said, taking a seat to get a better view of my computer screen. I scrolled past a picture of Colt at a dressy event, wearing his usual suit and bolo tie.

"You know Colt Canuso?"

Brianna bounced on the second not-so-good office chair, making it squeak. "Not personally, but I thought he looked familiar. I just saw this guy in the coffee shop. Like five minutes ago." She pointed at the screen excitedly. "This guy. With the bolo tie and everything."

"He was at House of Bean?" I hadn't seen him there before, or around the downtown core for that matter.

"This guy was totally in the line in front of me," Brianna said. "His hair's long in the back, and he had it tied with a leather strap. He was wearing a suit like that, with a bolo tie. What a character! I actually snapped a reference photo when he wasn't looking, because as soon as I saw his look, I knew I had to put him in my web comic." She pulled out her phone and showed me a blurry picture of Colt Canuso in profile.

"Brianna, you shouldn't put real people in your comic. If your website gets popular—I mean *when* it gets popular—people will try to sue you. It doesn't seem like a big deal now, but you need to think about your future." I shook my finger at her. In an exaggerated parental tone, I said, "You must think about your future, young lady. The internet is forever!"

"Whatever," she said, just like the bratty kid she was.

Brianna had recently turned twenty-two, but in many ways she resembled a teenager. She'd never lived on her own or had a serious relationship. She even looked like a kid, with her round face and big eyes. I had "acquired" Brianna along with my purchase of the gift shop. To my relief, she was an ideal store manager. Behind that cute face was a sharp mind. Not only was she quick enough to keep up with my witty banter, but the cash drawer always balanced to the penny whenever she was on the register. I couldn't say the same for our other casual and part-time help.

Brianna leaned over and clicked the arrows on the computer keyboard to scroll through Colt's posts. Her glossy dark-brown hair swung back and forth energetically.

"What exactly are we looking for, boss?" She scrolled the page down, all the way to pictures from five years ago. "Isn't that the gymnasium at the high school?"

"Those must be pictures from my ten-year reunion. Don't get too excited about seeing me with bad hair. I wasn't there. I didn't make it home for that one."

"I know a lot of these people," she said. "There's my second-cousin, Chip, and his wife, Quinn. Oh, and there's the real estate lady. Samantha. Did I ever tell you about the time Gloria made her cry?"

I turned my chair around so I could face Brianna. Gloria was the original owner of Glorious Gifts. She'd listed the business for sale through Samantha Sweet's real estate office, which was how we'd originally met.

"Gloria made Samantha cry?" And here I thought I was the only difficult client who brought the nervous realtor to tears.

Brianna made a flat line with her mouth. "I shouldn't talk trash about my old boss, but Gloria could be mean."

Mean. I frowned. Jessica had called me mean on Saturday. Was it just a word people used without considering how it might hurt someone's feelings? Or was it inevitable that any woman would get one label or the other, either *nice* or *mean*, with no middle ground?

The door chimed to let us know someone was opening the front door. We weren't supposed to be open for a few more minutes, but apparently Brianna hadn't turned the latch on her way back with our beverages.

Brianna groaned. "Someone has made it through our defenses."

"That's what happens when you don't lock the door behind you."

She grabbed her takeout cup of mocha and headed toward the front to greet our first customer of the day. She might groan to me in private, but she was always polite and sincere with our customers.

A minute later, I heard a man's voice. "Is the owner here? I need to speak to the store's owner. She's in big trouble."

CHAPTER 11

I came out front to find a dark-haired man leaning casually against the store's front counter.

"There's that manager," he said, smiling.

It was none other than the man I'd been cyberstalking all morning—Colt Canuso.

I let out a chortle of relief. "You had me worried for a minute," I said. "I was about to call in my big, tough security guards to kick you out on your tush."

Brianna, who stood behind the counter, struck a pose, flexing her biceps. "Boss, do you want me to toss this fella out?" She looked extra comical with her red Librarian Chic cardigan still buttoned crookedly.

"I'll deal with this surly customer personally," I told her. "Go finish drinking your mocha and open all that mail on my desk. You can even use the pointy mail opener."

She saluted me and went back to the office. We had several running jokes at the store, and one of them was about the hierarchy of staff members and which ones were allowed to use the pointy mail opener and the good scissors.

After she'd left, Colt asked, "Has she been working for you long? And by *working for you*, I mean spying on people."

"She's my manager here at the store, but she doesn't work for the investigation agency. Any spying Brianna does is strictly personal."

He raised his dark eyebrows and fixed me with his deep-brown eyes, just like he had in my dreams.

"Come on, Stormy. It's just us." We were alone in the store. Monday mornings weren't usually busy, which made it a good day to do orders and take deliveries. But after the dreams I'd had, I found myself hoping for an interruption.

"You sent your employee to do surveillance on me," Colt said. "She's not very subtle. I heard her phone click when she took my picture." His forehead wrinkled with worry. "What's going on? Has Michael hired your boyfriend the lawyer to sue me for giving him what he deserves? We carry insurance, but you should know, we've got some real tough-as-nails lawyers of our own."

I smiled to set him at ease. "Colt, I swear Brianna wasn't acting on my orders. You're not being sued—as far as I know. Brianna was taking your picture for her own nefarious purposes."

"Nefarious? You and your big words."

"You'll see what I mean when a dark-haired man with a bolo tie suddenly shows up in her web comic."

"Oh? That girl is Brie the Distractor? She works for you?" He blinked rapidly. "If that girl in the red sweater is Brie the Distractor, and you're her boss, that means you're... *her*." He laughed. "You're Whirlwind. I can't believe I didn't put that together before now. Stormy is Whirlwind."

I shook my head. "I'm not Whirlwind, trust me. Any resemblance to real people in her web comic is strictly coincidental." I tried to strike a casual, non-Whirlwind-like pose with my elbows resting on the counter. "And since when did Brianna's web comic get so popular?"

"I've been reading it for a few years now."

"Great," I said. "I'll get you an autographed calendar for Christmas."

He stared at me and sent me a warm feeling without saying a word.

I felt the urge to rearrange the stapler and other items on the counter. "So, what brings you here, anyway? Can I help you pick out a gift for someone?"

"I was just running some errands in town when I noticed your lackey taking my picture, so I thought I'd pop in and say hello." He cleared his throat. "Stormy, I'd like to apologize for my behavior on Saturday."

"Which part? Kissing a married lady? Flirting with me? Or punching a guy in the stomach, right in front of a whole bunch of families?"

"I'm a lover, not a fighter, so I'm only apologizing for the last one."

"I read the press release. It was pretty vague."

His dark-brown eyes glistened. "I'm a pacifist. It was wrong of me to punch Michael Sweet. Even if he did deserve it."

"What was he even doing? Did he confront you about"—I lowered my voice to a whisper—"kissing his wife?"

Colt's head jerked up, and he gave me a startled look. "Did you tell him about that?"

"No. I believed you that it was a one-time thing. But you promised me you were going to back off." I poked my finger at him. "But you did the opposite of backing off. So, if it wasn't Samantha that you two were fighting over, what was it?"

Colt rubbed his temples. "This and that. Did you know he used to date my sister, Trigger?"

"Ew."

"Mikey's not that well-liked by my family, but I don't think his own family likes him much better."

"Is it true his niece works at the casino?"

"Apparently. I didn't know, until I caught him pushing the rules at the roulette table. Plus he was soliciting. He's been asked repeatedly to stop hustling my customers, but we still catch him handing out business cards for his real estate business. I always tell him, people come to the casino to relax, not get a sales pitch."

"That's all there was to it? You wanted him to stop placing late bets and handing out business cards?"

"That's all, I swear. Stormy, I'd never lie to you." He bit his lower lip suggestively. "I admire you way too much." He lifted his chin and looked down at me with interest. I didn't need to have read three books on body language to understand what he was thinking about, much less admiring.

I checked the top buttons on my blouse and took a step back. The previous night's dreams had been vivid, but reality was even more intense.

The door chimed, and another customer entered. I breathed an actual sigh of relief.

It was a petite blonde with a familiar face. At first, I thought it was Samantha, but this woman was wearing a sexy black cocktail dress, and Samantha always wore bright colors and white blazers. But I *did* know this woman. I'd been so focused on Colt that it took a few seconds for my brain to switch gears and cough up a name.

"Quinn!" My arms flew up in the air girlishly. The arms-in-the-air move had to be a muscle memory from high school and the enthusiastic way we cheerleaders always greeted each other in public.

"Stormy-poo!" Quinn threw her arms in the air as well. She ran toward me, saw Colt, and did a double take. "Colty-poo!"

Colty-poo? I'd completely forgotten about the head cheerleader's diminutive nicknames for everyone.

I'd circled around the counter to give her a hug. Colt had his arms outstretched as well.

Quinn laughed and hugged both of us at the same time. Her arms weren't very long, so it felt less like a group hug and more like I was being purposely crushed against the front of Colt Canuso, like a child's Ken and Barbie dolls being forced to kiss.

This is life in your hometown, I told myself. Every day was an opportunity to reunite with high school friends, for better or worse.

Quinn must have been thinking a similar thing. She squealed, "It's like a miniature high school reunion happening right here."

I broke away from the squishy embrace and looked my old girlfriend up and down. She was smaller than I remembered. Even in spiky black heels, her eyes were barely the same level as mine. Quinn Baudelaire had seemed larger than life when we were teenagers. The bossy head cheerleaders in teen movies had seemingly been inspired by our own Quinn, a true queen bee to the rest of the squad.

Her blond hair was now styled in a sensible mom haircut, but her enviable figure remained unchanged by time and motherhood. Beneath the hem of her short black cocktail dress were the legs that couldn't possibly be as long as they seemed.

"Look at you," I said with genuine admiration. "Nothing but legs and boobs and a smile."

She squealed in delight and kicked up a heel. "Pilates five times a week!"

"I believe it," I said.

"You should come, Stormy! I do a cardio funk class twice a week as well. It's like cheerleading, but for older gals like us."

"Older gals." I snorted. "Speaking of cheerleading," I waved at Colt, who'd been standing by patiently, "Colt was just telling me on Saturday morning that he should have been on the squad with us."

"Saturday *morning*? You were together in the morning, as in...?" She glanced between the two of us and let out a bubbly squeal. "I knew it!" She made the shame-shame finger gesture. "Shame, shame. Stormy, now I know your new boyfriend's name." She stopped the gesture and put her hands on her petite waist. "It's about time you ditched the weird lawyer with the hipster beard and got yourself a *real* man."

A real man?

Colt grinned and waggled his eyebrows at me.

"Actually, I'm still dating the lawyer with the hipster beard," I told Quinn. "I just happened to bump into Colt the other day at—"

"Did you see him punching Michael in the guts at the casino?" She shook her head but kept smiling. "You boys and your scuffles. You're so silly." She reached up and bopped Colt on the nose. "Silly Colty-poo. You know Michael's harmless."

"He's not harmless," Colt growled. "And don't call me that." He straightened his bolo tie and gave me a formal bow as he took a step back, toward the exit. "Stormy, I'll be seeing you around. Next time you want to go for a swim, try the pool."

"Ha ha," I said.

He winked at me and then left.

Now I was alone with Quinn. What other unwanted surprises did that Monday have in store for me? I glanced over at the back hallway, hoping for Brianna to emerge and save me before Quinn signed me up for Pilates and cardio funk, whatever that was.

Quinn gave me an openmouthed smile. We both looked each other over once more.

She said, "At least your bearded guy's a lawyer. I hear they make good money."

"They can," I said. "And you married a mailman. I hear that's secure."

"Chip?" She covered her mouth and giggled. "I did always love a man in uniform."

"Congratulations," I said. "I met your daughter, Quinby, on Saturday. Very charming, just like her mother. So confident."

"And ambitious," Quinn added. "She's going to be a big star."

"Did the talent scouts at the casino give her some encouragement?"

"Oh, yes," she breathed as she leaned forward and bounced up and down on the balls of her feet with excitement.

"Quinn, I don't mean to be a killjoy, but promise me you'll be careful around those entertainment people. They're only in it for themselves. They want nothing more than for every proud parent to drop a thousand bucks on professional styling and photographs, from their approved vendor list, of course."

The smile fell off her face. "Jessica's right. You have changed. You've become so jaded and cynical."

"Come on, Quinn. We're all a few years older now. We've both changed." I leaned forward and sniffed her. "You don't smell like watermelon lip gloss anymore." I sniffed again. "Are you wearing perfume? It smells expensive. And nice."

She giggled. "It should smell nice, because yes, it *is* expensive." She tilted her head to the side and narrowed her eyes as she scrutinized me. "And you've let your hair go... natural?"

I fluffed my pixie cut self-consciously. "I'm a low-maintenance kinda gal."

"Sure you are," she said. "Just keep telling yourself that, Stormy. Never mind that low maintenance is just another word for *lazy*."

And there it is, I thought. The note of condescension. The Quinn bossiness that was more than simple enthusiastic support. Back in high school, we secretly called her the Queen of another B-word. Nothing was ever good enough. If we did five perfect cartwheels, she insisted we do six. If we stayed an hour late for cheer practice, she demanded we skip dinner and stay for two.

I let her veiled insult of my hair hang in the air and didn't respond.

Brianna walked past us, back from her break in the nick of time.

"Hey, cousin," Brianna said to Quinn. "I mean cousin-in-law."

"That's right! You're related," I said. "We're all related."

"Not really," Quinn said. "My husband, Chip, is second-cousins with your employee."

I gave her a big smile. "But we're all one big, happy family here in Glorious Gifts."

Brianna said, in a little-girl voice, "I'm allowed to use the sharp mail opener."

"You goofball," I said, cracking up.

Quinn gave us a disgusted look. She'd never been a fan of antics.

"I hope you're both coming to the big party I'm hosting."

"Wouldn't miss it for the world," Brianna said.

The conversation ground to a halt. Brianna walked away and busied herself with the window display, seemingly having no interest in further conversation with her second-cousin's wife.

Quinn pursed her lips and looked me up and down. "Speaking of big families, I hear you've been spending time with Samantha Sweet and her family." She pursed her lips until they were sharp enough to pop balloons. "Who knew Michael Sweet could be housebroken, right?"

"You know, Quinn, I always thought you two would end up together. You really did make a lovely Homecoming King and Queen."

She sighed and got a faraway look in her eyes. "We really did create something wonderful together." She shifted her attention back to me. "Thank goodness Samantha got him house-trained. He was running around climbing on half the girls in town like it was his job. Even a couple of the Canuso girls." She raised her eyebrows. "I'm surprised he didn't get himself killed."

"There's still time," I said with a dark chuckle.

The door chimed with an incoming customer. Thankfully, it wasn't anyone I went to high school with. It was a retired couple, Canadian tourists by the flag pins on the man's fanny pack. The last stragglers of the summer tourism rush.

They leaned over our sparse candles display, which reminded me, I had candles to order.

I rearranged the stapler and pens on the counter. "Quinn, I've got some work to do."

She made a disappointed sound. "Boo. I wanted to catch up. But I guess you only have time for Danish royalty. It's a shame Countess Whats-her-face had you tied up on my birthday."

Ouch. She was the Queen of Passive Aggression.

I sighed. "If you're still downtown around lunchtime, let's get a bite to eat and catch up."

"Maybe," she said with a yawn. "I've got a bunch of boring housewife errands to run first."

I looked her up and down. "Boring housewife errands? You look like you're dressed for something more exciting than that, in your little black dress and your come-get-some heels."

She covered her mouth with her hand and giggled. "A girl needs to keep things interesting."

The way she said it, I pictured her ambushing her husband Chip somewhere along his route and dragging him into the bushes. It was a startling daydream that was hard to dismiss.

We said goodbye, she hugged me again, and I watched her leave, walking away in the spiky high heels as easily as some people walk in tennis shoes.

* * *

Later that Monday, at 1:47 p.m., my phone rang. That was when I realized that not only had Quinn not come by to take me out for lunch, but I'd forgotten about eating lunch entirely.

The incoming number wasn't programmed into my contact list. It came up as PRIVATE CALLER.

My stomach grumbled. I wanted food, not another distraction. I was tempted to let the call go to voicemail, but I knew it could be an investigation client, and I did need to grow my business. In a town as small as Misty Falls, investigation cases didn't grow on trees.

I answered with a professional, "This is Stormy Day."

There was no response except for heavy breathing. "Hello?"

More heavy breathing.

I was about to end the call when a trembling female voice came through. "Stormy? It's me. Samantha."

I took in a deep breath and steeled myself to deal with another of Samantha's crises of confidence. From the sound of it, she was crying. Again. How could I have made her cry? I'd been safely in my office all day, having no contact with the outside world except for with the wholesales department at our scented-candle supplier.

"Samantha, tell me what I can do for you," I said gently.

"Is Logan there with you?" Her tone sounded robotic and urgent at the same time.

"No. Logan's not here. I'm at the gift shop. What's wrong, Samantha?"

"Michael," she said, and she started to say more, but it broke off into a sob.

"Did he hit you?" I put together a scenario instantly. "Listen, Samantha. Stay where you are. Tell me your location and I'll be there as soon as I can to pick you up. We can go to the police station and make a report."

"What?" More sobbing.

"Never mind the details. Where are you?"

She gave me the address. It was the house she was trying to sell, the one we'd been to the open house for on Saturday.

"Stay right there," I said. "I'm on my way."

I grabbed my purse and ran toward the back door, calling out to Brianna that I was dashing out to help a friend. She yelled back something about the candle order but I kept going. Samantha's phone call had me riled. I'd heard the woman upset before. This was different.

I drove fast enough to get a speeding ticket—if they'd caught me, which they didn't.

When I got to the house, I found Samantha Sweet trembling and incoherent.

Now I understood why she'd sounded so strange on the phone.

She was covered in blood, yet she had no wounds.

CHAPTER 12

Samantha's white blazer was smeared with blood. Her skirt and legs had only minor transfer stains. I got her to take the ruined blazer off so I could check her for injuries. As I expected, the blood hadn't come from her.

She didn't say a word to me.

I put through a second call to Logan, telling his voicemail it was urgent, and then I called 9-1-1.

Samantha swayed on her feet, as though she could fall over in a strong gust of wind. I led her over to the home's small dining room and sat her on a wooden chair. She folded her bloodied hands neatly on her lap.

After a minute, she spoke softly, asking me about Logan, muttering, "He's a lawyer, right? I think I need a lawyer. That's what they always tell you." She continued rambling incoherently.

I held the phone away from my mouth and told her Logan would be there soon.

Samantha looked up at me and right through me with an eerie emptiness.

"Everything's going to be okay," I told her.

The woman on the phone asked me to speak up and clarify the nature of my emergency. I gave the dispatcher on the other end of the call as much information as I could, as I ascertained it.

"There's a woman here, Samantha Sweet, and she's got blood on her clothes, but no injuries that I can see."

Samantha's eyes flickered at her name and went blank again. The dispatcher asked more questions.

"No, she hasn't told me what happened, but I'm looking around now." I patted Samantha on the shoulder and ventured into the other parts of the house. When I'd arrived, she'd been standing inside the front doorway. I told the dispatcher, "I can see one set of bloody footprints coming down the stairs. The footprints match the shoes that Samantha is wearing. It looks like the source of blood is upstairs."

The voice on the line continued, but the words blurred together as though she was speaking another language. I swallowed and closed my eyes, which didn't help. I opened my eyes and found the room was swimming. Time pulled away and stretched out.

"Yes, the source of the blood is upstairs," I repeated.

The dispatcher said more words. I struggled to stay present.

Upstairs.

This moment felt so much like the time I'd discovered a con artist dead in her rented home. The self-styled fortune-teller hadn't been able to foresee the future after all. She'd been shot by someone she knew well, with an antique pistol borrowed from the Koenig Estate. I'd stumbled across the scene in her house not long after the incident. Her blood was still warm. And as I walked through her house, the killer may have been watching me.

Was it happening all over again? No, it couldn't be. The killer had been caught and jailed. Logan still had the scars from the confrontation.

"Ma'am," came the voice over the phone line. "Are you still there?"

"Barely," I said. "I just realized something. I need to secure the premises."

"Ma'am, please stay by the front door to let in the paramedics."

"I left the door open," I said.

She protested my plan, suggesting instead I go outside and wait on the sidewalk with neighbors, but I ignored her. I headed up the stairs, stepping along the side of the staircase to avoid treading through Samantha's bloody shoe prints.

I tucked the phone into my pocket without switching it off. I slowly opened my purse and pulled out some personal self-defense items. I'd gotten in the habit of being over-prepared, with more goodies than hands. I selected my top two picks from my EDC. First there was the *kubotan*, also known as a ninja spike, that connected to my keychain. Second, and relatively new to my kit, was the monkey ball, a steel ball bearing wrapped in a cord.

They say the safest fight is *the one you run away from*. I had every intention of running if someone scary jumped out at me, but I could still run with a kubotan in my hand. I carefully wrapped my fingers around the base of the spiky object some people referred to as the "attitude adjuster." I'd only practiced striking a dummy, but the concept was simple: introduce the pointy end to something bony, fleshy, or sensitive.

Feeling just a teensy bit like a ninja, I reached the upper floor.

"Hello," I called out. "The police are on their way now."

I held steady, listening for signs of movement.

The upper part of the house was still. It felt empty, yet not empty.

The air was moist.

A tap was dripping.

I could hear Samantha downstairs, still rambling semi-coherently to herself. I wanted to sit beside her and be a source of comfort, but there'd be no comfort if an assailant was still in the home.

I checked the first bedroom, where I'd seen Samantha talking with Colt two days earlier. Empty.

Second bedroom. Empty.

The lack of closets made the home a tough sell with home buyers, but it did speed up my search.

In the silence, a small, tinny voice called out. "Ma'am?"

I wheeled around, ready to stab with my ninja stick, strike with my monkey balls, or run.

There was nobody behind me.

"Ma'am? Are you still there?"

As my heart rate settled down, I realized the tinny voice was the 9-1-1 dispatcher trying to talk to me on the phone, which I'd put on speaker mode.

"I'm still here," I said loudly. "Just have to check the bathroom. That's the room with the bloody footprints leaving it." I cursed under my breath. "And the door is closed. Of course."

The dispatcher said, "Ma'am, did you say bloody footprints? Ma'am, do not go into that room."

"The footprints are coming out," I said. "Someone might be hurt in there."

"Are they calling out for assistance?"

"No."

"Ma'am, you should go wait outside, with a neighbor." After some heavy breathing, she broke away from her script. "Lady, you need to get outta that house! Use your head, girl! If I walk in some place and see bloody footprints, I'm gonna bust my way out, not keep goin' in!"

"Well, I'm here already," I said bravely.

I pulled a fresh handkerchief from my purse and delicately turned the door handle

I kicked the door open with my toe and then took a few steps back. If someone had been trapped in the room and wanted to escape, they could do it right past me rather than through me.

Nobody ran out.

The only sound was water dripping.

I steadied myself and looked in.

There was a man lying in the tub, staring lifelessly back at me.

Michael Sweet.

Someone had stabbed him.

Someone had stabbed him *a whole bunch of times*.

CHAPTER 13

"Stormy Day, don't talk to me like I'm a bonehead. You know a heck of a lot more than you're saying."

Officer Peggy Wiggles gave me one of her no-nonsense looks, her cobalt-blue eyes piercing into me.

I tore my gaze away and looked out the passenger-side window. We were sitting in her police car, parked in front of the house where I'd discovered Michael Sweet's body an hour earlier. The whole team had swarmed the house. Crime scene investigators had fastened yellow crime-scene tape to the base of the home's For Sale sign and encircled the yard.

"Taping off the yard seems excessive," I said. "Poor Samantha will never be able to sell this house."

"She should have considered that before she killed her husband."

I whipped my head around to face the officer. Peggy Wiggles looked as serious as her name was playful. The woman was in her early fifties, and she was a rookie cop—as new to the badge as she was to the town of Misty Falls, but she brought with her a wealth of life experience. She and I sported the same sensible short haircut, though hers had blond highlights mixed with gray. Her angular face shape was rarely softened with a smile, except when she was talking about her cat. That Monday afternoon, she was not in the mood to talk about her cat.

"Samantha wouldn't hurt a fly," I said. "Or even a spider. I've seen her use a sheet of paper to pick up a spider and take it outside."

"Did a spider give her that bruise on her eye?"

I answered her question with a question. "Have there been reports of domestic violence?"

"You tell me," she returned coolly.

I glanced out the passenger window again, watching the crime scene investigators perform a grid search of the home's entryway.

"I can tell you Samantha didn't kill her husband."

"Oh? How can you be so certain? Did you volunteer to kill him for her?"

I whipped my head back again. There was a trace of amusement in her piercing cobalt-blue eyes. She might not enjoy having another homicide in town, but she was getting a kick out of rattling my chain. It was the kind of dark-humored ribbing that police officers gave each other. I decided to take her accusation as a compliment. Back in February, I'd served as her right hand at the Flying Squirrel Resort, when the mountain pass had been blocked by a snowstorm.

"Hang on," Officer Wiggles said. "If you're going to confess to being a hit woman, I should probably write something down." She held her finger in the air while she pulled out a notepad and pen with her other hand. "Now, how much did she pay you?"

"Very funny," I said. "It's good to see that working under Tony Baloney hasn't destroyed your sense of humor yet."

"He tries," she said plainly. "Now, what makes you so sure Samantha didn't snap and kill her husband?"

"The smell of bleach," I said.

"I'm listening. Tell me more about the bleach."

"I didn't notice it at first. You know how panic shuts off some of your senses. It wasn't until I heard the sirens that I smelled the bleach. I found the home's washing machine, which is in a closet on the main level, and I very carefully opened it, using the edge of the lid plus my handkerchief."

She shook her head. "You can't go tampering with a crime scene like that."

"Fine. Get people in this town to stop killing each other and I'll stop touching things in crime scenes."

She waved her hand impatiently. "Go on."

"The owners of the house are out of town, but there was a wet load of laundry in the machine. The load had finished a thirty-minute cycle before I arrived, but it was still wet. It reeked of bleach, and the only thing in the load appeared to be men's clothes. A shirt, a pair of jeans, socks, and underwear. The killer tried to destroy evidence by washing everything."

"We don't know that," Wiggles said. "Michael could have tossed his clothes in the wash before he took a shower."

"Don't be sexist," I said with a twisted smile. "Even a man as dumb as Michael would know not to put a bunch of bleach in with dark clothes. I didn't pull the jeans out, but I bet they were ruined."

"And the bleach did a good job of removing evidence," she said with a sigh.

"We're looking for a scary, cool-headed killer."

"Cool as a cucumber."

"Exactly," I said. "Which completely rules out poor Samantha. She's a blubbering mess. She wouldn't have had the presence of mind to put in a load of laundry and then get blood all over her hands and call me. Not unless she was a devious criminal mastermind. She's a hard worker, but she's no mastermind."

"They never are," she said flatly. "I'm sure your thoughtful testimony of Mrs. Sweet's innocence has nothing to do with her being a friend of yours. I'll just make a note in my book here that we shouldn't bother looking into her alibi or motives, since you vouch for her."

"I'm just trying to help."

"If you really wanted to help, you'd tell me who killed the guy. Who hated Michael Sweet enough to stab him in the chest and neck twenty-three times?"

"Twenty-three stabs?"

"Plus a few slashes." She paused to wave at Captain Tony Milano, who was staring at us through the windshield. He nodded back, pointed his finger at me accusingly, and walked away.

Officer Wiggles shifted in the driver's seat, her utility belt and equipment squeaking with her movements. She watched and waited for Tony to disappear into the house before she spoke again.

"Stormy, I do have your discretion, right? This information I'm providing is not for public consumption. We'll keep these details out of the news."

"I counted twenty-five stabs."

"Of course you did." She sighed. "Well, we're done here. I trust you'll give me a call when you're ready to ambush the killer with one of your devious little whodunit schemes. You can take all the glory and leave us dumb cops scrambling to get some real evidence that the district attorney won't throw out while laughing hysterically."

"Nope," I said. "This has nothing to do with me." I summoned up a phrase I'd been repeating to myself recently as a mantra. "If I'm not getting paid, it's not my case, and if it's not my case, it's not my business."

"How much do you charge for five minutes? I'll hire you now, and you can cough up whatever it is you're not telling me."

That again. She was a good cop, and she wasn't wrong. I did know something I hadn't shared. Namely that the most obvious suspect was Colt Canuso.

"I would never obstruct justice," I said. "If I knew who killed Michael Sweet, I'd tell you."

"You have a theory, don't you?"

True, I had some suspicions, but the killer hadn't exactly left a calling card. "Officer Wiggles, I was in the house maybe twenty minutes before you showed up. I looked over the body, and I peeked into the washing machine downstairs. That's it."

"That's it?" Her cobalt-blue eyes remained steady. "If you know more, spit it out now so I don't have to haul your hiney down to the station."

"Don't waste your time with me. I don't know anything." I tried to relax my throat so my voice wasn't squeaky. I also tried not to think about Colt Canuso, and where he might have been between the time when I'd seen him at Glorious Gifts and the time Michael Sweet got himself stabbed between twenty-three and twenty-five times.

Wiggles narrowed her eyes and clenched her angular jaw. "No, I suppose twenty minutes wasn't enough time to do much investigating. But it's a good thing we got here as quickly as we did, before you could start your autopsy on the victim."

I had to laugh. "A visual inspection of a body is not the same as an autopsy."

With a casual tone, she asked, "How long had the victim been dead when you arrived on the scene?"

I cleared my throat. "How would I know?"

"Stormy."

She had me. "Based on temperature, I'd say about two hours."

"Do I want to know how you took his temperature?"

"Probably not." I fidgeted with the strap of my purse.

She eyed my purse. "You keep a meat thermometer in that bag of yours?"

"No." I shook my head. "But the homeowners, like most people, keep a thermometer in their bathroom vanity."

"Please *tell me* you didn't stick the thermometer into one of the stab wounds."

I blinked innocently.

She shook her head.

I asked, "Was it fast? Did he die quickly?"

"What do you think?"

"I didn't see very much blood on the walls of that tiny bathroom. Some spray from the blade, but it seemed he went down without much of a fight."

"The killer got lucky and nicked some major arteries. There would have been a hell of a lot more blood on the scene if he hadn't been stabbed in the tub."

"He was killed in the tub? Not transferred there?"

She looked away from me and started rubbing her temples. She muttered, "Why am I telling all this stuff to you? Milano's going to bite me on the hiney."

"Peggy," I said softly. "Am I still allowed to call you Peggy?"

She kept rubbing her temples. "I don't know. Are you going to tell me who stabbed Michael Sweet?"

"I want to cooperate with the investigation, I really do. But I don't want to be responsible for ruining the lives of innocent people who may or may not be involved."

"One name," she said. "Give me one person to look into."

"Start with Samantha. Rule her out first and see if she has any ideas."

Wiggles leaned to the side with a squeak and pulled her phone from her pocket. "Want to see something cute?"

"Is it cute enough to wash away the image of Michael Sweet dead in a bathtub?"

"Temporarily, yes. This is what Peekaboo has gotten into."

She set a slideshow of cat pictures running and handed me the phone.

Peekaboo was a well-fed orange tabby with hypnotic orange eyes. He'd been a scrawny rescue kitten when Officer Peggy Wiggles had adopted him, before she moved to Oregon and joined the Misty Falls Police Department. The little guy had been skittish, almost feral, and spent the first few weeks hiding in tiny spaces and burrowing into piles of laundry.

Peekaboo was no longer the tiny orange bit of fluff that Peggy had to be careful not to dump into the washing machine. But his cat brain hadn't gotten the memo that he now weighed close to twenty pounds and didn't fit into small shoeboxes.

I giggled at the images of chubby Peekaboo trying to fit himself into a series of smaller containers. The final three photos were Peekaboo sitting on a kitchen table wearing a square Chinese-food takeout container as a helmet.

"That cat is a superstar," I said. "I'd suggest a play date between him and Jeffrey, but with all that cuteness in one place at the same time, it might cause a rift in the space-time continuum."

"Plus they'd just hiss at each other."

"True," I said. "Jeffrey is not very fond of other creatures encroaching on his kingdom, unless they have two hands for petting."

"Pictures?"

"I thought you'd never ask." I pulled out my phone and showed her pictures of Jeffrey Blue's recent antics. "He's stopped drinking out of the toilet," I said. "We put a big bowl of water on the edge of the tub, and he prefers that, as long as it's fresh. *Really fresh.* You have to fill his bowl with cold water while he's watching you, so he knows it's fresh. And it has to be right up to the brim."

"Peekaboo has a fountain. It's actually nice to have a running water feature inside the house." She turned her head and looked up at the house.

Officer Kyle Dempsey, also known as Dimples, was adjusting the yellow crime-scene tape strung across the front porch. He saw us looking and gave us a wave. The expression on his face was so serious that none of his infamous dimples were showing.

"So?" Officer Peggy Wiggles turned to face me again. "Are you going to give me a name or two?"

"Have a look at the visitor log from Saturday's open house," I said. "Samantha found a strange man in the kitchen, holding a big knife. He claimed to be cutting a tiny cupcake in half, but it sounded fishy to me."

She grinned. "There. Was that so difficult?"

I smiled back at her. Actually, it had been difficult. Since the moment I'd seen Michael Sweet's lifeless body, I'd been thinking about my friend Colt, and how bad the situation looked for him. A lot of people had witnessed him punching Michael Sweet on Saturday and threatening him. It was a small miracle that Officer Wiggles hadn't yet learned of that altercation.

Or did she already know? Had she invited me to sit in the car with her as a means of softly breaking me?

Had I accidentally incriminated my friend? By *not* mentioning him as a name for her to look into, had I all but driven the investigation straight at him?

"You've really been a big help," Wiggles said, still grinning.

"Oh, I wouldn't say that," I said. "You aren't looking for a cupcake killer, and that's all I've given you."

"Actually, it's more about what you haven't given me," she said. "I know all about what happened at the casino on the weekend."

A thousand swear words went off in my head at the same time. She did have Colt as a suspect.

I gave her a weak smile. "Everyone loves frolicking in a water fountain."

"One more thing," she said. "An alarm reminder came up on Mrs. Sweet's phone. Somebody needs to pick her daughter up from school and the baby from daycare."

I stammered, "A-a-and you think that somebody should be me?"

"Just until other arrangements have been made."

I felt a heavy thud in my guts, like I'd been punched. "Poor Sadie."

"Her name is Sophie."

"Poor Sophie. Someone needs to tell that girl her father's dead."

"Can you keep her calm and entertained until her mother can tell her?"

"I'm not great with kids."

"You're great with people. Kids are just people," she said, and she gave me the address of Sophie's school.

CHAPTER 14

I had only met Samantha and Michael's daughter, Sophie, a handful of times. I'd accidentally called her Sadie or Sofia or even Sammy Junior on a few occasions. The last one had been intentional, but she'd acted mortally wounded. I wondered, would she even recognize me, let alone get into my car?

This was exactly the kind of Stranger Danger scenario that we, as a society, educate our children about. I'd never expected to be on this side of a potential learning lesson. Normally, if a stranger, or even a vaguely familiar acquaintance, gets sent to pick a kid up after school, saying there's been an emergency involving the child's parent, there's supposed to be a password. But I didn't know Samantha and Michael's password, assuming they had one.

If little Sophie Sweet had good sense, she'd turn right around as soon as I approached, and go straight to the principal's office to report me for attempted child abduction. Then the police would be called in, except they wouldn't be available, due to the small matter of the town's latest homicide.

What I wanted to avoid was another phone call to the Misty Falls Police Department, not to mention further traumatizing the poor child who didn't yet know she'd lost her father.

I approached the girl's school and followed the signs directing parents to the pickup area.

I parked my car and quickly checked myself for blood. I'd been cautious around the body, but

Samantha had already gotten Michael's blood smeared all over herself before I'd shown up, and she had grasped my hand and arm a few times.

It turned out I did have blood on me, on the edge of my shirt sleeve. I swallowed down my revulsion and quickly rolled up both my sleeves. *Is this just normal for me now? Seeing corpses and casually checking myself for transfer stains?*

Other than the wave of queasiness I'd felt upon seeing the blood on my sleeve, I'd been feeling okay, considering. I hadn't even been sick at the crime scene. It certainly helped that I'd skipped lunch and didn't have any stomach contents to throw up. But I did wonder, was this part of the change other people saw in me?

I pushed open my car door and stepped out into the afternoon sunshine. It was the first week of October now. We'd been having such a mild autumn, it felt as though summer had been extended indefinitely. A cool breeze made the trees next to the school rustle peacefully.

What a perfect day to abduct a small child, I thought darkly.

I scanned the playground for Sophie and spotted a familiar face by the swings. It wasn't until I reached the swing set that I realized the little girl wasn't Sophie. She was Quinby, the daughter of Chip and Quinn. On the plus side, at least she knew who I was and could vouch for me to her best friend.

"Hi, Q," I said, waving. "Sophie's mother sent me to pick her up."

"You're late," Quinby said, her expression serious. "Sophie decided to walk home." She jumped off the swing and twirled around the support post.

"Oh?" I turned and looked around for signs of Sophie.

With a tattletale tone, Quinby said, "It's not the first time her mom has forgotten her, you know."

"Is that so? How often does Mrs. Sweet forget?"

Quinby rolled her eyes. "All the time. My mom says she's not the sharpest knife in the pack. Or is it the roundest marble?" Quinby wrinkled her small brow. "I can't remember, but what I'm trying to tell you is my mom says she's stupid."

The pint-sized future head cheerleader twirled once more around the support post then returned to the swing. She parked her butt on the U-shaped seat, walked it back, and kicked off swinging. The squeak-squeak of the chain supports made me long for carefree younger days.

"It's not very nice to call someone stupid," I said.

"What if it's true?" She grinned, showing her perfect teeth. Darn it if she didn't look angelic, despite insulting my adult friend.

"You know, it's not your fault you're this way. That sounds exactly like something your mother would say. She used to call me lazy."

Quinby pumped her legs, swinging higher and higher. "You're not lazy. My mom says you're busy." The chains on the swing squeaked as though in protest as she soared high above my head. "Busy, busy, busy. You're a real *busybody*."

"She's not wrong," I said, turning to leave. "Tell your mother I said hello."

Quinby abruptly launched herself out of the swing and landed beside me. "Tell her yourself." She grabbed my hand and tugged me back toward the parking lot. "She's standing over there staring at us like a weirdo. Maybe she has to use the bathroom. She has the ABS. Angry Bum Syndrome."

Quinn McCabe was up ahead, standing next to a Range Rover. When she saw us looking her way, she waved and quickly turned around to open the vehicle's rear door.

"Q, I think you mean IBS. Irritable Bowel Syndrome."

"No, Stormy, it's called ABS. It means you get to yell at people if they don't let you use the staff washroom. Angry Bum Syndrome."

"You learn something new every day," I said as we reached the parking lot and her mother. "Hello again, Quinn. Funny how we haven't seen each other in a decade, and now we've bumped into each other twice in one day."

She buttoned her oversized sweater over her little black dress. She crossed her arms over her stomach and looked at me while lifting her upper lip in a chipmunk gesture that reminded me of her mail carrier husband, Chip.

Her eyes had a glazed-over appearance. "Twice in one day?" Her head tilted forward slowly and then jerked up again. "Oh! We were supposed to have lunch. Stormy, I'm so sorry. I got so busy, and I forgot to come see you." She patted her daughter's blond head. "I got busy with important meetings for Q's career. We have to get head shots and a website. I'll make it up to you, I swear. I'll buy you lunch at the best place in town."

"Don't worry about it," I said. "It's been a crazy day, and it was for the best I didn't eat lunch, as it turns out."

"Oh?" She raised one eyebrow and grinned. "Have you got any hot gossip for me?"

"Not today, Quinn."

Her daughter looked up at her. "Mom, I told Stormy about ABS. She didn't know what it meant."

All the color went out of Quinn's face. She pulled the front of her cardigan tight across her front and hissed at her daughter, "Sweetheart, we don't discuss these things outside the family."

Quinby made two small fists and stomped her foot. "There are so many secrets, I can't keep track of all of them!"

"Kids," Quinn said to me with a twisted smile. "When are you going to start popping some out?" She squinted at my midsection. "In about six months?"

"Ha ha." Luckily, my cycle had been regular so she didn't scare me. I backed away, toward my car. "I'm really sorry but I have to run. I'm picking up Sadie on behalf of Samantha. I mean Sofia. Er, Sophie. Do you have any idea what street she would have started walking down?"

Quinn looked over her shoulder, eastward. "I have a good idea where she'll be. You can go home,

Stormy. I'll pick her up myself. Is Samantha at the house?"

"Long story, but I'll be getting Sophie."

She uncrossed her arms and bunched up the front of her sweater. It was a men's sweater, dark gray, and quite bulky for such a warm afternoon.

"What's going on?" She opened the back door of the vehicle and ushered her daughter into the seat. She closed the door and whispered, "Does it have something to do with those two security goons from the casino? I saw them skulking around downtown. The big one and the bigger one."

"What makes you say that?"

She shrugged. "I don't mean to be prejudiced, but some of those people Colt has working for him are super sketchy. A lot of them have criminal records and can't get work anywhere else."

"Good to know," I said. "Which street would Sophie have taken? I really should go. Even in Misty Falls, a little girl shouldn't be on her own at a time like this."

"That street." Quinn turned and pointed. "Then left on Laurel and right on Gumdrop."

I thanked her and jogged toward my car. I kept my face calm, but on the inside I had a new thing to panic about.

Quinn was a snob, but she'd still given me some valuable information. Two of Colt's security guards had been seen in town today.

My small list of suspects had doubled. There was Colt, the stranger who'd been cutting a cupcake, and now the two security guards. Samantha wasn't on my list, no matter what the statistics said about homicide by spouse.

CHAPTER 15

I found Sophie a third of the way to her house. She had her pink backpack strapped on and was dawdling along in no particular hurry. When she slowly turned to look in my direction, I was reminded of my sister, Sunny, at that age. She'd always been the slowpoke, stopping to smell every flower or to "rescue" snails by helping them cross the sidewalk.

Had my sister and I ever been as small as eight-year-old Sophie, with her dainty pink shoes and her child-sized backpack? It didn't seem possible.

I pulled the car over, jumped out, and jogged up to the sidewalk with a friendly smile. Sophie barely noticed me. I knelt before her on the sidewalk and delivered the speech I'd been preparing on the drive, about how her mother really had sent me, but I didn't know the family password, yet I wasn't a stranger because I'd been to their house before and she'd shown me her butterfly collection and so forth.

She cut me off. "You're Stormy Day," she said. "Everyone knows who you are."

"Everyone?"

"Duh." She flashed me a charmingly crooked, gap-toothed smile. Jessica was right about Sophie Sweet having some steep dentist bills in her future.

She looked at my car. "Your car's dirty. Can I write my name on the dust?"

"No. You'll scratch the paint."

"No, I won't." She ran at my vehicle with her finger outstretched. Again, I was reminded of my sister. Sunny used to draw snails and flowers on dusty cars, which was how I learned about the tiny scratches such activities left.

She finished drawing a smiling sun on the door.

I let her admire her work before I grabbed the door handle for the passenger side and opened the door. "Sophie, it's a masterpiece. Now get in the car so I can drive you home. We'll find some art supplies at your house and have a craft night. How would you like that?"

"You're going to kill me," she said ominously.

I laughed self-consciously, unsure if I could believe my ears. "What makes you say that?"

"The airbags are in the front," she said. "I have to ride in the backseat until I'm twelve years old, and *then* I can ride in the front with the grownups."

"Oh." I clicked the button to tilt the seat forward. "I knew that," I said defensively. "Get in the back and buckle up." With a professional air, I said, "Your safety is my top priority." I put my hand under her backpack as she wiggled her way in.

I closed the door and circled around to the driver's side, glancing around to see if anyone was watching. *Way to look guilty*, I told myself.

I got in and started the car. In the stillness, I realized my heart was pounding, and I felt the first signs of dehydration. I made eye contact with Sophie in the rearview mirror. "How are you doing back there?"

"I'm hungry. Can we get fries at the drive-through?"

My first instinct was to say no, but then I remembered the sight of Sophie's father, Michael Sweet, lifeless in the tub at a client's house. Sophie would never have to see that, but she'd hear about it, and she'd think about it. Her imagined version could be just as terrible as what I'd seen.

Now what? I wanted to get out of the car again and hold her in my arms, hug her and tell her that this day would pass. This life-changing moment would always stay with her, but it would get smaller and smaller with each new experience. Even though it wouldn't feel possible, someday she would smile again. She would be okay, even happy.

But the kid barely knew me, and the last thing she needed right now was for me to start crying. I clenched my jaw and fought my emotions back down again, down into a little box.

"Fries at the drive-through," I mused. Right on cue, my stomach growled. The last thing I'd ingested had been a vanilla latte, and that had been hours and hours ago.

"And chicken nuggets," Sophie said. "Because I'm a vegetarian."

I smiled at her in the rearview mirror. "Sophie, chicken nuggets aren't vegetarian."

She made an exasperated sound. "When we go to the drive-through, that's when I don't have to be vegetarian, because the meat's already cooked."

"Ah," I said. "Now I understand. Totally." *Kid logic.*

I checked to make sure she had her seat belt on, and we drove to the fast-food place.

Misty Falls doesn't have a McDonald's, but it does have a Goodie Burger.

We ordered fries and chicken nuggets, plus milkshakes and a burger. I was really hungry.

While we ate in the car on a side street, Sophie told me more about her personal vegetarian rules.

"Bacon is not vegetarian," she said. "It comes from a pig. Did you know that?"

"I may have heard that before."

"Same with sausages." She made a world-weary sigh. "All the most delicious meats come from a pig. But not a guinea pig. Not in this country."

"Good to know." I dipped my chicken nugget into the container of honey mustard sauce we'd been sharing.

Sophie squealed, "Double Dipper!"

"That doesn't count," I said. "I turned it around, so it was the bread-crumb side that I dipped."

"My dad is a Double Dipper," she said. "Mom says he does it just to be gross and make everyone mad at him. He thinks it's funny."

"Does your dad do a lot of funny things around the house? To make people mad?"

"Not really." She didn't elaborate, but she did watch my next nugget dip like a hawk.

"This is fun," I said. "I don't usually let people eat in my car, but this is fun."

Sophie let out a big burp, and we both laughed.

"That's my stomach saying thank you for the food," she said.

"Better your stomach than your butt."

Her eyes widened, and she made a gasping sound. I panicked, thinking she was choking on a fry or having an asthma attack. But then she started laughing.

It turns out that, to an eight-year-old, there are few things in this world funnier than a grownup saying the word butt.

Her laughter cheered me up so much that by the time we wiped away our tears, the guilt I felt about what was yet to come was crushing.

* * *

Our next stop was picking up the baby, her little brother, from the daycare.

As soon as I picked up the kid, I realized I didn't have a safety car seat in my vehicle.

The woman at the daycare assured me it wasn't the first time it had happened. Parents sometimes sent friends to pick up kids. Luckily, the daycare had some loaner car seats.

She offered to help me get everything set up in my car.

"Michael has been a good boy today," the woman said as I unlocked the car doors.

Michael? I was thrown off by the name for a second, then I remembered the baby was Michael Junior. Samantha usually referred to him simply as the baby.

We got the borrowed car seat as well as Michael Junior into my vehicle.

The woman spotted the fast-food bags from Goodie Burger and gave me a judgy look.

"It was just for today," I said. "Things are topsy-turvy." She continued the judgy look. "It was Sophie's idea," I said. "Right Sophie?"

I turned to see Sophie pick up a loose fry from the floor and eat it.

The daycare lady gave me a grim look. "Tell Michael Senior I hope he had a great day on the green."

"On the green?"

"Golfing," she said slowly, as though I was not very bright. "That's what it means when you're *on the green*."

I smiled politely. I knew what she meant but had been surprised to hear of Michael's plans for the day. If he'd been scheduled to golf, how had he ended up at the house?

"Yes, golfing," I said. "It's certainly a nice day for being outside." I glanced around guiltily. This wasn't my investigation or my business, but I couldn't help myself. "Did you chat with Michael very long this morning?"

"Just a few minutes, when he dropped off Junior. He was meeting some business contacts at the Misty Pines and playing golf all day." She picked at a fleck of dried vomit on her shirt. "Must be nice!"

"Are you sure he said he was playing golf today?" I looked at the daycare's open door, which was letting out all manner of chaotic sounds. "Things can get a bit hectic with so many kids around."

The woman frowned at me. "I have an excellent memory. You need to be on the ball when you're responsible for this many children. Mr. Sweet was golfing today at the Misty Pines, all day."

Except he wasn't, I thought.

I thanked her again and got into my car. She hadn't asked for identification. Having the older sibling with me had been enough proof of my legitimacy, as far as she was concerned.

The baby made some fussy noises, but his big sister knew how to get him settled.

Good, I thought. *Samantha will need all the help she can get.*

I wanted to call Officer Wiggles right away with the information about Michael's planned day of golfing, but I couldn't do it in front of the children.

CHAPTER 16

We got into the Sweet residence without needing to use a key.

I poked my head in, while holding Michael Junior. The interior of the house smelled like an active family lived there—not bad, but it was the general sort of "lived in" smell Samantha tried to get rid of in the homes she was showing.

The furnace wasn't running, and the house was quiet. Maybe too quiet. The skin on the back of my neck prickled.

The front room looked disheveled, with cereal strewn across the coffee table and sofa cushions jutting out at messy angles. Was this how the home normally looked, or had someone been ransacking the place, looking for something?

Whoever killed Michael Sweet could be there now, waiting inside the house.

I hesitated in the doorway and asked Sophie, "Do you always leave your front door unlocked?"

Sophie strode in past me and raised her hands in the air. "How should I know?" She tossed her pink backpack and her purple jacket on the floor, a mere foot away from an array of child-height clothes hooks on the wall.

I shifted the baby to my other arm so I could pick up her gear and hang it on the hooks. "Sophie, didn't your parents teach you to hang up your things? When I was your age, my sister and I got banned from using the front door. We had to come in through the back door and hang our stuff in the porch. My sister used to—"

Sophie interrupted. "Can I watch a movie?"

The baby clamped onto my ear with one hand while attempting to poke out my eyeball with the other.

"Sure," I said, and I got her set up on the couch with her movie playing. "Is this the way your living room normally looks?"

She stared at the TV and didn't answer.

I tried to put the baby down on the couch next to her, but he clung to me like he was made of Velcro.

Over the sound of the television, I could hear a scratching noise. I lowered the volume. It was coming from somewhere inside the house.

For a second time, I tried to put the baby down. He screamed like a banshee. I picked him up, and the screaming stopped immediately, like a tap being shut off.

"Neat trick," I told him. "I guess I'm stuck with you. Or, rather, you're stuck to me, Mr. Velcro."

He lunged for my ear happily.

The scratching noise started up again.

"Sophie, do you guys have a dog?"

She didn't answer until I used the remote control to pause the show. I repeated the question.

"Mom says we're not allowed until I'm twelve and I'm more responsible."

"Then do you have a cat?"

"Dad says cats are disgusting because they poop inside the house."

"Uh, humans poop inside the house, too, Sophie."

She covered her crooked-toothed-smile with her hands and giggled. "I made you say poop."

"Humans go to the washroom inside the house."

"No, they don't," she said matter-of-factly. "They go in the toilet." Without taking her eyes off the paused cartoon princess on the TV screen, she reached in between the sofa cushions, pulled something out—a granola bar—and started eating it. She'd eaten a huge meal in my car, and she wasn't a big girl. Where the heck was she putting all the food? It had to be some sort of child magic.

"Anyway, dad says cats are gross," she said.

"Your dad is wrong, as usual, because cats are awesome."

She took her gaze off the screen and turned to me, still munching the sofa granola. "My dad is wrong?"

Oops. Now that I did have her attention, I wanted her to go back to her movie. I clicked the button to get the movie playing again.

While I was leaning over, the baby arched his back without warning, pulling away from me and pushing me off-balance. I quickly shifted my center of gravity to get under him. He ricocheted off nothing but air and gave me a solid head butt, right on the side of my face.

I actually saw stars—spots of light in my vision.

Sophie laughed. "He does that."

"Michael Junior hits people in the face with his head?"

"All the time."

I turned to the little guy and asked, "Is that true? Are you the big brute who tried to give your mommy a black eye?" Michael Junior gave me an innocent look while cramming his fingers into his tiny nostrils.

Sophie was engrossed in her show again.

I walked over to the living room's front window. The baby was getting heavier by the minute, but his warmth was soothing, and the top of his head smelled nice—when he wasn't head-butting me with it. Outside, the quiet residential street looked normal enough. I didn't see any suspicious vehicles or people. I got a chill down my back, just thinking about nightfall. It wasn't even five o'clock yet, and it wouldn't be dark for hours, but I closed the curtains and walked around the living room turning on every lamp anyway.

The scratching sound hadn't happened in a while, but I couldn't shake the feeling someone or something was in the house with us.

Maybe mice, I thought. *Or rats.* There was certainly enough loose bits of food around to attract rodents.

I wanted to sit on the couch and keep Sophie company, watching whatever she wanted to watch and eating whatever she wanted to eat, right up until she received the worst news of her young life. But first, I had to secure the premises.

With the baby in one arm and my ninja stick in my other hand, I started a search of the house.

The scratching sound started again.

I actually smelled the culprit before I saw him.

I found him in Sophie's bedroom.

He was a wild-eyed guy, with big front teeth and patchy brown and white hair. He was startled by me pushing open the door, and froze.

Then we just stared at each other, each of us daring the other to make a move.

He squeaked first.

"So, you're a tough guy," I said to him. "What do you weigh? A whopping two pounds?"

The guinea pig flashed his big, scary chompers at me in what appeared to be a knowing smile.

I had only myself to blame. I'd asked Sophie if she had a cat or a dog, but I hadn't specifically asked if she had any other pets.

"Today might be a long day for this family," I said to both the guinea pig and the baby in my arms. Michael Junior stared at my mouth. "A really long day," I said as I sunk down to the floor to sit across from the cage. "You guys have to stick together."

The guinea pig made a noise that sounded like WHEEK!

I looked down at Michael Junior, who wasn't smelling so fresh anymore.

"Neither of you can understand a word I'm saying, but you're still good listeners."

The baby squealed.

The guinea pig went WHEEK!

It would be a long day, for the Sweet family, and for me. At least these two wouldn't understand what was going on. They were the lucky ones.

CHAPTER 17

SUNDAY

(SIX DAYS AFTER MURDER)

"A guinea pig," my father said. "The scratching intruder was a guinea pig?"

"His name is Higgins," I said. "After the British sergeant major on Magnum P.I."

My father took a sip of his cheap beer and then licked his lips. In a near-perfect English accent, he replied, "Stormy, I know very well who Jonathan Quayle Higgins is."

"That's a good accent," I said. "Almost as convincing as your Irish."

"Says the woman who was terrified by a guinea pig."

I laughed. "In all fairness to me, Higgins is a really big guinea pig. Over two pounds."

Finnegan Day grinned. "Glad to see you can laugh at yourself." He lifted his can of beer. "A good laugh and a long sleep are the two best cures." He nodded at the six-pack of beer on the kitchen table. "Go ahead."

I pulled a can from the beer package and cracked it open. I clinked my can to his and took a sip. It wasn't bad.

"Heaven help me," I said. "I'm starting to enjoy the taste of your cheap beer. How much was this? Or do they pay you to take it away?"

"If that's not good enough for your refined palate, Dimples left some of his fancy bottles in the fridge."

"This'll be fine," I said with a grimace. "When was Dimples over?"

My father raised an eyebrow. "Since when do you care?"

"Dad, I know Kyle Dempsey tells you everything that's going on at the department. And I also know he's over here two times a week, minimum. And since it's been nearly seven days since someone made shish kebab out of Michael Sweet, that covers at least one visit, if not two. You're as up to date on the Sweet homicide as anyone."

"Perhaps not," he said. "Until tonight, I haven't heard a single word about your brave confrontation with a two-pound guinea pig."

"Speaking of confrontation, that kid has a head like a bowling ball. Michael Junior is a regular one-man wrecking crew. He screamed if I set him down, so I had to keep holding him, which was how he was able to do the most damage. He bopped me on the chin, the cheek, and even the side of my eye. I'm lucky he didn't give me a shiner."

As I described the baby's head-butting abilities to my father, he nodded knowingly. "I'm familiar with that particular maneuver. Both you and Sunny got in a few baby love taps on me as well."

"Enough baby talk," I said, and then, "Now there's a phrase I *never* thought I'd be saying, especially not to you."

"Just because the little gaffer caused some bruising, that doesn't mean the husband wasn't taking his fists to the wife as well."

"I know, I know," I said. "But it does provide an alternative story."

"Aye," he said with an accent. *"Aye, it surely does."*

I finished the can of cheap beer and went to the refrigerator to raid the supply left behind by Kyle Dempsey, a.k.a. the cop son my father never had.

"Please catch me up," I implored. "I'm trying to keep my nose out of it, but I'm dying to know. Are they any closer to arresting whoever killed Michael Sweet?"

"They followed up on your tips. They checked out the open house visitor who'd been handling the knives. There were a few men who came through on their own that day. One name in particular stood out. A fellow named Dwayne Efrain Greer. Have you come across him?"

"Dwayne Efrain Greer? Not that I know of. Should I?"

"I'd steer clear. He's not without his issues—a few priors for public indecency and intoxication—but he does have an alibi for Monday. He was up in Seattle on Monday, all day, wrapping up some business. He didn't recall picking up a knife in the kitchen and giving your friend Samantha a scare, but guys with a record get careful about what they admit to."

"But he's totally cleared? He couldn't have killed anyone on Monday?"

"Not in Misty Falls, anyway."

"That's a shame," I said. "It would have been awfully neat and tidy if the killer had signed his name on the guest log."

"And it wouldn't have been the first time," my father said. "Most criminals aren't masterminds." He added, smiling, "As you know."

"How about Michael's meeting at the golf course?"

"He was never there. And there weren't any parties booked who were missing a player. He must have lied to the daycare."

"Why would someone lie about going golfing?"

"Image," he answered. "Most people associate golfing with the rich and well-connected, even though it's more affordable these days. It probably made him feel sophisticated to tell people he was going to be on the green that day."

"The daycare lady did seem in awe of him," I said. "What did the tech guys turn up on his phone and email?"

"There was one text message they found suspicious. What was it now?" He scratched his chin. "It was from a guy named Binky."

"Binky?"

"Something about meeting at the house at eleven o'clock to practice their knife-throwing act for the upcoming Misty Falls Talent Show. Binky the Clown. Binky said he had his knives all sharpened for their act. I told Kyle not to bother with that lead. Clowns never harmed anyone."

"Very funny." I shook my head. It was Finnegan Day's way to never give a straight answer when a circuitous story could be worked into the conversation.

"Clowning is serious business."

"I'm sure it is, Dad. I guess that's your hilarious way of telling me the tech guys found nothing on his accounts?"

He looked down, frowning as he reached for another can of beer. "I'm afraid things don't look so good for your friend Colt."

"No alibi?"

"He said he visited a certain gift shop in town, but his whereabouts are a mystery after that." He slowly looked up and met my eyes. "He needs your help, Stormy."

I leaned back and held my hands out. "I'm just a private investigator. I'm not a homicide detective. The police need to do their job."

"That's not what I meant. You can help by getting Colt to cooperate with the investigation. He lawyered up, and he won't talk about where he really was on Monday morning."

"What about the other two guys? The security guards Quinn saw in town?"

"They're each other's alibis."

"How convenient," I said.

"What do you think happened?"

"He was taking a shower in a client's house when someone came into the tiny upstairs bathroom and killed him. It sure doesn't sound like he startled someone during a robbery."

"It was a crime of passion," my father said. "People shower after sex."

I stared at him. "Yes. I've heard of such things."

"Did you ever...?"

"I hated Michael Sweet in high school."

"There's a fine line between love and hate. Haven't you ever watched a romantic comedy? They always start out hating each other."

"Dad, I've never had any sort of passionate contact with Michael Sweet. The first and only time I saw him naked was after he was dead."

"I know I'm your father, but you can talk to me about anything."

I shook my head. Me and Michael Sweet? "I'm not even going to dignify that with a response."

"How about Colt?"

I looked away quickly, feeling guilty about my dreams.

My father made a knowing sound. He'd caught me.

"He flirted with me the last few times I saw him," I said. "That's all. Just flirting. And if you're picking up on my guilt, it's because I do feel guilty. I enjoyed the attention, and things with Logan have been weird lately."

He coughed into his fist. "The homeowners are cleared. They were, indeed, out of town. Still are."

I fidgeted with my beer's label. My father might talk the talk and tell me I could talk to him about anything, but in reality I couldn't. Whenever I mentioned Logan, he'd change the subject.

"Next theory," he said.

"Michael was sleeping with someone he wasn't supposed to be with—a married person—and their spouse caught them."

"Very good," he said. "That's a valid theory." He paused. "But on the other hand, it might have been a thrill kill." He looked down at the table and swept away some stray crumbs. "You know, the movie *Psycho* comes to mind."

"As it should." I rubbed my chin thoughtfully. "The police need to round up all the local serial killers who run dodgy motels."

After a minute, he asked, "How well do you know Samantha?"

"How well does a person know anyone?" I looked into his eyes. "Sometimes we're sharing a roof with a killer, and we don't even know it."

He didn't react, except to not react at all, which told me a lot.

After a long silence, he said only, "One who lives in the past does not live at all." He pushed his chair back and stood. "Ready for meatloaf?"

CHAPTER 18

MONDAY

ONE WEEK SINCE MURDER

My father might cite *a good laugh and a long sleep* as being the two best cures, but there's nothing quite like the comfort of routine. Or so I hoped. I really wanted to think about something other than a murder investigation.

By Monday morning, a full week since I discovered Michael Sweet's body in his client's tub, I was happy to be heading in to Glorious Gifts nice and early to embrace the routine of working on orders and receiving inventory.

Once I was in the office, I resisted the temptation to snoop around online for clues about the Sweet homicide investigation. I wasn't getting paid to investigate the matter, therefore it wasn't my business. *No money, no worries.* That was my mantra.

I worked on the banking reconciliations for a full ten minutes before I got insanely bored and needed a break. I went out to the front of the store to look at the window display Brianna was changing around. She barely noticed me there, due to being entirely focused on the simple task at hand. Why couldn't I be more like her? She looked so content, in a happy "flow" state, rearranging new tableware on a display table decorated with acorns, pine cones, and other natural autumn accessories. She was humming along with a catchy tune.

I asked her, "Who is this?"

"Barenaked Ladies."

Was she pulling my leg? "Who?"

"Barenaked Ladies," she repeated. "BNL for short. You're not a fan of the most celebrated Canadian alt-rock band of the midnineties? They're triple platinum." She self-consciously smoothed her straight dark hair over her ears. "That's a quote from *Community*."

"You and your pop culture references." I listened for a bit. "They're growing on me. Is this the radio?"

"It's a new option from the licensed music service. This one meets the CRTC guidelines for thirty-five percent CanCon." She explained, "CanCon is short for Canadian content."

"Is Oregon no longer part of America? I know things get a little weird sometimes, politically, but did I miss a major development?"

"We're still in America, boss. I'm just feeling nostalgic for the Canadian tourists now that summer's over."

"Their geese are still here. You can go visit them at the lake."

"Not the same thing." She returned to humming along with the Barenaked Ladies tune, which was about the wild things they might purchase if they had a million dollars.

I was still thinking about the geese. "Fun fact," I said. "The Canada goose produces two pounds of you-know-what per day."

"But they do it politely," Brianna said matter-of-factly. "And if they get some on your shoes, they apologize, on account of being Canadian." She spritzed the window interior with cleaning spray and started wiping it clean. "Since when did you become Glorious Gifts' leading expert on the waste production of Canada Geese?"

"Since Creepy Jeepers cornered me at the post office to tell me all about the local goose overpopulation problem."

"Leo Jenkins from the Masquerade Shop? That guy is obsessed with poo."

"I hadn't noticed," I lied. "He also wants me to join the local Chamber of Commerce."

"So? Why haven't you joined already?"

"Ah, I'm glad you asked. You see, once upon a time, your boss had a swanky job in venture capital. Great pay. Excellent travel opportunities. But long hours, and many, many boardroom meetings. So many. If I never have to sit through another long meeting, it'll be too soon."

"Because you can't sit still, right? You're only happy when you're whirling around. Like a whirlwind."

I narrowed my eyes at her. She might have based a character named Whirlwind on me, but I wasn't going to admit the name suited me.

Instead, I said, "Why are you looking at me like I'm a bug and you're about to pin me to a specimen board?"

"No reason," she answered breezily.

"Is there something you want to confess? Perhaps something cheeky that you've done without my permission?"

"Uh." She spritzed the cleaning spray on the window all over again. "Have you got that candle order done?"

"What? I just ordered candles last Monday."

"Yes, but we need the other ones now. The unscented, soy-based candles."

"I'll get right on it," I promised.

Right then, someone walked up to the front door and yanked it. We hadn't opened yet for the day, so the person only succeeded in rattling the front of the store. The noise made Brianna drop her bottle of window spray.

I avoided eye contact and hoped they would read the hours on the sign before they tore off the door.

"Hey, it's my cousin," Brianna said, and she ran to unlock the door.

Her cousin Chip McCabe came in, dressed in his US Postal Service uniform. As usual, he wore shorts instead of pants.

She launched herself at him and gave him an enthusiastic hug. At a glance they didn't look like cousins, since half of Brianna's family was Chinese American, but I did pick up on the familial warmth between them.

Brianna pulled away and said to him, "Don't you have some mail to lose? What did you do, throw it all in a recycling bin so you could take the day off?"

Chip frowned at his younger cousin. "What about you, Monkey Ears? Why aren't you up in a tree throwing bananas at people?"

"Nice haircut," she said. "Nice and straight. Where did they find a salad bowl big enough for your giant head?"

"They borrowed the water bowl from your cage. Speaking of which, when did they let you out of the zoo?"

"They freed us all because soon the spaceships are coming to take you back to your real home."

"Not happening. The aliens came already, but then they saw you and got scared and went back to their planet."

Brianna held her hands up. "You got me, Chip. Sick burn!"

"I still love ya, Shrimpie Chimpie." He gave her another hug, which she pretended to despise.

After they pulled away a second time, Brianna told me, "Chip was my babysitter when I was little."

"You're still little," he said. "Why doesn't your family feed you?"

She eyed his stomach and smirked. "No comment."

Chip turned away from his cousin, his expression growing more serious. "Miss Day, can I, uh, talk to you?"

"Sure. Do you need help picking out a gift for Quinn? She can be picky, but I know her taste pretty well." I rubbed my hands together, relishing the idea of selling him the most expensive item in the shop.

He glanced at Brianna, blushed, and then looked back at me. "In private? It's about your *other* business."

Normally, I didn't see private investigation clients at my retail store. I paid a monthly rental fee to a packaged office space company so I could use their private meeting rooms. I should have insisted Chip make an appointment. However, my curiosity got the better of me. Plus I really didn't feel like putting in another boring candle order.

"Sure," I said. "We can talk in my office, but you should know the walls are pretty thin."

Brianna chimed in, "I'll turn up the music." She winked at her cousin. "Plus Stormy will tell me everything after you leave."

"No, I won't," I said, shaking my head. To Chip, I said, "I won't. It's confidential."

He seemed hesitant, but he followed me back into the office. I gave him the good chair, because I didn't think the other one would hold his weight.

I closed the door and asked what I could do for him.

"I hear you can dig up dirt on people," he said. "Like for blackmail."

I held my hands up. "Whoa there, Nelly. Blackmail is a crime. A federal crime."

"So, you don't dig up dirt on people?"

"Chip, I can do a background check on someone, if you'd like. In the business, we don't call it *dirt*."

"Then what's the point?" He attempted to lean his elbow casually on the armrest of the chair, but the chair had no armrest, and he nearly fell off. "What I mean is, what exactly comes up in a background check?"

"Well, a potential employer might request a background investigation on an individual before employment, or security clearance. If that were the case, I would then look up and compile various records—criminal, commercial, financial, academic verification, citizenship, and so forth. All the information that's perfectly legal for me to collect."

He stared at me with his big, blue eyes. A bead of sweat dripped out of his fair, fine hair and down the side of his temple. If I didn't know he was always sweaty, I might have thought he was extremely nervous.

He crossed his arms. "What about following them around town? Like for protection?"

"That can be arranged, on an hourly or a per-day basis. Perhaps you could give me some more details?"

"I'd rather not," he said. "I just want my family to stay intact."

"Is someone threatening you? If you're being threatened, you should go straight to the police."

He snorted. "I'd rather not bother them while they're trying to catch a killer. Have you heard? They haven't even made an arrest. We might never know who killed Mikey Sweet."

"I'm sure they're working on something."

His eyes widened. He uncrossed his arms and leaned forward. "What have you heard? Is it true you saw the body? Was his head hacked right off?"

"What? No! I mean, who told you that?"

"All the rumors," he said, his eyes bulging and spit flying from his mouth. "But it makes you wonder, doesn't it? My wife used to date Mikey in high school. What if there's someone out there who's obsessed with Quinn? She was really popular, and she's still so beautiful. What if I'm next?"

I was so relieved, I nearly laughed. "Is that why you're here, Chip? Are you worried you might be the next victim of a serial killer?"

"No," he said, a little too vehemently. "But what would you charge to follow Quinn around town? You know, just to make sure she's safe."

"Something tells me Quinn can take care of herself."

"Are you saying you won't do it? I'll have to get someone else." He looked down and muttered, more to himself than to me. "Actually, that might be better, because if it's a stranger, then she won't know she's getting followed."

"I could refer you to another service provider," I said. "Or—and please forgive me for being presumptuous about your situation—there's a group therapy session for anxiety that's quite affordable. Since last week's events, a lot of people around town have been on edge. There's no shame in getting some help."

The sweaty mail carrier pulled a checkered handkerchief from his pocket and mopped his brow. "Never mind," he said. "I should be on my route right now, anyway. It was stupid of me to come here. Can you do me a favor and not tell Quinn about this?"

"This meeting was strictly confidential," I said.

He stared at me with bulging eyes. "Was his head cut right off?"

Normally, I wouldn't have said anything, but since I thought it might help Chip's anxiety, I said, "No. Not at all."

He let out an audible breath, thanked me, got up from the chair, and left with surprising speed.

A few minutes later, Brianna sauntered into the office. "Everything okay?"

"My meetings really are confidential," I said. "And they would be even if you weren't a soon-to-be-famous internet cartoonist who draws from real life for inspiration."

"I understand," she said. "But I can tell you stuff, right?"

"Maybe. What kind of stuff?"

"It's probably nothing." She looked down at her feet. She was wearing mismatched novelty socks with vintage dancing shoes.

I waited and let the silence do the coaxing. Most people can't handle dead air and will cough up all manner of secrets just to alleviate the quiet.

"Quinn keeps talking about this photographer guy," she said. "She keeps sharing his photos on social media and talking about how talented he is. And there's one picture in particular that's got everyone in the family talking." She used her phone to pull up a photo to show me.

In the image, Quinn's daughter Quinby was sitting on a stool in the background, and Quinn was in the foreground, filling the frame. Her chest in particular. The picture had a caption reading, *A divine outtake featuring the flower from which the petal was plucked.*

"Quinby's the petal and her mother's the flower?" I made a gagging face. "Ew. This photographer's a bit much."

"And he charges a bit much," Brianna said. "But Quinn thinks her daughter's going to get that big TV role, so she doesn't want to spare any expense."

"That sounds like our Queen Bee."

"Except the photographer didn't charge anything at all. I think she might have paid him in... another way. As in, another form of currency." She winked twice. "Like money, but not money. Like—"

I cut her off. "Yes, Brianna. I get the picture." I chewed my lip and put the pieces together. Chip didn't want me to follow his wife around for protection from a serial killer. He wanted me to catch her in adulterous activities. Hah! Why hadn't he just told me the truth? I might have done it for free.

CHAPTER 19

"Lasagna?" I'd just walked in the door of my house and kicked off my shoes. "What have I done to deserve your amazing vegetarian lasagna?"

Jessica looked up from the sink, where she was scrubbing a pan. "I thought you could use a hot meal that didn't come from the gas station."

"My father did make me his famous meatloaf last night. Which he served with potato chips." I knelt in front of the oven and peered at the bubbling cheese through the round-cornered window. "I'm actually looking forward to eating some vegetables." Jessica's lasagna was usually meatless but filled with every kind of roasted vegetable, from mushrooms to peppers and even eggplant. Jeffrey came over to see what I was looking at.

I asked, "How was your day?"

My red-haired roommate didn't answer. My gray-furred roommate rubbed against my leg before walking away.

I stood up again and took a seat at the table. "Was your day that bad?" I tapped my fingers on the table. "Jessica?"

"Huh?" She turned from the sink and blinked at me. "Oh. I thought you were talking to Jeffrey."

"Really? I don't talk to Jeffrey that much."

She laughed. "Sure."

"What's been happening with Mitch the Fireman?" I heard the phrase *Mitch the Fireman* come out of my mouth. Jessica was right. I did say his name like he was a character in a children's book. "I mean Mitch, who happens to be a firefighter?"

Her shoulders crunched in with body tension as she screwed up her face. "He sent me some text messages but I don't know what they mean."

I held out my hand. "Let the private investigator see."

She got her phone from the charger and held it to her chest. "Okay, but promise not to send a reply."

"Come on. Would I do that to you?"

She gave me a look that said she wouldn't put it past me. I rolled my eyes as I took the phone from her.

I scrolled through Mitch's messages. He'd said things like, "Watching TV with the guys," and, "Gotta do laundry. Learning how to separate."

"That's sweet," I said.

"Did you read them? They're all like that. He actually sent one yesterday to tell me it was raining. We live in the same town. I can tell by looking out the window that it's raining."

"He's letting you know that he's thinking about you. I know it seems like he isn't saying anything, but honestly, I *wish* I could get messages like this from Logan."

She sat across from me, her face still pinched with worry. "You don't have to lie to make me feel better." She picked up the phone and frowned at it. "Is his phone missing the question mark key? He never asks me a single question."

"That doesn't mean he doesn't want to know," I said. "This regular everyday stuff is how guys let you know they're thinking about you."

"Does Logan send you messages like this?"

"No," I said. "But that's different. His personality is... intense."

"Yes," she said, still frowning. "Logan is more to the point. He doesn't understand that sometimes an invitation to do something doesn't mean you actually do the thing. Like watch a video, for example. He gets antsy if we take an hour to make nachos and then another hour to pick out a movie."

I glanced over at the wall separating my half of the duplex from his rented half. "You're right," I said. "Like how Sunday before last, he cooked three steaks and he couldn't relax until he'd lined up three people to eat the steaks. That was when the Lubbesmeyers came over."

"Guys are weird," she said.

Jeffrey jumped up on her lap and rubbed his head on her chin.

"Present company excluded," she said.

I leaned over and peered through the oven door at the lasagna. "That's a big pan of food. Do you want to invite Mitch the Fireman over for a bite? They say the way to a man's heart is through his stomach."

She picked up a butter knife. "Not through the chest?"

"What?"

Jessica's eyes widened. She gasped and set the knife down. "I'm so sorry, Stormy. That was awful of me. You know, this whole week, I keep catching myself making comments like that. It's almost like the more I try not to think about Michael Sweet getting stabbed, the more it bubbles up in my subconscious."

"It's affecting everyone," I said. "Let's hope they catch the person soon."

"I sure hope so. Harper has been a wreck."

"Harper that you work with?" Harper was in her midtwenties and new to Misty Falls. She lived with her younger sister in the apartment building where Jessica used to live before moving in with me. She also worked at the Olive Grove with Jessica. "Why would she be worried?"

"I didn't tell you? She's been working part-time for the Sweets, doing some administration for the business. She's thinking about getting her real estate license, so she's been getting job experience. I guess she's jumpy because it could have been a client or another realtor in town. Maybe a competitor. The killer might be a person she talks to regularly."

"Or maybe Harper knows something."

Jessica picked up the knife again and made a stabbing motion. "Ree ree ree," she said, grinning and imitating the iconic soundtrack from the movie *Psycho*—composer Bernhard Hermann's screaming violins. "Or maybe *Harper* killed him. She didn't have a lot of respect for Michael."

"Does she have an alibi for Monday?"

Jessica set down the knife and rolled her eyes. "I'm just joking. Harper wouldn't hurt anyone. Don't take everything I say so literally."

"To quote my father, *where the tongue slips, it speaks the truth*."

The timer on the stove started beeping. The subject quickly turned away from homicide and toward lasagna.

I tried not to think about Michael Sweet and all the reasons someone might want to kill him, but if there was one person who would have known where he was that day, it was his office assistant. Whenever I needed to track down Logan and he wasn't answering his phone, I'd ask Corine, the receptionist at his law firm, Tyger & Behr.

I couldn't stop wondering what Harper might know about the case.

"We should hang out with Harper again soon," I said.

"Promise you won't interrogate her?"

"I'll buy her a drink. That's all."

Jessica poked at her lasagna and narrowed her eyes at me. "Okay. I'll set something up." She looked down at her phone. "We've got the funeral Thursday, so how's Friday for you?"

I'd forgotten about Michael Sweet's funeral. We had to go to support Samantha and the family, even though it would mean being stared at by people.

"Set it up for Friday," I said. "After Thursday's funeral, I'll need a drink."

"Are Logan's parents coming?" Logan was Samantha's cousin, so his parents were her aunt and uncle.

"No. They're busy."

She sniffed. "Runs in the family."

I dug into my lasagna. It was a masterpiece, as usual.

"Don't fill up," Jessica said. "Dean Lubbesmeyer is coming over with some new potato chip flavors he wants us to taste test." She gave me an ultra-serious look. "It's a dirty job, but somebody's got to do it."

CHAPTER 20

"Stormy, I need to make a confession."

I looked across my kitchen table and its silver bowls of flavored potato chips at my next-door neighbor, Dean Lubbesmeyer. His hair wasn't as colorful as his wife's purple locks—in fact, he didn't have much hair at all—but his cheerful tropical-print shirt matched his zesty, always-joking personality.

Tonight, however, his expression was serious for a change. Were we not giving him the feedback he was hoping for? We'd been crunching on new flavors of potato chips for the past thirty minutes, and enjoying them immensely. I'd thought doing a buttered popcorn flavor on a potato chip would be gross, but the resulting chip reminded me of my favorite road trip travel snack, Old Dutch Popcorn Twists.

I glanced over at Jessica and then back at Dean.

"Go ahead," I said. "What's this confession you need to make?"

"First of all, these aren't zero-calorie diet potato chips."

"No kidding," I said flatly. "Don't worry, Dean. You didn't fool me for a minute."

"And also, I think some of my DNA might be at a crime scene." He scrunched up his rubbery features. "Like on the murder weapon?" His voice pitched up at the end, as though he was asking a question.

My lovable neighbor's DNA was on the murder weapon that killed Michael Sweet?

"That's not funny," I said, pushing the bowl of buttered-popcorn-flavor potato chips crumbs away from myself. "Or maybe it is, but I'm not really in the mood."

"I'm dead serious," he said. "You know the house where that man was found killed last week?"

I glanced over at Jessica again to see if this was part of a prank. I knew the Lubbesmeyers loved to joke around, but this didn't seem like a typical Dean and Eve gag. Was it possible Dean without Eve was like a bicycle missing a tire? Jessica looked as stunned as I felt, at hearing Dean talk about his DNA being at last Monday's homicide. The look on Jessica's face reminded me of another night, when I'd made the horrible mistake of confronting a criminal over dinner at that same table. The evening had ended with Logan being rushed to the hospital. He still bore the scars on his stomach, but Jessica's were invisible. Except times like this, when I saw the trauma surface on her face.

I gave Dean a stony look. He'd better have a good reason for being so dramatic.

"Yes," I answered slowly. "I'm familiar with that particular house." Did he not know I was one of the people who saw the body? How could he have missed that bit of gossip? He had to be messing around. I glanced around for signs of his wife, Eve. Surely the woman with the spiked purple hair was about to pop out from behind my sofa with some wisecrack.

"I toured that house on the Saturday before the homicide happened," Dean said.

"So did we," Jessica said. She took a large potato chip and crunched it noisily. The room was so quiet, I could hear every chew.

I sighed and shook my head at my overly dramatic neighbor. "Is that all? Dean, a lot of people toured the house."

"But did they all handle the knives?"

I kept shaking my head, but for a different reason. "Dean Lubbesmeyer. Tell me you didn't handle the knives."

"Sorry." He hung his head. "I'm a bit of a knife nerd. I found myself alone in the kitchen, and I noticed the homeowners had some good ones—Henckels chef knives, and also some Messermeister cleavers—so I took them out and I'm afraid I handled all of them."

"That's a bit strange," I said. "But anyone who knows you would believe it. You do love your kitchen equipment, and industrial potato slicers and peelers."

"I believe it," Jessica said brightly. "The first time we met, you offered to sharpen all of our scissors."

I reached across the table and patted his hand. "Dean, if there's a legitimate reason for your epithelial cells to be found on the murder weapon, the police aren't going to come after you. They want to close the case, but they're not going to pin it on an innocent man."

He looked straight at me, his big brown eyes extra serious-looking due to the new dark circles underneath them. "Should I turn myself in?"

Jessica laughed nervously. "That's funny."

I slowly withdrew my outstretched hand. Jessica was a gentle soul who always saw the best in people, but I'd learned to pay attention to the smallest signs of guilt or shame. And the fumes coming off Dean Lubbesmeyer were pretty strong.

Casually, I said, "We could call the police right now to come take a statement." I paused. "That is, if you think you might have done something wrong. Maybe by accident."

Dean pushed his chair back and stood quickly. "Never mind." He started stacking the stainless steel serving bowls of potato chips on top of each other, crushing the chips carelessly.

Jessica asked him, "Did you cut a cupcake in half that day?"

He paused in his stacking of bowls. "A cupcake? Yes, I do believe I did. I was testing the knives when the blond realtor came in and screamed. I was too embarrassed to say I'd been playing with the knives, so I made up something stupid on the spot. I think I told her I was on a diet." He stared at Jessica, his eyes bulging. "How did you know about that?"

"Oh, Dean," Jessica said warmly. "You silly goose. You scared the dickens out of Samantha that day. She actually told us about it. I guess she hasn't met you before, so she didn't know who you were."

"No," he said plaintively. "No, no, no," he cried. "This is bad, right?"

"It's not bad," I said calmly. I was feeling more confident about his innocence by the second. If he'd made Samantha scream that day, it had probably made him feel awful. That could be what he was feeling guilty about now.

Jessica looked at me and flashed her eyes for me to fix the situation.

I told Dean, "It's good, see? You have an eyewitness who *saw you* touching the knives on Saturday. You're actually better off than if you hadn't frightened poor Samantha."

He squeezed the bowls in his hands, crushing more potato chips audibly. "So, I don't need to hire Logan to defend me?"

Jessica let out a loud, high-pitched laugh. "Not unless you killed someone! You didn't stab Michael Sweet to death in a tub, did you?"

More potato chips crushed under pressure. "Of course not," he gasped. "No, no, no."

"You could talk to Logan if you want," I said. "Just to be certain." I used one hand to make a sweeping gesture between myself and Jessica. "Neither of us is qualified to give legal advice."

"But you know stuff," Dean said. "You know about epi-feel-y-alls"

"Epithelial cells," I said.

"Exactly," he replied, and he sat in his chair again. He set the bowls on the table and covered his face with his hands. "Ugh, what a mess."

"Dean, why were you at the open house anyway? You guys already bought a house, and a potato chip factory."

He kept his hands over his face. "I was thinking it might be a good starter home for one of the kids when they get done with college. I could rent it out for the time being, as an investment."

Jessica said soothingly, "That's a very generous and kind thing to do for your children. Lucky kids."

"This is not legal advice, but you probably have nothing to worry about," I said. "Did you sign the visitor log that day?"

"I think so," he said.

"Then the police already have your name. If they recovered DNA from something and wanted to exclude people, they would have been in contact. I know they reviewed the visitor log."

He peered at me from between his fingers. "They did? How do you know?"

Oops. I wasn't supposed to tell people that Dimples fed information to my father who fed it to me.

"I'm assuming they did," I said quickly. "They're good cops. Very thorough. They've got this one under control, I'm sure."

Dean slowly lowered his hands. "If you say so." His eyes weren't as bulging, and his eyelids looked almost sleepy. He yawned. "I think I'll finally be able to sleep tonight. Thanks for letting me get that off my chest. I'm going to tell Eve about it now. I've been keeping it to myself all week, but she always knows when something's up." He yawned again. "The spouse always knows."

"Go home and talk to Eve," I said.

He grabbed the bowls and got to his feet again.

"Hang on just a minute," I said with a slight growl.

His eyes bulged guiltily and he gasped, "What?"

"Those are my bowls," I said.

He let out a high-pitched laugh. "Of course they are." He set the bowls of crushed chip samples on the table. "Keep the chips."

* * *

As soon as Dean Lubbesmeyer left, I called my father and gave him a summary of what had just happened.

"They should have some results back on the knife," he said. "The lab's always backed up, but this should have been a high priority." He muffled the speaker and spoke to someone else in the room. When he came back, he said, "Dimples wants to talk to you."

"I don't want to talk to him," I said. "I don't want anything to do with this case."

"Then why'd you call?"

"Dad, tell Dimples it's nothing. I'm just being paranoid."

"He's waving his hand for me to give him the phone."

"I gotta go," I said. "Jessica just put dinner on the table."

"At eight o'clock?"

"Love you, Dad." I ended the call.

Jessica made a tsk-tsk sound. "Lying to your father?"

"No," I said sullenly. "If I take a second helping of that lasagna, it's technically not a lie."

She gave me an amused look and pulled the wrapped-up lasagna pan from the refrigerator.

* * *

At eight-twenty, there was a knock at the door.

"The movie," I said with a start. "I'm supposed to go see that new horror movie with Logan at nine o'clock."

"You forgot?" Jessica gave me a crooked smile as she looked over my lounge outfit. "If you're going on a date wearing pajamas, you should at least make sure the top and bottom match."

I ran toward my bedroom. "Can you stall Logan while I get changed?"

"I'll do my best," she said, laughing. She yelled at the door, "It's not locked!"

The door opened and someone in boots came in. "Hello, Ms. Kelly."

"Officer Dempsey!"

I groaned, and not just because someone had shrunk my favorite jeans in the wash and I had to wiggle to get into them. Officer Kyle Dempsey must have left my father's house and come straight to mine right after my phone call.

When was I going to learn to stay out of investigations that weren't my business?

CHAPTER 21

"Dimples, talk fast," I told Officer Kyle Dempsey. "I've got a date tonight."

His sky-blue eyes fixed on my shirt, which was still the pajama top I'd changed into after dinner, before I'd realized I had plans to see a movie with Logan.

"Stormy, you don't have to lie to me," he said, looking straight at my flannel shirt.

"I'm not dressed yet," I said.

"Ah," he said, as though he didn't believe me. "Either way, I won't be long. I'm going to see that new sci-fi horror movie everyone's talking about."

"Hah! That's where I'm going, too."

"Great. You can sit beside me and share my extra-large tub of popcorn."

"I'm going with Logan."

"Oh." Kyle grinned, the dimples in his smooth, young-looking face deepening. "Then I take back my offer. It's bad enough I have to see Logan with *you*. He's not getting any of my popcorn." He turned toward Jessica, who was making a cup of chamomile tea in the kitchen. "How about you, Red? I've got a spare ticket."

"Thanks, but I don't do horror movies." She dunked the tea bag three times. "Real life is plenty scary."

"But that's the whole point of horror movies," Kyle said. "It's controlled fun, like being on a roller coaster."

"Not really," she said, shaking her head. "I love roller coasters, but I hate horror movies."

"Only because you haven't been to one with me." He grinned and waggled his eyebrows at her.

"Stop hitting on Jessica," I said. "She's got a boyfriend."

He turned back to me. "Mitch the Fireman? How's that going?"

"You tell me. Isn't he a friend of yours? I know you uniform types all hang out at the Loose Moose."

"I see Big Mitch around," Kyle said. "He's so large and muscular. Girls don't like that, do they?"

"Some girls like that."

"Girls like you?" He leaned casually against the kitchen counter next to where Jessica stood. "Should I be hitting the gym a lot more?"

"Only if you think it will help you catch more bad guys," I teased.

Jessica interjected, "You two are so weird." She tossed her used tea bag in the compost bucket under the sink. "I'm going to read a book in my room. Feel free to continue discussing my love life without me."

After she left, Kyle asked, "Am I in trouble?"

"No more than usual," I said. Loudly, for the benefit of my roommate down the hall, I added, "I'm glad we're done talking about other people's romantic lives now, so we can get down to discussing homicides, as usual, Officer Dempsey."

"Maybe I'm here on a social call." He sniffed the air over the sink. "Is that tea a legal substance?"

"Just chamomile," I said. "The last time Jessica took drugs was during the Great Smoothie Incident."

"How about you?"

"High on life." I took a seat at the table and kicked out a chair for Kyle. He took off his leather jacket and hung it on a hook by the door, revealing a very form-fitting, pale violet T-shirt with a deep V-neck.

"Nice shirt," I said. "Do they make it in men's sizes?"

He took a seat and quirked a light-brown eyebrow at me. "Is this your sibling rivalry coming out? Are you feeling snappy because I've been spending so much time with Finn?"

"No," I lied.

He gazed at me steadily, his sky-blue eyes only darkened slightly by being indoors. "Let's get to it. We don't have long until your boyfriend gets here."

"What?" I pulled together the upper front of my pajama top as I blushed. Too late, I realized he was referring to the movie start time.

He grinned knowingly. "Why were you asking your dad about knives and DNA?"

I quickly explained to him all about the concerns my neighbor Dean Lubbesmeyer had about skin cells containing his DNA being found on the knife.

"It's a moot point," Kyle said when I was done. "You didn't see the murder weapon in the bathroom, did you?"

I pulled up a mental image I wished I didn't have. "No. There wasn't anything sharper than a pair of nail clippers in that washroom. Did the killer take the murder weapon away?"

"We found the knife that matched the wounds. The assailant gave it a good cleaning, with bleach, and tossed it into the washing machine with the clothes for good measure." He leaned forward, resting his forearm casually on my kitchen table. "But you can't tell your neighbor about that. It's one of the details we're keeping out of the news."

I promised to keep the murder-weapon detail to myself.

We talked for a few more minutes about the case. There'd been some people calling in tips, but nothing concrete.

Finally, I said, "I hope you make an arrest soon. That'll put everyone at ease."

"What we need is physical evidence. Something connecting Colt Canuso to the crime scene."

"Colt?" It was the first time Kyle had mentioned a suspect by name, and I didn't like it. "No. He didn't do it."

Kyle made a too-casual, forced shrug. "Then find me someone else. Work your magic. Get me a name."

I sighed. "I'm not on the clock. Even just talking about this case with you is costing me money, Dimples. This is time I could be spending thinking about something that actually is my business."

I would have given him more heck, but my phone alerted me to an incoming message. It was Logan.

Logan: *Have to run out for one more stupid waste of time meeting. Can't make the movie tonight. Sorry. Love ya.*

I glanced up at Kyle. "Love ya," I said, mystified.

"Don't tease."

"No, it's just—never mind." I sent Logan back a quick text response and put my phone away. "Do you still have that extra ticket?"

"Only if you change your shirt. That flannel thing looks something a grampa wears to mow the lawn."

I snorted. "You're one to talk. How about we trade? You give me that V-neck and I'll find you something more appropriate, like a burlap sack."

"Okay." Kyle got up from his chair and pulled off the pale purple shirt in one smooth motion. His body was smooth and rippled in all the right ways over his stomach, like buttercream frosting.

I squeaked. And I stared at his bare abs just a little too long before I wheeled around and ran to my bedroom, calling back for him, "Kyle, put your shirt back on! I was just kidding!"

I quickly pulled on a dark- gray, scoop-necked shirt and ran to the bathroom to check my hair. It was flipping up at the back in a way that looked intentional. Good enough.

I popped my head into Jessica's room. She was sitting on her bed cross-legged with Jeffrey on her lap. He kept reaching up and batting the pages as she turned them.

I asked, "Are you sure you don't want to come to the movie? It's more sci-fi than horror. Not too scary."

She wrinkled her nose. "Did I hear something about Officer Dempsey having his shirt off?" She put the paperback down and waved her hand. "Never mind. I don't even want to know."

"Will you come see the movie?"

She pointed to the dark gray cat on her lap. "Can't disturb His Royal Fluffiness, sorry. And I don't watch horror movies."

I fidgeted by the doorway for a minute. I wanted to tell her how Logan had signed off his text message with a casual *Love ya*.

It was not the first time Logan and I had used the word "love." He'd made a few heartfelt speeches about loving me, but it was usually within the larger context of loving his new life in Misty Falls, as though I was part of the New Life package he'd ordered. So, he'd said something to the effect of "I love you" a few times, but it hadn't yet made it into our daily greetings. Until tonight.

Was my bearded lawyer boyfriend Logan Sanderson signing off his text message with *Love ya* because he was genuinely missing me, or because he was overcompensating for something?

I wanted to get Jessica's take on the situation, but that would mean opening up a whole big discussion, and Dimples was waiting to take me to the movies.

CHAPTER 22

It was a good thing Kyle had pre-purchased two movie tickets, as the show was a hit and every seat was sold out.

The crowd in line for the nine o'clock show was mostly teens and younger folks who were more concerned with each other. We had to line up outside the small theater, as the seven o'clock showing hadn't let out yet. The theater, like many in small towns, had only one screen. Most movies showed for one week only, which I didn't mind, because it made for more of a big event when everyone in town had to go at the same time.

Once we joined the line for ticket holders, I scanned the line. There were a few familiar faces in the crowd, but thanks to the youthful audience the film had drawn, I had the rare experience of feeling anonymous.

I shared my thoughts with Kyle, who said, "That's why I wear things like this V-neck shirt when I'm off duty." He looked at a group of kids off to the side and pointed at them with his chin. "For example, if I was wearing a dark button-up shirt with a collar right now, that smart-mouthed dipwad over there with the skateboard would recognize me as that jerk cop who busted him for underage drinking last week."

We watched the kids for a few minutes.

I confessed, "I don't know if I'm getting old or what, but I don't like the way that dipwad is talking to the girl with the half-shaved head. She looks like a shy kid who's lost in the world, and I don't like how she's looking at him like he's her new role model."

"That dipwad never had a chance," Kyle said. "But you never know. He could turn himself around, the way my brother Julian did."

"Julian Dempsey," I said, and the name conjured up old feelings. I used to look at Kyle's older brother the way the head-shaved girl was looking at the dipwad with the skateboard. Julian had gone through a pyromaniac phase, but he'd straightened his life out eventually. The last I'd heard—from baby brother Kyle—Julian was a pyrotechnics expert working in the film industry.

Kyle frowned at me. "Did you have a crush on my brother?"

"Me?" I laughed. "Gross. No way."

"Mm hmm."

The doors of the lobby cracked open, and the crowd from the early show began pouring out. A minute later, our line started shifting forward quickly.

I went ahead to find two seats while Kyle stayed behind to get the snacks.

The movie was as good as the reviews promised, and Kyle Dempsey shared not just his tub of popcorn with me but also his large bag of almond M&Ms.

After the film, Kyle had to visit the restroom, thanks to his extra-large tub of iced tea.

I stood alone in the lobby while the teenage staff walked around cleaning up.

There was a large cardboard cut-out display advertising a package combo deal for "date night." The couple pictured was shown sharing a large root beer with two straws.

The boy in the picture looked so much like Colt Canuso that I almost couldn't believe my eyes.

I took out my phone, snapped a picture of the cutout, and sent Colt a friend request through his social media account, along with the picture, captioned, "Can you believe this?"

Kyle came out of the men's room, apologized for taking so long, and we walked outside to his car.

On the drive back to my place, we only discussed the movie and how good it had been.

I'd all but forgotten about sending the picture to Colt until I was climbing into bed. My phone buzzed with an alert.

It was Colt, and he'd apparently taken my message as an invitation.

Colt: *Sure! I'd love to buy you that root beer, Stormy. Thanks for asking! What are your plans for lunch tomorrow?*

I wrote back: *I'll be at my store, if you want to meet me there.*

Colt: *It's a date.*

Me: *It's lunch between two friends, not a date.*

Colt: *Tell it to my hopeful heart.*

I set the phone on my nightstand, turned off the light, and snuggled up to Jeffrey, who was hogging my pillow as usual.

CHAPTER 23

"One root beer, two straws." Colt smiled down at the drink between us.

He'd picked me up from Glorious Gifts ten minutes earlier, and we'd beat the lunch rush to the cafe. The restaurant was a small place I didn't usually go to, but Colt seemed familiar with the staff.

The drink was, indeed, a single root beer with two straws.

"You finally get your teenage wish," I said with a smile. "And it only took you, what, twenty years to break me down?"

"It hasn't been that long," he scoffed. "Then again, hold your horses a minute while I do the math. I would have been about fourteen, and now I'm thirty-four, so..." He trailed off into chuckling. "Damn, Stormy. Twenty years. We're both getting old."

"Speak for yourself. I'm skipping all birthdays from now on."

"Good idea." He shifted in his seat, unbuttoning the jacket of his western-style suit. "You can skip birthdays by refusing to answer their call. Like how the process server can't serve you papers if you don't answer the door."

I held my finger in the air like a lecturer. "Actually, that's a common misconception."

He raised his eyebrows, his dark eyes dancing. "Tell me more, Ms. Private Eye."

"If an investigator wants to serve you papers, she will find a way. My personal favorite is to knock on the door, and then, when they don't answer, I go to their vehicle, assuming it's parked in front of the house or at least within view. As I walk away, I know they're watching me from the window, because, well, who wouldn't? Then I hand-write a note on bright pink paper and leave it under their windshield wiper."

"Does that count as being served? I don't get it. Do you put the court papers underneath the note?"

"Nope." I grinned, proud of myself. "I get in my car and drive away, but only as far as around the corner. Then I park again, get out, and come back quietly." I paused, relishing how interested Colt was in my story. "You know that saying, curiosity killed the cat?"

He smiled, catching on. "I do run a casino, Stormy Day. I'm familiar with many aspects of human nature, including curiosity."

"Nobody can resist a handwritten note on pink paper. The guy—or gal—goes up to their car and pulls off the handwritten pink note. While they're reading my love note, I tap them on the shoulder. Bingo. Papers served."

"What do you write on the note?"

"It doesn't matter." I grinned. "But usually I write something clever like, *Look out. She's right behind you.*"

"Hah!" Colt leaned back and slapped his knee. "What if they lie about who they are, and throw the papers in the street?"

"I've already taken their picture from a distance. Plus I've made my own visual identification. My word and judgment do count for something. I certainly don't need to swab for DNA or even get them to respond in the affirmative to their name." I gave him a knowing look. "Unlike what you see on TV."

"So, they don't *have to* give you their name?"

"It's a nice bonus if they do, but it's optional."

"You're so devious." He reached out and drew a heart in the condensation on the side of the root beer glass. "You must love your job. I haven't seen you this energized since your cheerleader days."

"How about you? Do you feel fulfilled by your line of work?"

His shoulders slumped, and he visibly flattened. "I'm responsible for a lot of people and their families."

"You didn't answer my question. Is your work fulfilling?"

"Let's put it this way: I get to shower *before* I go to work, unlike my father and grandfather, who both used to shower *after* they came home from a shift at either the mines or the old pulp mill."

"Still not much of an answer. And coming home clean isn't everything. Take it from someone who regularly gets herself soaked in lukewarm garbage juice."

The restaurant got quiet, and the words *lukewarm garbage juice* hung in the air.

We both looked down at the root beer on the table between us.

"Don't be grossed out. It's not that color," I said, which wasn't entirely true. Lukewarm garbage juice came in all sorts of colors.

The waitress, a thin woman with silver-streaked hair, came to check on us.

Colt looked at me expectantly. "I'm not hungry yet," I said.

"You haven't touched your root beer," the waitress said. "You two must have a lot to catch up on."

Colt grinned up at her. "I went to school with this young lady. Twenty years ago. Can you believe it?"

The woman winked at him. "You must be mistaken. Twenty years is a long time."

"Thanks, Melody." He winked back. "Are those grandkids keeping you busy?"

"Not too busy for my slots. I'll be seein' you at the casino again soon." She took a step back and tilted her head to the side. "A lot sooner if you leave me a big tip."

Colt chuckled and assured her he would.

"I'm scandalized," I said once she was gone. "That nice grandma just shook you down for money."

"It's the world we live in," he said. "So, what do you really want?" Colt kept his gaze on the glass of root beer as he trailed his finger through the condensation. "The scrawny fourteen-year-old sci-fi-reading nerd inside me was hoping you sent me that picture last night as a precursor to a make-out session today, but based on your choice of clothing, I'm guessing seduction wasn't your intention."

I looked down at my sweatshirt. It was something I'd yanked out of my drawer on the way out of the house. As far as sweatshirts went, it wasn't the most sloppy. It was dark blue, and relatively new, so the collar was still round. However, it had a fuzzy gray pattern down the front that hadn't come from the store.

"Jeffrey," I said, looking down and trying to brush the fur away. "He pulls my dresser drawer open and climbs in to sleep on my sweatshirts. Honestly, I don't know how someone with no thumbs can get himself into so much trouble." I kept wiping at the gray fur but it was no use. "Jeffrey's my cat," I added.

"Figured as much." Colt watched me with amusement. "You need one of those sticky rollers. I've got one in my truck, if you want me to run out and get it. I probably have a spare I can give you. I buy those things by the caseload."

"You have a cat?" My voice rose up to a squeak.

"Two dogs," he said. "Sisters. They're mutts, a few breeds mixed together, but mostly Siberian husky."

"With blue eyes?" He nodded. "They sound adorable," I said.

"Want to come out and meet them? They're in the truck. I told them I'd take them for a walk in Central Park if they came into town with me."

I looked at the untouched glass of root beer between us. I'd sent Colt Canuso the photo of the movie theater advertisement the night before, simply because it had made me think of him.

Then I'd accepted his lunch invitation without thinking it through.

As much as I'd promised everyone from Jessica to my father as well as Kyle Dempsey that I wasn't going to get myself involved in the Michael Sweet homicide investigation, here I was, hanging out casually with one of the suspects.

Could I use this casual get-together to help clear Colt's name? All I'd heard against him was that he didn't have much of an alibi for that Monday, and he wasn't being very cooperative.

I might be able to get more out of him. He certainly seemed relaxed around me.

They say that to get someone to participate with an investigation, the best approach is to earn their trust and become a friend. Unless, of course, you're Jack Bauer in an episode of *24*, in which case you torture it out of them. But I was never big on torture. Never mind what might be said by one gray cat who was going to get himself permanently banned from my sweater drawer.

I agreed to a walk in the park, and Colt overpaid Melody for the untouched root beer by a factor of a thousand percent.

"I'll get it all back thanks to the slot machines," he told me as we left the restaurant.

"And you said I was the devious one," I teased.

He linked his arm with mine at the elbow. "We make quite the pair," he teased right back.

CHAPTER 24

The official name of the fenced-in park running through the middle of town is Pacific Pine and Cedar Grove. There was a vote on the name, between pine and cedar, but the results of the vote were inconclusive. It hardly matters, since everyone in Misty Falls calls it Central Park, inspired by the larger and much more famous park in New York.

At Glorious Gifts, we have mugs and fridge magnets that read, *Get your bark on at Central Bark, Misty Falls, Oregon.* The word *Park* is intentionally spelled *Bark.* Visitors find it squeal-worthy, and we do sell a good number of the mugs. The fridge magnets never took off the way I'd hoped, possibly because the background color was a shade of milky puce not unlike the color of lukewarm garbage juice.

Central Park was busy that Tuesday afternoon, full of people taking in the last sunny days before winter arrived with our first snowfall, which was due any time, as it usually snowed in early October.

Colt and I walked around the outer perimeter.

His dogs were adorable. I instantly fell in love with the two huskies. How could I resist? They had lovely blue eyes and white, heart-shaped markings on their faces. Both were very well-behaved and gentle, listening attentively to Colt's short verbal commands.

"I'm glad you like my girls so much," Colt said as we strolled along in the autumn sunshine. "Can I ask you a favor?"

"You can always ask."

"Would you take them if something were to happen to me? Would you be their godmother?"

"Why? Are you sick?"

It took him a while to answer. "No," he said. "I just worry about the future. I don't have a wife anymore, or kids, and my brother's got no energy for anything outside of the casino. There's my sister, but I'm afraid she'd teach them bad habits."

I bit down a wisecrack about his sister and bad habits. Now wasn't the time for it.

"Colt, you're going to be around for a long time." I leaned down while walking and scratched the girls' ears while they climbed over each other to get a prime scratching spot. "Your papa is talking crazy talk," I told them.

"Maybe I am talking crazy," Colt said. "It's just that after what happened to Michael, a person really can't take anything for granted. Such as being alive at all." He lifted his chin and gazed off into the distance, east, in the direction of the factories.

The wind had changed direction, and the scent of potato chips drifted over us in the park. The factories were located on the east side of town, so their smell and smoke usually drifted away from town, but that day was one of the rare exceptions. Smelling the chips made me think of my next-door neighbors. I was about to tell Colt about the Lubbesmeyers when he said something startling.

He said, "Who knew Samantha had it in her?"

"What?" I jerked my head to stare at his profile. "Don't tell me you think Samantha killed her husband. You're as bad as the gossipy old ladies at my hairdresser's."

"Well, she did it. And she's probably going to get away with it, too. Nobody likes to see a pretty, blond mother of two get put behind bars."

"Those are strong allegations," I said. "A person who overheard you casting blame on someone else right about now might wonder if you were trying to cover your own butt."

"Me? I've got an alibi."

"Plus you didn't do anything wrong," I said.

"Right," he agreed. "That, too."

"What were you doing on Monday last week? I overheard you telling Samantha you were free all day to look at properties. Did you see her at all?" I hesitated before asking, "Or Michael."

"After I saw you at your shop, all I did was drive around town." He reached down to pat the huskies. "And then I took the girls for a walk."

"Dogs aren't great witnesses," I said.

He chuckled. "I also met up with some of the guys from work. They can vouch for me. We got some steaks and had a good time that night."

I walked quietly, thinking about how Colt had been enjoying a steak dinner at the same time I'd been hanging around at the Sweet residence, waiting for Samantha to get home and explain to her daughter that Daddy wasn't going to be tucking her into bed that night. Samantha was going to keep her daughter home from school and gradually break the news to her. My heart was breaking for both of them, pulling me away from the sunny fall day in the park and down to a dark place.

After a few minutes, I asked Colt, "Were you hanging out with those two security guys who tossed me out of the casino Saturday before last? Those guys aren't very reliable. It's already been established those two will roll over for forty bucks, cash. That's how much I paid them for information."

"Ouch." His stride faltered. "Stormy, if you really think I'm capable of murder, why would you meet with me in private? Why would you get into my vehicle with me?"

"I just want to make sure your backside is covered," I said. "Plus we're in the middle of town, surrounded by dozens of witnesses."

He stopped walking. I stopped as well and looked into his eyes.

He said, "Deep down, in your heart of hearts, you know I'm not capable of violence." He blinked. "I'm a lover, not a fighter."

I almost smiled. "You're not the *best* example of a pacifist. I did see you punch Mikey Sweet in the stomach."

"I barely hit him. It was the surprise of it that made him double over. He was up and swinging within seconds, but you didn't see that, because you were in the fountain. What were you doing in there, anyway?"

"The pool looked so refreshing. Plus I saw a lucky penny."

He grinned. "The security footage of your refreshing swim has been very popular with the staff."

"Nice." I glanced around the park. A few people were looking our way, but that was nothing new for me. "Are you going to tell me what you and your goons were doing in town that Monday?"

He looked away from me. "Just driving around. My brother is looking to pick up some more properties in town, so we were scoping out that new subdivision."

"Did you go back for a second tour of the tiny house?"

He was quiet for a long time.

Finally, he spoke. "Stormy, you're barking up the wrong tree. After I punched Michael that day, I went to my office, closed the door, and did something I haven't done in a long time. I got down on my knees and I prayed."

I felt a chill snake up the back of my neck. I didn't hear people talk much from day to day about praying, except as a joke. Colt was dead serious.

"What? No snarky comment?" He elbowed me. "Aren't you going to tease me about praying, or hearing voices talking back?"

I rubbed my arms. The sun had disappeared behind a cloud, and the air had turned crisp and autumnal. Over half of the leaves in the trees surrounding the park's looping walking trails had turned yellow or red. Time was always marching forward.

"No snark," I said. "I promise."

I waved for Colt to continue telling me about his experience, and he did. After punching Michael Sweet, Colt had felt himself hitting a new low. He looked around at the horrified faces of families, and felt deep shame.

Alone in his office, he hadn't exactly gone straight into prayer mode. First, he'd unlocked his personal liquor cabinet and started a conversation with a bottle of whiskey. After a few hours of that, he fell asleep on the rug in his office. In his dreams, he'd been visited by his dead wife, who'd given him a very motivating pep talk.

When he woke up a few hours later, he locked the liquor cabinet and flushed the key down a toilet. And *then* he'd gotten on his knees and prayed. Nobody had spoken to him, not God and not his deceased wife, but he'd received an inner peace that he'd been lacking, and he knew he had to change his life. He didn't know how he was going to change, or how he could purge the anger that had burned inside him for so long, but he was going to try.

Going for long walks in the woods with his two dogs was how he found his inner strength, so he'd been out practicing his new-found peace that Monday.

"Good for you," I said. I felt a warmth in my heart, which made me realize how chilly the wind had gotten. I pulled the sleeves of my cat-fur-covered sweatshirt down to cover my hands as makeshift mittens.

"You're freezing." He whipped off his suit jacket and had it around my shoulders before I could argue.

"Thanks," I said, and we continued walking.

The dogs suddenly took off. We were on a leashes-optional section of the walking path, and the dogs ran freely, chasing a squirrel up a tree. The squirrel got up to a branch that was just beyond the reach of the dogs, and began angrily berating the blue-eyed huskies.

We watched, laughing at the excited dogs and the mouthy squirrel.

"That is one cheeky squirrel," I said.

"She reminds me of you," Colt teased.

"No way! I only climb trees on rare occasions, such as when my roommate has accidentally taken psychedelics."

"Your life is far more interesting than mine," Colt said.

We watched the dogs whimper and circle the tree fruitlessly.

"That's enough," Colt finally said to the dogs. "Leave Miss Squirrel alone. She's not doing anything wrong."

"Yeah," I agreed. "Pick on someone your own size."

The dogs started barking again.

Colt said, "So much for our nice, peaceful walk." He apologized to people walking by for the noise and went to retrieve the dogs.

While he was leaning over the two dogs, fastening the leashes to their collars, I noticed something on the back of Colt's shirt. Dark spots, like dried blood spatter. It was exactly the kind of evidence that might be left in a hard-to-see spot following an angry altercation involving stab wounds. When the assailant raises the knife in between stabs, a stream of blood flies off the blade, flying to places where it might not be noticed.

"Hey, Colt," I said, leaning forward to look at the dark spots. "How did you manage to..." I stopped myself from finishing the sentence.

I wasn't a homicide detective. I was a private investigator. My domain included weighing bags of garbage and serving summonses. Not tricking killers into making confessions—never mind that I'd been successful at that task before.

I had to think fast and figure out what to do. Shifting gears hurt my head as much as my heart. I didn't want to believe what I was seeing, but there it was.

If Colt Canuso was walking around town wearing evidence from Michael Sweet's homicide, it wasn't up to me to trick a confession out of him right now.

I had to be smart, no matter how I felt about Colt. If he was a killer, and he knew that I knew, I could be in danger.

Amidst some excited face-licking, he finally got the two dogs onto their leashes and under control. He glanced back at me and asked, "How did I manage to what?"

I put on a steady smile. "How did you manage to get such lovely dogs? Are they from the local rescue place, or did they come from a breeder?"

"Long story," he said. "One of the tenants at a rental property we own couldn't make rent, so he gave me the dogs in lieu of payment."

"That's not a long story."

"He tried to give me his sister first."

"Oh." I forced a laugh. The truth was, I could barely follow the conversation, because my mind was screaming about blood spatter and chain of evidence.

He frowned at me. "Everything okay? You look like you're still freezing, even with my jacket on."

"Low blood sugar," I said, my mouth dry and gummy. "I'm wishing I had that root beer right about now."

"Then we'll go back to the cafe and get another one. This time, we should actually drink it." He raised a finger at me. "No take-backsies. You promised to share a root beer with me, and I'll be damned if I don't hold you to your promise."

"Uh," I said weakly. I didn't want to sit across from Colt Canuso, but if he drove me directly back to the gift shop, he'd be gone. He might even notice the stains on his shirt and get rid of the evidence before the police could track him down. I had to agree to going back to the cafe with him if I wanted to keep him in one place.

I pulled the borrowed jacket tighter around myself. As I did, I looked down at the cuffs of the jacket. Was that another dark blood spatter stain, near the cuff button?

CHAPTER 25

The waitress at the cafe, slots-loving Melody, found it funny we'd come back an hour later for more root beer, considering we hadn't touched our drink the first time.

"Let's splurge on two glasses this time," Colt said, grinning. "With ice cream."

"Two root beer floats," Melody said. "Can I bring you something to eat, honey? We've got those curly fries you love."

Colt rubbed his hands together and looked at me. "That walk in the park really fired up my appetite. Two orders of curly fries, and a burger for me, hold the pickle. How about you, Stormy?"

I didn't feel hungry at all, but I ordered the chicken strips anyway.

I heard little Sophie in my head, telling me chicken nuggets were practically vegetarian. Normally, it would have made me smile, but seeing as I was sitting across the table from the man who might have killed her father, it only turned my stomach.

I took off Colt's jacket, handed it back to him, and excused myself to use the washroom.

When I returned to the table, he'd already started eating his root beer float. He made a joke about how my own float would be in danger if I left the table again.

I forced a laugh and kept my hands folded on my lap so I didn't nervously rearrange the cutlery.

After a moment of silence, he said, "They need to follow the money."

"Who? What money?"

He swished the air with one hand. "I can take a hint. If I keep talking about the Sweets, you'll say I'm gossipy."

"You got my curiosity," I said. "Finish the thought."

"Samantha Sweet is about to come into a few bucks. Rumor is, a million dollars. It might not be the sort of cash that would go far in a big city, but this is Misty Falls. She's going to be set for life."

"Are you talking about some sort of insurance policy? That seems a bit high to me."

"Mikey valued himself highly."

"That he did," I said.

Colt's dark eyes practically blazed. "Can you keep a secret?" He gestured for me to lean in. I did, and he continued in a hushed tone. "That morning in the house, Samantha offered to split the cash with me if I took care of the old man. She was going to hire a professional, but she figured why not get someone who'd enjoy the job?"

I pulled back and crossed my arms. He had to be messing with me.

Colt laughed and smacked the table, open handed. "Gotcha! Oh, Stormy. The look on your face is priceless. I wish I'd taken a picture."

"You shouldn't joke about stuff like that," I said through gritted teeth.

"Or what? Are you going to have me arrested for making jokes in poor taste?" He looked out the window at the parking lot, where a marked police cruiser was pulling into a spot.

"Come on," he said. "Would it kill you to lighten up? I've got a news flash for you about this whole business we call life. None of us is getting out of it alive."

I reached for my root beer float. I could feel my hand trembling with nervousness, so I didn't dare lift the glass. I slid it toward myself, leaving a trail of condensation on the shiny table. I leaned forward, closed my eyes, and sipped the ice-cream-infused root beer.

When I opened my eyes, the police were there, asking Colt if he would cooperate with their investigation and provide them with the shirt he was wearing, as well as his suit jacket.

Colt gripped the edge of the table with both hands as though it might fly away. He gave me a bewildered look. "What should I do?"

"Give them what they want," I said with a detached coolness.

The police officers who'd responded to my report were two men I wasn't very familiar with, which was somewhat of a relief. I didn't want to face Dempsey or Wiggles or especially Milano.

They asked Colt if he would come to the station to answer a few questions.

Again, he gave me a bewildered look. "Should I go? My lawyer told me not to talk to anyone."

My stomach flip-flopped. He hadn't yet figured out that I'd been the one who called the police; I'd done so on my trip to the washroom.

"Call your lawyer on the way over," I said.

"Okay." He pulled his vehicle keys from his pocket and slid them to me across the table. "Would you be a pal and babysit my girls for as long as this takes?"

I wrapped my sweaty fingers around the keys, which were still warm from his pocket.

"Sure," I said, my voice croaking.

The police started taking him away. Colt kept pulling back, fussing about paying for the meal, and worried about giving me instructions for what to feed the dogs.

I nodded and clenched my jaw through all of it.

"Everything's going to be okay," I kept saying.

Melody and the rest of the staff at the restaurant watched from behind the bar counter with wide eyes.

I had to keep reminding myself to breathe. I felt as though I'd been holding my breath since seeing the spots on Colt's shirt at the park.

After, once I'd paid for the uneaten meals and let myself into Colt's truck to get the dogs, I finally let go.

I put my face in my hands and cried.

CHAPTER 26

"Listen, I'm not happy about this situation, either."

Jeffrey flattened his ears back against his head and hissed at me. I was on my tip-toes, trying to pry him out of the space he'd wedged himself into, which was the negligible area between the top of the refrigerator and the bottom of the upper cabinets. The more I tried to get him out, the further back he wedged his little gray body.

"They're nice dogs," I said. "Very well behaved. I'm sure they wouldn't eat you."

I turned and looked at Echo and Juno, whose names I had learned from the tags on their collars. The two huskies were sitting on the kitchen floor and watching the top of the fridge with a patience and focus that would make any vigilant private investigator jealous.

"They're probably just curious," I said to Jeffrey. "Curious about what kind of squeak sound you'd make if they got hold of you. Get it? Because they think you're a squeakie toy."

Jeffrey took a break from hissing at me to make a moaning sound straight out of a horror movie about exorcisms.

"Are you sure you want to stay up there? I could move you to the bedroom, or you could go skulk around in the basement for a while."

More otherworldly moaning.

"Okay, buddy. I hear you. It's been a long day. Maybe you can make a getaway if I distract Echo and Juno by taking them for a walk."

At the sound of me saying the word *walk*, both dogs let out happy whimpers.

That sealed the deal. I was taking the huskies for a walk, heading straight out again not ten minutes after getting home.

As I turned away from the fridge, I saw stars floating in my vision.

Dehydration, I realized. I'd been feeling shaky for hours, ever since I'd spotted the stains on Colt's shirt. That had been midafternoon, and now it was—I checked the time on the stove and then looked out the window, because I couldn't believe it—7:15 pm, twilight.

I poured a glass of water, downed it, and then another. The dogs were on high alert, watching every move I made. One of them walked over to the front door, whimpered, and gave me a heartbreaking look, complete with the saddest blue eyes. And here I thought Jeffrey was the master of the guilt trip. My cat had nothing on this fluffy dog with the heart-shaped white face.

I rummaged in the cupboard for something I could eat while walking. We were out of granola bars, but we did have crackers. I grabbed a three-quarters-full sleeve, tucked it under my armpit, and started putting the leashes back on the dogs.

Unfortunately for me, Echo and Juno knew a rookie when they saw one. When it came to dogs, I was a rookie. Echo moved toward me in what appeared to be an affectionate nuzzle, but then she deftly nosed the closed end of the sleeve of crackers. The plastic sleeve pushed through my armpit and fell. The other dog, Juno, snapped the bag from midair and then shook it like she was snapping a weasel's neck. Crushed bits of whole-wheat crackers sprayed everywhere.

But I didn't have to worry about sweeping up the crumbled mess, because the dogs lapped up every last crumb within seconds. And then they sat on their fluffy butts and quietly gazed up at me with the sweetest expressions, as if to say, *more? Please?*

"I would be mad if you weren't so cute," I said. "Let's go for that walk, straight to the store to get you some dog food. Assuming you haven't been too spoiled by Jeffrey's tasty cat kibbles."

Juno and Echo licked their lips. They'd been distracted by the cat food just long enough for Jeffrey to get himself on top of the fridge.

Juno kept glancing over at the dark space above the refrigerator, which had two shining eyes and moaned like an old ghost.

I shook my finger at the dogs. "No. I will not leave you alone in a room with Jeffrey on ground level," I said. "Not after I saw what you did to those crackers. Jeffrey is not a squeaky toy."

I finished getting their leashes on and scrawled a quick note for Jessica. She wasn't home yet, as she was working a late shift at the Olive Grove.

I wrote: *I'm out walking two dogs. If you hear a moaning sound from the fridge, it's not broken. Jeffrey's hiding on top. If he comes out, please tell him I'm sorry.*

With the dog leashes firmly in hand, I stepped outside with the girls.

I noticed there was a light on inside Logan's side of the duplex. My hopes rose and then sunk just as quickly. He wasn't home. He'd just left the light on inside his kitchen before leaving that morning. I hadn't seen him the night before, either, as he'd come home and gone straight to bed by the time Kyle drove me back after the movie.

I checked my phone again. My handsome lawyer boyfriend hadn't updated me since his last message, two hours ago, when he'd warned me he might be working late yet again on a last-minute brief.

He didn't know about my meeting with Colt earlier that day. I hadn't burdened him yet with the whole situation. Mostly because every time I tried to type out how terrible it had felt for me to turn in an old friend, the waterworks had started up anew. No wonder I was so dehydrated.

The dogs, however, knew nothing about what was going on. As far as they were concerned, their master was at an extra-long meditation class, getting in touch with his pacifistic feelings. The huskies tugged on the leash for me to walk faster, so I walked.

With each block, I felt my head becoming more clear. It wasn't that I had a better perspective on everything that had happened. It was more that it all seemed so distant and unimportant. Right now, there was a breeze, and so many smells in the air.

Whatever Colt Canuso did or didn't do, it was between him, the police, and his lawyers now.

I would carry on with my life.

I pushed away my worries and focused only on the dogs, who were enjoying the moment.

Dusk was approaching, and streetlamps were switching on overhead. I had to stop and check the street signs a few times so I didn't wind up lost. I wasn't far from the house where I'd lived for nearly a year, yet I didn't know this neighborhood very well.

I should get out and walk more, I thought.

The people I encountered kept smiling at me and waving hello to the dogs. A few people stopped to pet the girls and ask what breed they were.

People in Misty Falls are always friendly, but they'd never been as friendly as they were that night, when I was walking two adorable husky sisters.

I should get a dog, I thought. *Or two.*

My happy thoughts were shattered by a truck skidding to a stop on the street next to me. The driver's side door opened, and a petite woman with long, black hair pulled up in a ponytail jumped out.

"There you are," she said angrily, and she started cursing me out. With every name in the book.

Oh, no.

Trigger Canuso.

I hadn't seen her since she was a young girl, but I recognized her by the twist of her crooked chin and nose. Trigger was Colt's baby sister, named after the palomino horse made famous in Western films starring Roy Rogers.

Trigger had been born with hemifacial microsomia, a genetic condition that caused tissue on one side of her face to develop more slowly. It gave her the appearance of scowling angrily, even when she wasn't.

However, based on the word choice she was now using to describe me, the scowl on her face was absolutely real.

The dogs greeted her with happy tail wags.

"Trigger, calm down," I said.

She screeched back, "Why should I calm down?!"

Trigger had an excellent point. Her brother had been taken in for questioning on a homicide case. By now, he would have figured out I'd been the one to call in the report about the blood spots on his clothes. Then he must have told his sister. And now she was here to do grievous bodily harm to me.

Or not.

She was a tiny thing, barely five feet tall. She was, as the casino security guard had described her brother, *a little dog who barks a lot.*

"You're right," I said. "Why be calm? This whole deal truly is messed up. All I can say is, I'm really sorry."

"Why'd you send the cops after Colt? You know he wouldn't hurt nobody!"

"They just need to rule him out," I said. "They have to be careful."

The dogs stood between us, their tails wagging more slowly now as they looked from one of us to the other. They probably didn't know what to think. Trigger was their friend, but she was yelling. I was their new friend, since I'd given them crackers. Who were they more loyal to?

I could relate to the dogs, because I didn't know whose side I was on, either. Especially now that I saw the girl, and memories of her as a child came back to me. Trigger had been a pint-sized brat when I'd been in high school. She'd followed her big brother around town on the weekends like a puppy. I'd always enjoyed seeing her. She'd shaken me down to buy her a chocolate bar or a burger more than once.

Inside me, I had a rush of conflicting feelings. She was still the grubby-faced child I'd taken under my wing. She was in her twenties now, but she was still so small, and the memory of her as a kid persisted in my mind. I wanted to walk up to her and hug her, but I knew better. You don't hug a rattlesnake.

Instead, I said, "Trigger, I'm sorry."

She spat on the ground. "Don't you dare say my name like you know me! You don't know me! You don't know my family!"

Juno whimpered, which made Echo whimper as well.

We both looked down at the dogs.

"They haven't had dinner yet," I said. "They worked up an appetite chasing my cat onto the refrigerator." I held out the leashes. "You did come here to get the dogs, right?"

"Yeah," she said.

She took the leashes from my hand, still glaring at me. The huskies began licking her free hand, and I saw the rage drain out of her.

"This is so messed up," she said, dropping in a few swear words as she patted the dogs.

"Your brother needs your support," I said. "No matter what."

"He's on his way home right now," she said. "The cops didn't hold him, because they know he didn't do nothin'."

"Good," I said, though I knew that releasing Colt didn't mean the police thought he was innocent. It just meant they didn't have the evidence yet to feel confident in arresting him. Even with a rush, it would take time for the crime lab to test the blood on Colt's clothes against Michael Sweet's DNA.

"Those cops need to go after the wife," Trigger said. "She's the one who's going to be getting all that money. Plus she's crazy. Cuckoo. Totally nuts."

"Samantha?"

"Haven't you heard? She lost her mind." Trigger let out a cruel laugh.

I hadn't heard about Samantha losing her mind, but I wasn't surprised to hear she was behaving erratically. She'd been dazed and sluggish the last time I'd seen her, as though heavily medicated.

"Some people behave strangely when they're grieving," I said. "It's different for every person, every situation. For some, confronting death makes them over-steer toward embracing life, seizing the day."

Trigger crossed her arms and told the dogs to sit. They didn't sit but continued to nuzzle her arms and lick her exposed skin, including her chin. Trigger was so short, the dogs barely had to jump to lick her face.

Ignoring the huskies as best she could, Trigger said, "That realtor lady is crazy. She doesn't even think her husband is dead."

"What are you talking about? She saw his body." *She had his blood all over her hands.* "Are you saying she's blocked the memory?"

"Yeah. Because she's *crazy*."

I rubbed my chin. It was possible for Samantha to disbelieve her husband was dead. "She could be in a disassociative state," I said. "I'm no psychiatrist, but I've been reading up on some of these things."

"Not that," Trigger said with a cold laugh. "She thinks the guy who got stabbed is actually someone who looks like her husband. A look-alike. A body double."

"That's crazy."

"I know! She's going to take the money from the insurance, and then, after it's all spent, she thinks Michael's going to come back."

"How do you know this?"

"You're not the only one in this town who knows how to get information."

"Come on, Trigger. We're on the same side. I don't want Colt to get caught up in this if he didn't do it."

She raised her voice. "He didn't do it! I told you, stupid!" And then she cursed me out some more.

I held my hands up. "Listen, I'll ask around, okay? I'll try to figure out what's going on with Samantha and this so-called body double."

"Don't you be comin' around the casino," she said.

"Don't worry. I promise I won't try to see Colt unless he wants to see me."

"No," she said coldly. "Never. Not ever."

"Are you banning me from the premises?"

She tugged the dogs toward her truck. The engine was still idling, and she'd left the driver's side door open. The dome light inside the cab of the truck gave it a warm, golden glow.

It was only now that I realized twilight was gone and night had truly fallen. All was dark around me. Darkness.

"You're dead," Trigger said as she backed away. "If I ever see you on my land, in my casino, you're *dead*." She switched the leashes to her left hand, pointed her right hand at me like a gun, and made a click sound as she mimed pulling a trigger.

CHAPTER 27

WEDNESDAY

Just when it seems like the sun will never come up again, it does.

Tuesday hadn't been so great. I'd turned an old friend in to the police, and then, because no good deed goes unpunished, I'd been reamed out by his sister. She'd tried to make me feel like dirt, and she'd been successful.

But Wednesday was a new day. Or so I told myself.

I woke up late, which wasn't the best start. I thought of that great Irish expression:*Lose an hour in the morning, and you'll be looking for it all day.*

I had a dozen pressing matters to deal with, yet I couldn't focus on my work. There was a heaviness in my chest that I couldn't chase away with coffee. Not even coffee plus Jessica's icing-covered cinnamon buns could lift my mood. I couldn't focus on anything except how lousy I felt.

My body ached, and the hard chair at the kitchen table where I usually worked felt harder than ever.

I moved over to the sofa, and the aches in my body moved to different regions.

I was two minutes into working on an insurance case when Jeffrey walked across my paperwork on the cushion next to me and then the keys of my laptop. I tossed his mouse toy across the room but he wasn't taking the bait. He walked across the keyboard again, making the screen do something I'd never seen it do before. I couldn't figure out what magical key combination he'd pushed with his paws. I had to reboot the computer to get the display back to normal.

As soon as my display was fixed, he returned to do his magical trick again.

"Jeffrey Blue, you're doing an amazing impression of a barnacle. Why are you so clingy? You've got both kinds of food, and I refilled your water dish on the tub while you were watching, so you know it's fresh. What's going on?"

I pushed the laptop toward my knees. He walked onto the available section of my lap and flopped down dramatically. He rolled his head back and gazed at me with slow-blinking affectionate green eyes.

"Is this about the doggies?"

His ears twitched in the feline equivalent of a frown.

"Those doggies aren't coming back here," I said. "It was just a one-time deal, I swear."

He opened his mouth and gave me a silent meow —the most heart-tugging of cat sounds.

"Let's say it is Michael's blood in those spatters on Colt's shirt. Let's say he does go to prison." I grimaced at the words, which left a bad taste in my mouth. "Just because he asked me to take care of his dogs yesterday doesn't mean I have to. I didn't even agree to be their godmother. Technically, we don't have a verbal contract, let alone a formal written one, like the type Logan would draw up."

Jeffrey rolled onto his back, exposing his tummy. I knew better than to take the bait and stick my hand in the fluffiest of feline traps.

"You're right," I said. "Logan hasn't been much help lately. He's always working at the office whenever I could use his help."

Jeffrey started purring.

"It certainly is a good thing I have you, and Auntie Jessica. Plus your grampa's been supportive through all of this, in his own way. He sent me a text message this morning with three stars and a frog. I don't know what it means, but at least he's checking in on me."

Jeffrey closed his eyes to focus on his rumbling purr. I carefully closed the laptop and set it beside me on the couch. I rearranged the cat so he was completely on my lap rather than draped over it, falling onto his head in slow motion.

"You're absolutely right," I said. "Why worry about all the things you need to do when you can take a nap and do nothing?"

I leaned my head back on the sofa.

The warm blanket of sleep came instantly, unlike the night before, when I'd tossed and turned for three hours.

* * *

The ringing of my phone woke me up. Jeffrey grumbled as I shoved him aside so I could grab my phone from the kitchen counter.

"This is Stormy Day," I said groggily, gripping the counter with one sweaty hand.

"Boss?" My employee, Brianna, was whispering. "She's here, and she's buying up half the store."

"The Countess?"

"No. Samantha Sweet. She keeps asking if you're here. She's asked me three times now. I swear she thinks I'm lying or something."

"Hang tight," I said. "I'm jumping in the car and I'll be there as soon as I can."

"Please hurry," Brianna whispered. "She's freaking me out."

* * *

I barely recognized Samantha Sweet. Gone was the bright, tidy wardrobe of citrus-colored dresses paired with crisp white blazers. She looked less like a working professional woman and more like a college coed on a reading break, with her tattered jeans and stained sweatshirt. Her blond hair was straight on one side and matted on the other, as though she hadn't brushed her hair or even showered since I'd last seen her ten days earlier.

As I watched her look over the store displays, I thought of what I'd said to Trigger Canuso the night before. *"Some people behave strangely when they're grieving. It's different for every person, every situation. For some, confronting death makes them over-steer toward embracing life, seizing the day."*

Samantha's behavior did seem strange, but how was a person supposed to act after having their husband murdered?

I'd entered the store through the back way, so Samantha hadn't seen me yet. Before alerting her to my presence, I caught Brianna's attention and met my store manager in the back hallway.

I whispered to Brianna, "Has she said anything to you?"

Brianna replied, "She just keeps asking where you are. That's why I called you." She nervously rubbed the red spot on her chin where she'd had a pimple the week before. "Thanks for getting here so fast."

She glanced guiltily at something in the middle of the store.

I followed her gaze over the counter, to the central display table. There was a conspicuous blank spot. "You changed the display? What's missing?"

"The *Laguiole* steak knives are gone," Brianna said. "When she was looking at the fairy figurines, I grabbed all of the knives and tucked them behind the counter."

I stared at Brianna's big, wide eyes. Should I give her heck for being paranoid, or congratulate her for protecting herself?

"Smart thinking," I said.

She grimaced. "I feel terrible. The poor woman's been through so much, but my imagination is really overactive."

I patted her on the shoulder. "It's okay," I whispered. "In the wake of a violent crime, we're all left with these broken pieces we have to shift around until life seems okay again."

Brianna looked down at her shoes. "Being an adult sucks. I want to make a blanket fort and hide."

"Make me one, too," I said through gritted teeth.

I gave her another shoulder pat along with a few words of encouragement, and ventured out onto the sales floor.

I put on a professional smile and said to the sweatshirt-wearing, disheveled woman, "I see someone's keen on redecorating."

Samantha spun around and gave me a wild-eyed look. "Stormy, don't sneak up on people like that!" She had a stainless steel paté knife in her hand, and she'd raised her fist in a defensive stabbing position. The short, round blade was designed for spreading soft paté, so it was no more than two inches long, and as blunt as a shiny penny, but the effect was still alarming. It would have been disturbing even if her husband hadn't been stabbed to death a week and a half earlier.

"I didn't mean to startle you, Samantha." I took a step back toward the office.

She lowered the gleaming paté knife and dropped it onto the cheese-serving accessories shelf, next to the marble cutting boards and the bamboo trays.

We stared at each other. The music was playing over the shop's stereo system, and the song at that moment was "Cuts Like a Knife" by Bryan Adams. The lyrics jumped out.

I turned my head subtly and gave Brianna a wide-eyed look. She lifted her hands and mouthed the word *what?*

I made a knob-twisting motion with my hand.

She lifted her eyebrows in acknowledgment and cranked the volume. Up.

I shook my head.

Brianna swore under her breath and shut the music system off completely.

"My bad," she said. To Samantha, she said, "I hate Bryan Adams. Canadians, right? Ugh. Canadians are the worst."

I smiled at Samantha and continued the lie. "Brianna hates Canadians. And their stupid geese."

"Yeah," Brianna said with false enthusiasm.

"The geese are awful," Samantha agreed. "I have a lake-front listing that would be an easy sell if the lawn wasn't covered in green goose droppings. That's not the sort of green lawn buyers are looking for."

With a casual tone, I asked, "How are things going with your listings? Is there anything I can do to help?"

"Everything's fine."

"How's your daughter doing?"

"Fine."

"Michael Junior?"

"Fine."

"How about Higgins?"

She blinked at me. "Who?"

"The guinea pig."

"Right," she said. "He's fine. He's a guinea pig."

"He's a little cutie pie. You must have your hands full. Do you have anyone staying with you?"

She ignored my question and picked up a heavy pewter candlestick. "Is this brass?"

"Pewter," I said.

"What is pewter? Whatever happened to brass, anyway? It's pretty, like gold. I like gold. I'm going to buy some gold earrings. Michael never bought me jewelry. Now I can buy whatever jewelry I want."

She continued to babble about jewelry and buying gifts for herself. The slightly obsessive part of my personality made me want to answer her question about pewter, because I knew it was a malleable metal alloy, mostly tin, mixed with copper, antimony, or bismuth. Older pewters exhibiting a darker silver-gray color might contain lead, so they shouldn't be used for food or come into contact with the human body.

But Samantha wasn't in the mood for a discussion about alloys or the history of tableware. She was in Full Shopping Mania Mode. She wanted napkin rings. And decorative key organizers. And an old-fashioned wooden sorting board for mail, decorated with a hand-painted rooster going COCK A DOODLE DOO.

If she'd had a shopping cart, she would have been filling it. But we didn't have big, rolling carts in the gift shop. Mostly people came in to buy only one or two items at a time. When people did go on sprees, they stacked things on the checkout counter, which was what Samantha Sweet was currently doing.

I asked her, "Are you picking up a thank-you gift for a family member? Maybe someone who's staying with you?"

She pointed to an octagonal mirror high up on the wall. "Is that for sale?"

"Sure," I said, even though the mirror wasn't for sale. It was there to cover an access panel. But I didn't want to say no to the woman. It would be like waking a sleepwalker.

For the next hour, I tried a few more times to find out how things were going at her house, but she kept ignoring my questions. She just wanted to shop.

Her behavior certainly matched with what Trigger Canuso had told me the night before, about how Samantha was going to be getting a big insurance settlement. But did she really believe Michael was still alive, and that the body was that of a doppelganger?

She was behaving erratically, for sure.

Brianna and I watched with equal parts horror and awe as Samantha Sweet stacked up for purchase a significant portion of our inventory.

I looked over her piles at the counter and said, "You can return this if you change your mind."

"Stormy, I wouldn't do that to you," Samantha said. "You've been such a help to me through this difficult time."

"I've helped?" I wondered if she'd heard about the police questioning Colt the day before.

"Sophie is always talking about you," Samantha gushed. "And your trip to Goodie Burger, and then how you watched princess movies with her, just like a true friend. You should come by and see her some time. She'd love to see you."

"I could do that," I said. "Are you sure it's a good idea? Kids might seem resilient, but they need time to grieve."

"Grieve?" Samantha blinked at me, her expression blank.

I didn't know how to respond, so I looked at the computer screen and read the total for her purchase.

She handed me a credit card without hesitation.

I swiped the card through the credit card machine. I hoped it would be declined. I didn't want to take Samantha's money, not like this.

To my surprise, the transaction was going through. I had just taken money from a woman who wasn't in her right frame of mind. It felt unethical, but I didn't know what else to do. If she was going to max out her credit cards, it was better for her to do it at my store, because I truly *would* accept back all the merchandise when she eventually came to her senses. I didn't know if the other local businesses would be so understanding.

Samantha took her credit card from my hand and tucked it away. "Sophie always misses her dad when he's away on business, but it just makes for a happier reunion when he comes home."

"But Michael's not coming home," I said. "Samantha, he's dead. We both saw him."

"That wasn't Michael," she said, scoffing. "It must have been a body he bought off someone at the morgue. Or from a medical school. Didn't you smell it? The thing smelled like pickles!"

"Pickles?" I was nearly speechless. "Do you mean embalming fluid?"

She shrugged. "How should I know? When Michael comes back, he can tell me exactly how he pulled it off." She looked at me and laughed. "He sure fooled you, Stormy! The look on your face that day!"

I nodded and decided to play along. "Yup. I was really fooled. Michael certainly was quite thorough with his plans. He even warmed up the body to make it seem like it had only just happened."

"I'm sorry if you were scared," she said. She glanced around to make sure we were alone. Brianna had gone into the office to take a much-needed break. The walls were thin, and she'd be able to easily overhear our conversation, but Samantha didn't know that.

"Don't tell anyone," Samantha said gravely. "Not until after we have that money from the insurance company and it's all hidden away where they can't touch it."

I mimed zipping my lips.

She looked down at the pile of housewares and tchotchkes. "How am I going to get all of this back to my house?"

"I'll help you," I said. "Whatever doesn't fit in your vehicle, we can put in my car. I'll follow you to your house, and then we can make a whole day out of setting everything up."

She clapped her hands girlishly. "That sounds wonderful."

I started boxing up the items in cardboard shipping boxes, since our bags would only hold a few items.

I decided I would follow her to her house, and then I'd conduct a search of her purse, her medicine cabinet, and her bedside table. She was, without a doubt, suffering a mental breakdown. Whether it was just a bad mix of medicines or something else was yet to be determined, and the diagnosis was not up to me.

Thanks for my investigative work experience, I had a few contacts in the social services field who could take my tip and deal with it discreetly.

It was with a heavy heart that I popped my head into the office and whispered my plan to Brianna.

"Someone's gotta do it," she whispered back. "You have to make sure those little kids of hers are safe."

"I really don't want to do this," I said.

"But you're so good at it," she said. "You'll do great. Call me with an update? I swear I'm not trying to be a *drama llama*. I feel kinda responsible, because I phoned you."

"I understand," I said. I really did appreciate her having called me at home to let me know about Samantha's strange behavior.

"Good luck."

"I'll check in with you," I said. "Brianna, you did the right thing by calling me."

Her eyes filled with tears. "How come the right thing feels so wrong?"

I felt myself channeling my father, speaking his words. "I'm sorry, sweetie. That's just how life is sometimes."

CHAPTER 28

I loaded the remaining boxes of Samantha's merchandise into my car and followed Samantha to her house. She parked in her driveway and went straight into the house, carrying in only one bag from her vehicle.

I parked on the street in front and stepped out. I was surprised by what I saw, at the transformation that had taken place over the last ten days. A pile of mail appeared to be bursting from the mailbox. The front step was strewn with wilting bouquets of sympathy flowers in a variety of containers. Some well-meaning neighbor had brought over a casserole, but it hadn't even been brought inside. If I hadn't already known, I would have been tipped off immediately that there'd been a tragedy at the Sweet residence. Two oily-black crows had easily removed the plastic wrap from the casserole and were now digging into the abandoned treasure. Human tragedy made for a tasty crow picnic.

The two glossy birds flapped their wings as I approached.

"Lunch is all yours," I told the crows. "That actually looks good. Is it lasagna?"

The crows continued pulling the casserole apart.

"I talk to animals now," I explained to the birds. "You see, I have a cat."

The crows paused and cocked their heads in an almost human gesture, as if to say they totally understood.

I entered the house.

"Where's Sophie?" I asked as I surveyed the mess in the entryway.

"At school," Samantha answered nonchalantly.

"And Michael Junior?"

"Um..." Samantha picked up a rumpled blanket from the sofa. "At the daycare?" Her voice inflected up at the end, as though she was the one asking me.

We finished picking up blankets and dirty laundry from the living room. I was relieved to not find the baby there unattended, but I was troubled by Samantha's lack of concern about where he actually was.

"We should tidy up before we bring more stuff in," I said.

"You don't have to help. Unless you want to?"

I gave her a warm smile. "I insist. Let's get things tidied up. It's always easier to think in a clean room."

She agreed. While Samantha went to the kitchen and started on the dishes, which I could smell as soon as we'd walked in the front door, I got to work on the rest of the house.

An hour later, I went into Sophie's room, where I found Higgins looking unhappy in a dirty cage. Or at least I assumed he was unhappy. If I were trapped in a cage that smelled as bad as his, I'd be grumpy.

"Hey, Higgins. I'm here to help. How would you like some new bedding in there?"

He stared at me with his big dark eyes. I'd never spent much time around guinea pigs, but he was a cute little guy, mostly brown with a white sash down the center of his face. The white sash had a zig-zag to it, like a lightning bolt. *Harry Potter*, I thought. Tony Milano's kids had a guinea pig they called Harry Potter because he or she had a lightning bolt. I wondered if their Harry and Higgins could be related. We only had so many pet stores and breeders in town, so it was possible.

I gave Higgins fresh food and water, and changed the stinky bedding in the bottom of his cage. I used the paper-based bedding material that was in a bag next to his cage. The writing on the packaging claimed it to be phenol-free and healthier than wood shavings.

"There you go," I said when I was done.

Higgins thanked me for my efforts by biting my finger.

You know what they say. No good deed goes unpunished.

Truthfully, it wasn't his fault. I'd spooked him with some sudden hand movements. At least he hadn't broken my skin.

"Sorry I scared you," I said.

He blinked up at me with big, frightened eyes. Or maybe I was projecting again. I was the one who was frightened. What was I doing there? What was I supposed to do about Samantha, who'd apparently gone a bit crazy?

I pulled a book about the care of guinea pigs off Sophie's shelf and sat down to learn more about the little critters. *One thing at a time*, I told myself.

Higgins gradually warmed up to my presence and hopped out of his cage to come check me out.

He meandered over to where I sat cross-legged on the carpet. After a few minutes, he eventually hopped up onto my leg and nuzzled my hand.

"Does this mean we're friends?"

He gazed up at me with big, black eyes. Was that affection?

"Sorry, I can't take you home with me," I said. "My cat is still very sore with me for bringing home two huskies last night."

He nuzzled my hand again and began vibrating.

Vibrating?

I checked the handbook.

Yes, guinea pigs purr. Who knew? Higgins definitely wanted to spend more time with me.

"Higgins, you don't know what you're asking for," I said softly. "Jeffrey Blue would try to eat you. I know you're bigger than his mouth, but he'd still try."

I handed him a leaf of lettuce I'd gotten from the kitchen, and he nibbled away happily on my lap.

"You're welcome," I said. "You sure are easy to please. Other than the time you bit me." I checked my fingertip. It was red but not bleeding. "No harm, no foul," I said.

The floor outside the room creaked, and a man appeared in the doorway. "Who are you talking to?"

"Tony Baloney!"

Captain Tony Milano grimaced at being called by his old nickname.

"That's weird. I was just thinking about you," I said.

"Of course you were." He looked around the little girl's bedroom. "This feels familiar," he said. "Me, you, the unicorn posters?"

I chortled. "I was a bit older than Sophie when we first met."

"Sweet sixteen," he said with a twist of a grin.

"That phrase always makes the person saying it look like a dirty old man."

He frowned. "It's hard to believe you were ever that young. You were just a kid."

"I was."

He'd been twenty-three when my father had taken him under his wing. As a young rookie cop, Tony had spent a lot of time at our house, including family dinners. Back then, he'd been so cute with his bronzed skin, cropped black hair, and big brown eyes. He was always flexing the muscles he'd built up at the academy. In his tight black T-shirts, Tony had been a bigger star than every famous actor and singer rolled into one. I lived for those nights he came over to see my father because he'd always spend a few minutes chatting with me. I loved how he treated me like an adult, like an equal.

And now, whenever I saw him, he made me feel the opposite. Like a kid. Not equal at all. And so I tried to poke at him, calling him Tony Baloney among other things, just to get a reaction. The truth was, I just wanted to see him smile. I'd loved him once, and a part of me still did. I wanted to see him happy, sometimes. Despite the other part of me that wanted to see him miserable. We'd dated in secret, when I was twenty-three, right before I left town. It was only supposed to be a fling, an experiment, yet I resented him for closing the door to me when his girlfriend got pregnant. He married her, and they had three kids.

And now here we were, years later, still feeling the past.

The only difference was a bit of gray hair, and bigger problems.

He leaned against the doorway and looked down at me on the floor. "What are you doing here?"

"Checking on Samantha. What about you? Did someone call in a ten-fifty-nine?" That was the Misty Falls Police Department's code for incidents involving yours truly. I was somewhat flattered to have earned my own code.

He didn't even twitch. "Who told you about the ten-fifty-nine?"

"I heard Dimples use it with dispatch a few weeks back, when we were in pursuit of suspects."

"You mean that time when you wrecked a perfectly good police cruiser?"

"Me? I wasn't the one driving."

"Maybe you should have been." He crossed his arms. "When are you going to give up on this private eye business and come work for the good guys?"

I felt my eyebrows rise in surprise. This was a new one. Usually, Tony tried to get me to stay far away from police business. Now he was recruiting me? I looked down at Higgins, who looked equally surprised. He'd paused in chewing his lettuce leaf to stare at Tony.

Tony was grinning, apparently pleased to have made me speechless for a moment.

"Captain Milano, you just want me working for the department so you can boss me around."

"Please," he said with a snort. "I may be slow sometimes, but I'm not an idiot. Nobody can boss you around, Stormy."

Just my cat, I answered in my head. *And my bossy redheaded roommate.*

"Are you going to tell me why you're here?" I asked. "You're not in uniform, so am I to assume this is a personal call?"

"Not that it's any of your business, *Miss Day*, but I'm here to keep Ms. Sweet up to date on the homicide case."

"Did you get a confession from Colt Canuso?"

"Do I look like I'm in a celebratory mood?"

"I can't tell, Tony Baloney. I haven't seen you happy in a long time."

"Ouch."

I shook my head and looked down at the guinea pig, who was casually distancing himself from a trio of suspicious-looking brown pellets on my jeans.

"I'm being pooped on," I said.

"Don't be so dramatic," Tony said with a sigh. "Fine. Since you were good enough to cooperate with the investigation, I can let you know there's been no confession yet."

"No?" I smiled as I gently scooped up Higgins and set him back into his cage. Tony had misinterpreted what I'd said about being literally pooped on. Who knew a little dramatic hyperbole would work so well at getting him to loosen up?

"Canuso is sticking to his story that he was walking his dogs outside of town at the time of the murder. We are, however, very interested in Tanner and the other Canuso, the security guards."

I closed the guinea pig cage and passed in a carrot stick between the bars.

"That would be great if it was one of those two," I said. "Or both of them."

"Anyone but your pal, right?" He uncrossed his arms and stepped into the room, where he looked large and masculine—out of place in front of the frosting-pink walls. "Is there something going on between you and Colt?"

"Yes, Tony. I'm sleeping with half the town."

He snorted. "No need to overreact."

"I'm with Logan," I said. "Not with Colt Canuso, or Kyle Dempsey, or any of the other men in this town between the ages of nineteen and ninety whom you *always* assume I'm sleeping with if you happen to see me having so much as a two-minute conversation with them."

He gave a nonchalant shrug. "I'm just looking out for you. You're like a sister to me."

"Ew." Suddenly, I wanted out of the small room. I got to my feet, and I couldn't resist giving him a bump with my shoulder as I moved past him, out of Sophie's bedroom.

He followed me to the bathroom and watched me wash my hands. The family's main bathroom was a mess, with towels on the floor, an overflowing laundry hamper, and what appeared to be a loose stack of used diapers forming a pyramid on the back of the toilet tank.

I whispered to Tony, "That's not a good sign," and nodded at the diapers.

"No," he said gravely. "I'm afraid I'll have to report this. We'll have a social worker pick up Sophie at the school. Any idea where the baby is?"

"At the daycare. I already called to check." I pulled out my phone and gave him the name of the place and the address. "What about Samantha?"

We both listened for a minute. She was now rearranging the furniture in the living room, talking to herself a mile a minute. By the sound of it, she was having a better day than us. In her own mind, anyway.

I explained to Tony what Samantha had said to me at my store, about how the body in the tub hadn't been Michael's and he would return to reunite with her, and life would be wonderful because they'd be rich from the insurance money.

"If only it worked that way," Tony said with sadness. "I'd fake my own death if I could."

I smacked him on the shoulder playfully. "Don't even joke. You're the one person in this town who could get away with it. Plus you have access to all the bodies."

He smacked me back on my shoulder. "So does Harvey Blight, the undertaker."

"Blight? I thought he was the manager of Accio Bistro."

"That's his brother, Howard Blight. The undertaker is Harvey Blight. Kind of an unfortunate name for the funeral business."

"Kind of an unfortunate last name for any profession, really."

"You would know." He grinned. "Stormy."

"Tony Baloney."

He breathed in deeply and glanced around. "Well, are we going to stand here all day trading insults, or are we going to make some phone calls and finish tearing apart a victimized family?"

I stared at him.

He broke eye contact, looking down at his feet. He'd taken off his shoes before entering the residence, and based on the number of children's Band-Aids that were now stuck to his foot, he was probably regretting his choice.

"It's just dark humor," he said. "We don't mean anything by it."

"I know," I said gently. "You can make amends by taking Higgins with you. He can play with your guinea pig, Harry Potter."

He looked up quickly, wide-eyed. "You remembered the name of my kids' guinea pig?"

I could have told him it had stuck with me, thanks to the anecdote he told me about it going missing, and how it was named after the boy wizard because it had a white lightning-shaped marking on its head.

Instead, I said, rather ominously, "I know *everything* about you, Milano."

CHAPTER 29

When I got home that Wednesday afternoon, I found a note on my front door. There were no words, just an arrow pointing to Logan's side of the duplex.

I walked over with the note in my hand, laughing to myself. He could be as cryptic as my father at times.

I let myself in and kicked off my shoes. "You summoned me?"

He turned around from his position at the stove and gave me the smile that could win over the toughest of judges, in spite of the dark beard so many people teased him about.

"You had a tough day," he said.

"You heard about that."

"My cousin called me, screaming that you were trying to take away her children. You wouldn't do such a thing, would you?"

I shrugged and went straight for the wine bottle on the counter. There were three glasses set out, which I found strange, but didn't question it.

"Those blond kids of hers are cute," I said. "My devious mastermind plot was to kill Michael, drive Samantha insane, and then take her children for myself."

He gave me a serious look, eyebrows raised. "There are simpler ways to get a couple of children."

I nearly spilled the wine I was pouring. Logan and I hadn't discussed having children, let alone a couple of them. I took a sip of the wine and waited for my thoughts to coalesce. The scene at the Sweet residence had been intense. Even without the kids there, Samantha had been a handful, hurling dishes at Tony as soon as he told her a representative from Child Protective Services was coming by for a "quick interview."

I'd locked myself in the master bedroom with the guinea pig for the better part of an hour, afraid to stay but more afraid to leave.

Samantha finally became more calm and agreed to be psychologically evaluated at the hospital. Some people came, helped her pack an overnight bag, and took her away. Tony and I did a quick check around the house before locking up. He agreed to take Higgins with him, informing me that I "owed him one" for taking temporary custody of the guinea pig.

Logan, being Samantha's cousin, had already heard about the afternoon's excitement from the opposite side—the point of view from which I was the evil enemy.

I must have been feeling guilty about something—perhaps how bad it looked for Samantha's car to be filled with merchandise from my store—that I gushed out the whole story in a stream of conscious rant, tripping over my tongue to make sure Logan had the full picture. The true picture. My picture.

I was pouring a second glass and still talking—I'd gotten up to the part about the Sweet family's next-door neighbor giving me royal hell for drawing crows to the street with food left out on the porch—when I noticed a third person quietly standing in Logan's kitchen.

She was younger than Logan, perhaps late twenties, with wavy auburn hair and big, doll-like hazel eyes. She was wearing flannel pajama bottoms and a sleeveless T-shirt with no bra. She looked really familiar, like an actress I'd seen on TV a million times.

"You're up," Logan said to her.

She made a gagging face. "Who can sleep with the smell of all that garlic wafting around?"

"Hello," I said, offering my hand. It wasn't the first time I'd come over to Logan's and discovered some friend or client of his—often a husband who'd been kicked out of the house—was bunking in his second bedroom. It was, however, the first time it had been a pretty young woman whose name I didn't even know.

"Stormy Day," she said. "I'm Jennifer."

I shook her hand tentatively. "You mean Jinx?"

She gave my hand a happy squeeze, and her face lit up. "Ah! So, my big brother hasn't been keeping me a secret."

"Yes and no. He doesn't talk about his family much."

Logan's sister, whom everyone called Jinx, wrinkled her nose adorably. "Can't say I blame him," she said. "Our family can be a bit trashy. And now poor Sam's getting her kids taken away, which is not unusual in the Sanderson family, I'm sorry to say."

"It's only temporary," I said. "Are you visiting for long?"

"I'm here for the funeral tomorrow, and then..." Jinx looked over at Logan, as though it was up to him.

He finished chopping and then swept a pile of chopped onions from a cutting board into the sizzling pan on the stove. The hot oil and veggies steamed noisily, filling the air with aromatics. Suddenly, I was so hungry, I felt hollow.

"As long as you wish," Logan said to his sister. Looking at me with a twinkle in his green eyes, he said, "Though my landlady might slap a surcharge on my rent for extra use of hot water and utilities, as per our tenancy agreement."

"She sounds like a tough lady," I said. "A real dragon."

"More like a tiger," Logan said. "But I know how to make her purr like a pussycat."

Jinx exclaimed, "Ew! Gogie!"

I smirked. "Gogie?"

Logan explained, "When Jinx was little, she couldn't pronounce my name, so she called me Gogie."

"Or Logjam," Jinx said. "I didn't know what a logjam was, but I must have heard it somewhere. That's what I called all jam. I used to eat a lot of peanut butter and logjam sandwiches."

Logan shook his head. "This is all so boring to Stormy."

"No, not at all," I said. "It's refreshing. Logan never tells me any of these things. It's like I'm suddenly seeing a whole new side to him. A cute side."

"I wasn't cute before?" He blinked at me.

I waved a hand at him, curling my fingers like a tiger's claws as I roared playfully. Normally, I wouldn't have been so flirtatious in front of someone I'd just met, but the wine was hitting my system, and it felt good to be silly after a rough day.

Jinx excused herself to get dressed for dinner.

I walked up to Logan and hugged him from behind.

"Mind the spatter from the stove," he said softly, but he didn't push me away. He arched his back to lean back and give me a kiss. "Don't mind Jinx," he said. "She likes to push people's buttons."

She hadn't bothered me at all, so I had to assume he was simply warning me. I slipped my hands into Logan's pockets. "Sounds like a certain lawyer I know."

He looked down at his pockets. "Are you conducting an investigation in there?"

"It's your fault for always having mints in your pocket." I pulled out his roll of mints and took two.

"That won't go with the wine," he said.

"I need sugar."

"They're sugar free."

"Why must you be so quarrelsome?"

"You would prefer a man who's spineless and jumps at your every command?"

I frowned, detecting a hint of acrimony in his question. I countered with another question. "How was your day?"

"I had to drive into the city and pick up my bratty sister from the airport."

"And how was that?"

"Long," he said.

I sighed inwardly. It was so like Logan to give me a one-word non-answer to any questions about his interior emotional life. Sometimes I wondered if he felt anything at all.

"Road trips can be fun," I said. "You should have asked me to go with you."

"You were busy getting Sam's kids taken away from her."

"And her guinea pig," I said. "Don't forget about Higgins."

"Release me," he said, looking down at my left hand, which was still tucked in his pocket. "I gotta put the pork in the stir fry."

"It's right there on the counter."

He breathed out audibly. "Stormy."

I pulled my hand away and held it up in the air. "Fine. I'll give you some space."

He frowned. "It's just that the pan is hot and there's oil spattering around."

"No need to explain," I said icily. "I understand. You've opened a nice bottle of wine, and you're cooking me a good meal. I can be grateful and give you the space you need to do it."

I retreated from the kitchen, taking the bottle with me to the living room.

"You've got stuff all over your butt," Logan said. "Is that a used Band-Aid? Don't you dare sit on my couch until you go clean yourself off."

"Okay, Dad," I said haughtily. Did he have to act so disgusted over a bit of lint?

I gave him a dirty look and sulked off to the bathroom.

Jinx was in the bathroom, putting on makeup with the door open. She nodded for me to come in anyway. She had her auburn hair pulled back with a clip and was applying liquid eyeliner. I hadn't noticed at first, but she had small wrinkles at the sides of her mouth, the kind of lines I associated with a young person who was also a smoker. She didn't smell of cigarettes, so either she'd quit or Logan wouldn't let her smoke around him. I wouldn't have been at all surprised if it were the latter.

Her auburn hair wasn't natural. The roots had a much darker tint, closer to the shade of Logan's hair. In the bright lights of the bathroom, the hair color wasn't flattering and gave her skin a sallow tone. But she was still a pretty girl, with the huge eyes and waifish look that was popular on young actresses lately, almost like a character in a Japanese comic book. I saw her resemblance to her brother in the way her eyes flitted between her reflection and mine while she smiled knowingly, as though we were the only two people who "got it." We were in on the same joke and everyone else around us was just playing a role, background actors in the main story, which was us.

I pulled open the drawer and grabbed one of Logan's many lint rollers. Sitting on the carpet at the Sweet residence had resulted in a lot of objects being transferred to the back of my jeans, including but not limited to guinea pig cage confetti, bits of crumbled food, and not one but two children's Band-Aids.

"You got in trouble," Jinx said with a teasing tone. "I heard him giving you heck. Do you always let him talk to you like that?"

"My father taught me to choose my battles wisely." I added, "As did growing up with a sister, actually." I finished removing the debris from the back of my jeans and carefully peeled away the sticky layer so it would be fresh for Logan's next use, just how he liked it. "Did you two get along when you were growing up?"

"As well as siblings in a dysfunctional environment can get along." Her expression changed, becoming sad and distant for a moment. "He got out as soon as he could, of course."

"Right," I said, nodding. Logan's home life was one of the many topics he only gave one-word answers about. "I hope you'll be around here for a while," I said. "I'd love to show you around the bustling metropolis of Misty Falls, Oregon."

"And for me to give you the dirt on Logan's old girlfriends, right?" Jinx gave me a mischievous smile. I could see how she'd acquired her nickname.

"There's dirt?" I blinked innocently.

"Don't worry," she said in a hushed tone. "You're not his usual type. I think he's finally broken the pattern."

"Good to know," I said. Was she pulling my leg or hinting at something I needed to know? Was this what Logan had tried to warn me about? Was Jinx a truth teller, or was she a troublemaker?

Logan called out that dinner was ready.

Jinx and I exchanged a conspiratorial look.

"We shouldn't make him wait," Jinx said. "Logan gets mad when he's ignored."

Neither of us made a move to leave the bathroom. We stared at each other without blinking.

"Girls!" Logan yelled.

We didn't move.

He yelled again, sounding more annoyed. "Come on! Your dinner's getting cold!"

"We're in trouble," Jinx whispered. She couldn't have looked more delighted if she'd been handed a stack of birthday presents.

"I'm used to it," I said with a giggle as we finally left the washroom.

CHAPTER 30

THURSDAY

I didn't want to attend Michael Sweet's funeral. Sure, nobody ever *wants* to attend a funeral, but I *really* wanted to sit this one out. Who wants to be near a mentally unhinged widow who's flinging pointy stuff around? Not me.

Logan and his sister tried to convince me it would be okay, and that I'd regret not going, but in the end, they both agreed that it might be fine for me to skip this one. I would avoid all the stares and whispers of people who wanted to talk about what I might have seen that day at the house, but more importantly, I'd avoid the angry recrimination of a mother who'd been—temporarily—separated from her children.

I was at home, alone because Jessica had gone to the service with the Sandersons, when I got a panicked phone call from Jinx. She needed me to run next door and grab her notes, then bring them to her at the funeral home so she could deliver her promised tribute to her cousin's deceased husband.

I put on an all-black outfit, like a ninja, used my landlady key to retrieve the notes, and sped off to the funeral home.

Jinx met me in the parking lot.

"You're a lifesaver," she said, and gave me a playful knuckle rub on the side of my head through my car window. I found it oddly familiar, yet it lifted my spirits for Jinx to be so accepting of me.

The night before, we'd consumed the better part of two bottles of wine, and we'd had a great time teasing Logan about his quirks, including how particular he was about the countertops being wiped down with a specific spray bottle and a different cloth than the one used for washing the dishes.

"I'm so hungover," Jinx groaned. "You shouldn't have made me drink all that wine."

I laughed. "Excuse me? You were the one pouring." I unbuckled my seat belt and leaned forward to look past her, at the groups of darkly clad people entering the funeral home. By the look of it, there'd been a huge turnout. As much as most people in town didn't love Michael, they did care for Samantha and were attending the service to support her—as it should be.

"How's it going in there?"

"Little Sophie's here," Jinx reported. "With a social worker. Poor thing." She scrunched her face and blinked away the beginnings of tears. "But she'll be okay," Jinx said, lifting her chin resolutely. "Kids are resilient. She's probably better off without him. No father at all is better than a lousy one." She leaned close to my open window. "Just between us, Michael was kind of a jerk. He grabbed my butt at their wedding."

I didn't know what to say to that, and then I did. "Don't walk too close to the casket."

Jinx stared at me for several seconds before she finally cracked up laughing. She had to pull a tissue from her pocket and dab the corners of her eyes before she ruined her professional quality makeup.

"Thanks. I needed that." She shook a finger at me. "You're a naughty one, Stormy."

"Thank you."

She glanced back over her shoulder at the funeral home. "We should be back out again in an hour. Do you want to get a late lunch with us?"

"Sure." I didn't have any other plans for the day. We talked for a few minutes about where to meet and what time. I wasn't sure which restaurant would be best. The good spots were near the funeral home, which meant that the crowd attending might pick the same places, and we'd be in for a big wait plus staring. Finally, I told Jinx I'd just stay in the parking lot and work on my laptop in my car. "It's no problem. I work in my car all the time," I assured her, pointing to my laptop case in the passenger seat. "Anywhere can be an office."

She reached in through my open window, gave me another playful head rub, and then walked away, waving without looking back as she walked up to the Blight Family Funeral Home doors.

"Jinx!" I waved her notebook out of my window. "You might need this."

She ran back for the notes, her loose auburn waves flying like flames, joking that she'd lose her head if it wasn't attached.

* * *

I waited around in the parking lot, in my car, for nearly an hour before I was distracted by a chattering sound. My teeth. The crisp autumn weather had turned shivery cold that week. My gas tank was low, so I didn't want to waste gas by idling my vehicle to power the heater. The service would be over any minute, but then we'd still have to figure out where we were having lunch, and I had to use the washroom now.

I locked up the car and casually slipped inside the funeral home to use the washroom and also linger a while to warm myself up.

While I was in my stall in the women's washroom, two women entered, talking quietly.

I recognized Samantha's voice immediately.

I froze where I was. I did not want to emerge from a stall and have an altercation with the grieving woman. Getting someone's kids taken away—even just temporarily and for their own safety—doesn't earn a person many friendship points.

Samantha called out, "Hello? Is anyone in here?"

Her voice echoed around the tiled room. I kept my mouth shut.

The washrooms at the Blight Family Funeral Home were semiprivate, with doors that went all the way to the floor. Unless she and her companion got right down on the floor, they wouldn't see my shoes under the stall door. I was reminded of a scene from the classic eighties movie, *9 to 5*, plus countless other comedies. At least I didn't have to pull my feet up onto the seat like some two-bit gumshoe or office snitch.

Samantha sighed. "Thank God it's just us. I'm so tired of having people stare at me."

I felt a twinge of guilt at hearing her repeat the same sentiment I had. She had far more to complain about than I did.

"At least you look stunning," the other woman said. "How much weight have you lost since the last time I saw you? Ten pounds?"

"I hope not," Samantha replied. "I should eat more. Michael doesn't like me to be too skinny."

"You're not too skinny," the woman said. "He'll be... happy to see you."

"Jinx, you're just saying that," Samantha said petulantly. "My boobs are deflated. They shrunk as soon as I stopped nursing Junior."

I nearly clapped my hand over my mouth. Samantha was talking to Logan's sister, and she was playing along with Samantha's delusion about Michael coming back from the dead.

"*Ain't no thaing* to worry about," Jinx said with an urban twang. "Michael will be happy to see your boobs, and the rest of you," Jinx said.

"Really?"

"Absolutely."

From my hiding place, I had to admire Jinx's acting skills. I was starting to believe Michael Sweet might be coming back any minute.

Members of both the Sanderson family and the Sweet family had been spoken to by the psychiatrist who was working with Samantha. I'd learned about this the night before, over wine and stir fry. The psychiatrist, who was an expert in disassociation, had asked that family members gently go along with Samantha's delusions for the time being. Confronting her would only make her lock in harder. I wasn't so sure about the psychiatrist's methods, but what did I know? I'd gained a lot of personal experience lately with abnormal psychology, but I was only scratching the surface of what made people tick.

"When Michael does come back, he's getting a vasectomy," Samantha said. "No more babies. That's what deflated my boobs."

I felt a tickle in my throat and attempted to cough silently.

"Right," Jinx said hesitantly. "Hello? Is someone else in here with us?" To Samantha she said, "I thought I heard something."

My skin prickled. She wouldn't be able to see my shoes or my shadow, but if she tried opening all the stall doors one at a time, she'd find mine locked.

Jinx and I had bonded the night before, teasing Logan as a team. Did our bond come with a psychic element? My sister and I noticed that the more time we spent together, the closer we got in our thoughts. I didn't believe in such things as psychic powers, but I tried it anyway, mentally willing Jinx to carry on with the conversation, carry on with Samantha's delusion.

Keep talking, I thought at Jinx. *Keep Samantha talking and then get her out of here. Definitely don't try to open stall number seven.*

"I guess we're alone," Jinx said with a light laugh.

I could see them through a slim crack at the edge of my door. They ran some water in the sinks, washed their hands, and then began touching up their makeup.

Jinx said, "You should put some face powder over that lipstick to set it."

"Oh? I usually kiss a tissue, like this." Samantha took a paper hand towel and pressed it between her lips.

"That just rubs it off. You want the lipstick to stay on your face." There was a clicking sound as Jinx opened her purse, which was a hard case with a buckle, like a toolbox. She patted the countertop. "Sit up here and let the professional makeup artist fix your face."

Samantha made an *oof* sound as she hopped up on the counter.

After a minute, Samantha asked her cousin, "Did you see the work they did on the body double? He looked exactly like Michael, lying there in the casket."

"Could have fooled me," Jinx said. In a less confident tone, her voice quavering and pitching up higher, she asked, "Are you sure it wasn't Michael in that casket? It sure looked like him, and I don't know if there's a makeup artist good enough to make someone look like someone else. I know I couldn't pull it off. What if your husband really is dead?"

"He'd never leave me," Samantha said with certainty. "Can you fix my eye shadow?"

"Uh, sure. Close your eyes and I'll fix it."

They worked in silence for a while. I could hear people milling around outside the bathroom's main door. It had been a large turnout, but most of the attendees were at the other side of the funeral home, at the post-service reception. This bathroom on the far side would be out of the way, which was I'd chosen it.

Jinx made a few comments about the makeup application she was doing, then asked Samantha, "So, if you don't mind me asking, what was it that tipped you off to Michael's big plan? Did he send you a note after the, um, staging at the house?"

"No, but I certainly would have appreciated a note," Samantha said with a snort. "He's never been the most thoughtful husband."

"Was he good to you?"

"Sometimes. Michael's full of surprises. And he's a tiger in the bedroom!"

"Good for you, honey! So, just between us, how'd you know he was planning to fake his death?"

I nearly stopped breathing. Jinx was relentless. She would have made a great investigator.

Samantha didn't answer for a minute. Finally, she said, "Just between us? Promise you won't tell anyone?"

"Cousin swear," Jinx said. "I never told anyone you stole the contents of Uncle Pete's liquor cabinet at the lake house, did I?"

"True," Samantha said. "Okay. How I know is: Michael slipped up on Sunday, the day before the whole thing. He told me that we were about to come into some money. A lot of money."

"Did he say how?"

"Nope. He said it was top secret for now, but soon I would understand everything. He said I'd be really angry at him at first, but then eventually I'd see how everything worked out for the best in the end."

"Are you sure he wasn't talking a business deal? Like a big sales commission on some property or business he was selling?"

Samantha snorted. "Yeah, right," she said sarcastically. "When it comes to the listings, I'm the one who handles the business end. He'd kill me if he knew I was telling you this, but he was basically a stay-at-home dad. I do all the real estate work, which is fine by me. As soon as our big insurance money comes in, I'm going to put my feet up and keep them up for a long time. Preferably on a sandy beach somewhere with a margarita in my hand." She giggled girlishly. "I could hire you to be my personal makeup artist."

Jinx laughed lightly. "If you can afford my fee, I'll take the job and fetch your margaritas as well."

There was the sound of makeup containers snapping open and shut.

Then Jinx asked, in a more serious tone, "Did you tell the police about what Michael said to you on Sunday?"

"No," Samantha snapped. "Why would I?"

"Uh..." Jinx was stumped. There wasn't much she could have said. If she pushed Samantha about talking to the police, it would go against Samantha's delusion that Michael had faked his death.

"The police need to mind their own business," Samantha said. "Besides, Michael already paid them all off. That's how he got the coroner to sign off on that other body. Michael took care of everything." She gasped. "Jinx, this is all very illegal. I could get him in big trouble. You won't tell anyone about this, will you?"

"Of course not," Jinx said. "Not even Logan."

"Good. He keeps asking me questions, but I won't crack. Your big brother thinks that he's the smartest person living in Misty Falls, but he's not that clever."

"What about his girlfriend? Stormy Day?"

"Oh, Stormy doesn't know half of what Logan gets up to. She should keep him on a shorter leash."

"Oh? I don't know her well, but she seems pretty clever to me."

"Too clever for her own good," Samantha said. Her voice had a vengeful tone that did not surprise me.

"Sam, she just wanted to make sure your kids are taken care of. She's worried about you."

"Whatever," Samantha spat out. "One of these days, Stormy Day is going to get what she has coming to her."

The skin all over my body prickled. I felt like I might explode or, at the very least, cough. I focused on relaxing my muscles and managed to keep myself quiet.

"Promise me you won't do anything you'll regret," Jinx said. "You always did have a short fuse."

"I'm okay," Samantha said softly, sounding frail. "I've got everything under control. Everything's going according to plan."

"Whose plan?"

"Michael's plan," Samantha whispered. "Shh. It's our secret."

"Our secret," Jinx agreed. She sounded so achingly sad, it made my heart break.

There was more snapping of makeup containers, water running, and then finally they both left.

I took what felt like the first deep breath I'd had all day.

My feet were somewhat numb from my not-so-dignified seat on the toilet.

I walked over to the sinks with an ouch-ouch-ouch from the pins and needles of my circulation returning.

Ah, the glamorous life of a sneaky sleuth.

Next, I had to slip back out of the funeral home and return to my car before I got spotted.

But before that, I had one small task to attend to.

I had to visit Michael's casket and make sure it was him inside, and not a body double.

Just to be absolutely, positively, one hundred percent certain.

Usually, when a person is dead, they stay dead. I'd seen Michael in the tub, and he'd appeared to be dead. But thanks to the strange events earlier that year at the Flying Squirrel Lodge, I knew there were certain chemical compounds that could make a person appear to be dead even when they weren't. While stranded at the lodge, I'd encountered one such "wandering zombie corpse," and so my suspicion about the state of Michael Sweet's body wasn't entirely unfounded.

CHAPTER 31

It's only because I'm a thorough and detail-oriented investigator that I find myself in compromising positions.

I've been busted in a few embarrassing situations before, but this one really took the cake.

Officer Peggy Wiggles, dressed in civilian clothes, walked into a private room in the back of the funeral home to find me standing over the corpse of Michael Sweet with two of my fingers stuck up his nostrils.

Peggy's jaw moved up and down, but no sound came out of her mouth.

"It's okay," I said in what I hoped was a soothing, take-charge tone. "I'm just checking to make sure he's dead."

She swallowed audibly then replied, "Stormy, putting the word 'just' in front of something doesn't make it acceptable."

I gently removed my fingers from the deceased's nostrils. "He's dead all right," I said.

"Are you sure? Did you check his neck for two small puncture wounds?"

"Not yet, but since you're here, you can guard the door while I unbutton his shirt." I moved toward the body but then stopped myself. "Wait. What? Puncture wounds on the neck?"

Peggy's thin lips twisted up at the corners the way they did whenever she talked about her cat. "I'm pretty sure we don't have a vampire on the loose," she said.

"Your jokes are so deadpan," I said. "You totally got me."

"Are you going to tell me what you're doing in here? Or am I to assume you have a thing for dead bodies?"

I closed the top of the casket to make the situation feel less creepy.

It didn't help much.

"You've heard about his widow's delusions," I said. "I heard a rumor he paid off the coroner to declare him dead when he wasn't. Plus, I was thinking about those chemicals that Benjamin Biggs knows how to make."

"What are you saying? Do you think Michael Sweet stored up a supply of his own blood for staging a crime scene, paid off multiple state and local authorities, dosed himself with some chemical compound Benjamin Biggs cooked up in his basement laboratory, then gave himself multiple fake stab wounds and crawled into a bathtub to wait for his vital signs to drop below detectable levels?"

"It sounds far-fetched when you say it out loud like that."

She raised her eyebrows and nodded slowly. "It does. And I've already questioned Benjamin Biggs. He assured me he had nothing to do with this."

"And you believed him?"

"He told me that arrogant jocks like Michael Sweet don't make friends with geeks like him."

"True enough," I said.

"And he's not hurting for money. His health-food company is worthless, but he sold a few of his chemical compounds to Big Pharma and made a mint." She rubbed her hands together as though brushing my far-fetched theory away for once and for all. "More importantly, Michael truly is dead." She glanced at the closed coffin. "They drained what was left of his blood and filled him with embalming fluid."

I turned and looked at the coffin as well. As part of the embalming process, the mortician would have jabbed Michael's body in the abdomen with a trocar to aspirate gases. If a person wasn't already dead, they sure would be after that. I could have checked the body for the trocar buttons that would have been used to cover the holes following this procedure, but sticking my fingers up the nostrils had seemed less invasive.

In hindsight, under the cold stare of Officer Peggy Wiggles, I probably shouldn't have touched him at all. But I had to be sure. That's just how I am.

I tried to look recalcitrant. "Peggy, am I in trouble?"

She frowned at me.

I smiled. "Do you need to call in a ten-fifty-nine?"

"You heard about that? We'll have to change the code." She shook her head. "You promised you weren't going to get involved in this case."

I shrugged.

Peggy took a step back, blinked twice, and glanced around the room as though confused. "This isn't the washroom," she said, as though talking to herself. "I guess I'll be exiting this room now, having seen nothing noteworthy."

"Before you go, there's one more thing."

She clenched her jaw, emphasizing the angular lines of her face. "Don't you dare open that coffin again."

"It's something else," I said. "I overheard something." I hesitated, even though I wasn't bound by cousin-swear confidentiality. Jinx and Samantha had a reasonable expectation of privacy. I shouldn't have listened to their conversation. But then again, they didn't check all seven stall doors. I had a reasonable right to be in there using the washroom.

"What did you"—she made air quotes with her fingers—"overhear?"

"The day before Michael was killed, he told Samantha he was about to come into a big windfall. Some big payoff."

Peggy lifted her chin. The tendons in her neck strained out, as though she was struggling to chew on this new information. If I had to guess, I'd say this particular bit of information was news to her.

She asked through her teeth, "Any other details?"

"Just that he was keeping the specifics from Samantha. You can try asking her about it, but I honestly don't think she knows anything. It does explain her hope, though. He planted the seed for her delusion."

"Thank you," Peggy Wiggles said with a nod. "I appreciate the information."

"You're not still looking at Colt Canuso for this, are you?"

She stared at me for a while, her cool gaze unwavering, before answering. "If you didn't think your friend did it, why did you turn him in?"

Good question. And I truly didn't know why until I heard the words coming from my mouth.

"Because it was what my father would have done," I said.

"He raised you right." Peggy turned back toward the door and slipped away discreetly.

I waited a few minutes and then did the same.

CHAPTER 32

FRIDAY

I entered the Fox and Hound, keeping my head down to avoid an exuberant greeting by Dharma Lake.

It didn't work. The white-haired older waitress accosted me by the front door and locked me into a hug. The woman had been friendly to me ever since we'd met, and after I helped the kind senior get out of a murder charge, she'd only become more friendly.

"How's Logan?" She waited expectantly, as though she alone was responsible for getting the two of us together. Dharma saw herself as a matchmaker and believed it gave her good karma to pair people up. As far as she was concerned, every loose sock had a match, and it could be found right there in Misty Falls. Working as a waitress in a bar that served plenty of alcohol must have made her matchmaking job as easy as shooting fish in a barrel, but I never mentioned that to her face. She was a generous woman with a sincere, loving heart.

"You know Logan," I said. "He's always busy, busy, busy." After the funeral the day before, I'd gone for lunch with him and his sister, and then they'd gone off together to attend some family functions without me. He'd finally gotten a few days off from his work at the law practice, but now he would be busy with his sister for a while. I wasn't one to complain. When Logan got busy, I just found my own things to be busy with. Tonight I would be socializing with the girls, and that was fine by me.

Dharma grabbed my left hand and made a hmm sound. I pulled my hand away self-consciously.

"No, I don't have an engagement ring," I said with a laugh. "Trust me. If Mr. Sanderson and I get engaged, you'll be the first person I tell, right after my father."

She made a tsk-tsk sound.

"Dharma, it's fine. I've been engaged before, and that was a disaster. Getting a ring on my finger is not the be-all, end-all, believe me. And besides, Logan and I have only been together about six months."

"That's half a year," she said. "You're not getting any younger, dear. What are you now, thirty-nine? Forty is right around the corner."

I made a shocked face. "I'm thirty-four. These bags under my eyes are because I didn't get much sleep last night, because I was working."

"I've worked late hours for many years. The secret is to take a nap in the afternoon. My husband John calls it my fountain-of-youth sleep."

I caught myself frowning and tried to relax my face so I didn't make myself look worse.

She continued, "The key to a good nap is to not sleep too long. Thirty minutes is perfect. Especially if your lover wakes you up with a kiss and a hot cup of tea."

"Ah. That's what I've been doing wrong. I'm usually woken up by either my phone ringing or my cat sitting on my face." I twitched my mouth from side to side. "This afternoon, it was both." I turned my head and scanned the crowded pub. "Have you seen Jessica? We're supposed to be having a girls' night."

"She's upstairs, by the fireplace. What can I bring you to drink?"

"Irish coffee, with an extra shot of espresso."

"We don't have an espresso machine, but I'll stir in an extra scoopful of the instant coffee mix we use."

"Perfect," I lied. I succumbed to another one of her friendly hugs and headed upstairs to find my friends.

I spotted Jessica by her red hair, which was twisted up in another of her elaborate braided hairstyles. My best friend always looked about one brocade vest short of being dressed up for a Renaissance fair.

Jessica was sitting with two blondes: Harper Hinton and Quinn McCabe.

I strode up to the table of three and said, "Looks like this girl group is missing their brunette."

Jessica whipped around on her chair and grinned up at me. "Stormy! I was just telling the girls I wasn't sure if you were going to join us. I thought you might be busy with your adulterers."

The other girls laughed as I took a seat in the fourth chair, facing the fireplace.

"Laugh now," I said with a mock-serious tone. "You won't be laughing when I catch one of you *in flagrante delicto*. That's Latin for 'in blazing offense,' in case you're wondering."

Harper, the youngest of the group, gave me a shy smile. She often wore lipstick that was a bit too dark for her skin, which made her look tired and a bit malnourished—not that I was one to judge, apparently.

Harper said, "Stormy, I'd need to have a husband first before I could get another one to *adulter* with. Wait. Is *adulter* a verb? Or even a word?" She glanced around at the other girls, who were a decade older.

Quinn McCabe started coughing into her fist. "How should I know? Why are you asking me?"

I took a good look at Quinn, who was still clearing her throat and avoiding eye contact with the group. I quietly put the clues together. On Monday of that week, Quinn's husband, Chip, had visited me at the store and asked about putting a tail on his wife. He'd said it was for her protection, but then, thanks to Brianna's family gossip, I'd figured out Quinn had something going with a photographer. It was no wonder the topic of adultery was making her uncomfortable.

"Adulter," Jessica mused. "Sounds like a word."

"It's not a word," I said. It was warm there by the fireplace, so I immediately slipped my jacket off and put it on the back of my chair. The girls were watching me expectantly, so I explained further. "In the private investigation business, we simply call it committing *adultery*. Interestingly enough, you can *adulterate* something, but that generally means adding cheaper or inferior material. For example, adding lead to pewter."

Dharma arrived with my Irish coffee, took drink refill orders from the other three girls, and left.

I continued explaining, "So, you could theoretically *adulterate* a marriage by adding cheap, inferior material such as another person's affection, but I wouldn't use that word in a client report. We prefer the term *indiscretion*."

Quinn was watching me with narrowed eyes. Did she know her husband was onto her, or was she suspicious of me due to her guilt? Perhaps a few drinks would loosen the truth out of her.

Harper turned to me and asked, "What about my boss, Michael Sweet? Would you call what he was up to adultery?"

I stared back at Harper, who'd clamped her dark burgundy lips together in a straight line. Why was she asking me? She worked for the Sweets part-time as an administrative assistant. She probably knew more about Michael's hobbies than anyone.

Quinn leaned in eagerly, licking her pink-hued lips. "Yeah, Stormy! Tell us what you know. Was Michael messing around? Is that why Samantha killed him?" She lowered her voice. "I mean, assuming it was her, and not a jealous spouse."

I took a slow sip of my Irish coffee and licked the whipped cream off my upper lip. The three women were watching me intently. They had no idea that this very moment was the first time I'd heard anything—outside of my own internal ruminations —about Michael Sweet committing adultery.

"You go first," I said slyly. "Tell me what you know, and then I'll tell you what I know."

Quinn elbowed Harper. "Tell Stormy what you told us."

Harper gave me an uneasy look. Her dark-hued lips were still pressed in a flat line. She was a recent transplant to Misty Falls, having moved there with her younger sister not long before I'd returned the previous fall. She and Jessica had become friends when they'd worked together and lived in the same apartment building, before Jessica had moved in with me.

Harper was a likable girl, but I'd noticed her acting skittish around me. I suppose the time I attacked her by throwing an industrial-sized jug of laundry detergent at her in the basement utility room hadn't helped our relationship. In my defense, I'd thought she might be trying to kill me. She hadn't been, but you can't be too careful.

Harper and I had seen each other around town since then, though we didn't talk about anything meatier than how much my father was enjoying the old green Ford Torino he'd bought from her in the summer.

Quinn kept urging Harper to tell me something. Jessica watched quietly, her expression neutral.

Harper shifted her chair to face me but a few inches further back, as though she preferred to keep her distance from me. Her mouth seemed to be getting smaller and smaller, her darkened lips rolling in until I couldn't see her lipstick at all.

"You can speak freely," I said to her. "This is all totally off the record." Inside, I gagged a little over using the phrase "off the record." It made me feel seedy and underhanded, yet it flowed so easily from my mouth. And it did the job. Harper's lips slowly reappeared, and she relaxed visibly.

Harper said, "Well, as you know, I've been working as an office assistant to the Sweets for a few months now. Just part-time."

Quinn waved her hand impatiently. "Tell Stormy the good part," she said.

Harper murmured something quietly. I couldn't hear her over the music and din of the busy pub.

Quinn put her elbows on the table hard enough to rattle our drinks. She exclaimed, "Michael Sweet was some sort of sex addict," she said. "He would disappear for hours at a time, and Harper thinks he was using their house listings for his sex romps."

I asked, "With who?"

Quinn leaned back contentedly, like a queen holding court. Just like old days. "We were hoping you could tell us," she said. "Surely you're the one person in town who knows all about who's zooming who."

I had to smile. Quinn had always referred to sex as "zooming." I hadn't heard the term in years, and it really brought me back to a more innocent time. I nearly forgot we were discussing the reputed sex life of a homicide victim.

"Quinn, I was never on the case. If Samantha had been suspicious enough to hire me to tail him, then I would know." I looked down at my Irish coffee. "In fact, it might have saved his life if he'd been busted sooner."

Jessica leaned across the table and patted my shoulder. "Stormy, you can't save them all."

I patted her hand and thanked her with my eyes.

"It wasn't another woman," Harper said, her voice quaking. "I mean, it might not have been."

We all exchanged wide-eyed looks.

Harper said, "A few weeks before Mr. Sweet's accident, a client found something he left behind at a house. It was a—"

Quinn interrupted, "I knew it! He was gay. That explains a lot, actually. When we dated in high school, I caught him trying on my cheerleader uniform more than once." Her hands fluttered excitedly. "Do you think his gay lover killed him?"

"That's not what I meant," Harper said, looking flustered. "If you would let me talk..."

Jessica stretched one arm across Quinn like the safety rail on an amusement park ride. "Go ahead," Jessica said to Harper, "I'll clamp my hand over the Queen Bee's mouth if she tries to interrupt you again."

"Please finish," I said to Harper, speaking slowly and trying not to spook her.

"The client found pornography magazines," Harper said. "I think he was using the houses for dates... with himself."

Quinn wrinkled her nose. "That's all? Phooey. That's boring. I bet it was hookers. This town is small, but it's not that small. I know there's a dominatrix in town, available for—"

Jessica made good on her threat to clamp her hand over Quinn's mouth. "That's enough," Jessica said. "The man is dead. He's not even been buried for a full day."

I raised my hand meekly. "Actually, there is more than one dominatrix in the local area." I waved my hand. "Which is a topic for another time." I gave Harper a friendly smile. "Do you still have those magazines?"

Harper shook her head vehemently. "I picked them up from the client and gave them some spa coupons to the Canuso Resort as an apology. Then I threw them in the garbage. I never told Michael or Samantha."

I asked her, "Did you tell the police?"

"Oh, Stormy," Quinn interrupted. "Don't be such a narc."

Don't be such a narc. The phrase stung every bit as much as it had in high school. Growing up the daughter of a cop in a small town hadn't been without its challenges.

"Never mind," I said. "I'm pretty sure Michael's porno magazines didn't kill him. Not even the sharpest paper can cut a man's throat."

Quinn laughed at my joke. Jessica raised her eyebrows and gave me an I-don't-know-what-to-do-with-you look. Harper hunched deeper into her chair, clutching her bottle of beer and watching me out of the corner of her eye.

I sipped my Irish coffee, let the conversation settle, and then asked, "What else is new?" I turned my head to check out our surroundings. "Is this place under new management yet again? Those light fixtures look different."

"New owners," Jessica said. "They got rid of karaoke night. Mainly to get rid of a certain singer, which is a shame, because she's really talented."

"They exorcised Della Koenig right out of here, huh? Probably for the best."

Quinn snorted. "That woman was a diva even before she got rich. Now she's a full-blown train wreck. I'm surprised we don't have paparazzi popping up in town." She tilted her head to the side and got a funny smile. "But the press will be coming, soon enough." Her smile got bigger and smugger.

Jessica took the bait. "Quinn, what are you talking about?"

Quinn breathed in the attention, sucking it all in like fuel for her ego. "Ladies, I'm not supposed to say anything until the big announcement tomorrow, but I'll give you a hint. It's big news."

Jessica punched her on the arm. Hard. Because that's the only way Jessica punches. Growing up the little sister to twin brothers made her tough physically, if not emotionally.

Quinn whimpered and rubbed her arm. "Easy, killer." She looked around the table with a sour expression. "I'll tell you guys, but only if you promise to come to the casino tomorrow. And you'd better act surprised."

Jessica asked, "Is this about your hootenanny next Friday?"

"Yes and no," Quinn said. "Are you coming to the casino tomorrow?"

Harper shuddered. "I'm out. That place gives me the creeps. Too much of the sort of element I moved here to get away from."

"Don't be a baby," Quinn teased.

I said to Quinn, "I can't go to the casino. I can't really get into the explanation, but I saw Trigger Canuso recently, she threatened to pull my legs off if she caught me on her land."

Jessica gasped. "Pull your legs off?"

"Not in so many words," I said. "But I don't want to find out how serious she was. She's tiny but tough. Like a wolverine."

Quinn said in a loud voice, "Michael actually went out with Trigger for a while. Did you hear about that? He said it was part of his personal sensitivity training program, to date *one of them*. I wonder where Trigger was the day Michael got killed."

Jessica elbowed Quinn. "Keep your voice down, Queen Bee."

In a hushed tone, I chimed in, "If you want to hurl accusations around, could you do it at a more discreet volume?"

Quinn shrugged one shoulder. "Oh, please. Like everyone in this Podunk little town isn't already thinking it. Look around. They're all staring at you, Stormy. They think you know everything."

I snuck a look behind me. She wasn't wrong. A few people were looking our way, but it probably had more to do with Quinn's volume, which was as loud and bossy as it had been during our cheerleader days.

Harper started pulling on her leather jacket. "Girls, thanks for inviting me out tonight, but I've got a busy day tomorrow. I'll be looking for a new job."

Jessica said, "I'm sure you can get your old shifts back at the Olive Grove."

"No offense, but it's not much of a career path," Harper said. "The next step up from waitress is manager, which is all the same drama minus the tips."

"Right," Jessica said through a tight smile. "Thanks for joining us tonight. It's certainly been interesting."

Quinn pushed her chair back and got up quickly. "Harper, I'll walk you to your car."

Harper wrinkled her nose and looked right at me. "I sold my car," she said.

"Then I'll give you a ride home, dummy," Quinn said in her bossiest Queen Bee tone. "I want to talk about some future job opportunities you might be interested in."

Harper brightened. "Can your husband, Chip, put in a good word for me with the post office?"

"Uh... sure." Quinn grabbed Harper's arm at the elbow and began steering her away from the table.

"Great to see you," I called after Quinn. "Really good quality time!"

She must have caught some of my sarcasm because she raised her free hand to give me the bird.

"Never change," I called after her, laughing.

I turned back around to face Jessica.

"Classic Quinn Baudelaire," I said. "Breeze in. Stir up trouble. Walk away as the bombs go off."

"You're the one who breezed in a full two hours after we were supposed to meet up," Jessica said. "And it's Quinn *McCabe* now. She's been warring with the other Baudelaires for a few years now and hates the sound of the name."

"Who would have ever guessed back in school that the Queen Bee would end up domesticated and married to a chubby mailman who I could have sworn wasn't into women?"

Jessica gave me a saucy look, batting her eyelashes. "Just because Chip McCabe didn't throw himself at your feet, it doesn't mean he's gay."

I rolled my eyes.

Our waitress, Dharma, appeared at that moment to whisk away Harper's half-empty beer bottle and Quinn's sticky martini glass. "Who's gay? I know a few single boys who'd love to meet someone. Really nice guys." She winked at us. "I'm an equal opportunity matchmaker!"

I shook my head. "We were talking about a famous actor. Nobody you'd know."

"Okay," Dharma said. "FYI, your blond friends stopped by the bar on the way, and the loud, bossy one told me you're picking up her tab."

"Classic Quinn," I said ruefully.

After Dharma left, Jessica and I spent the better part of an hour trashing on Quinn. I'd forgotten about some of her high school antics, but tonight's bossiness had brought back memories. Especially the part where she'd called Harper, a girl she barely knew, a dummy.

We eventually circled back around to the topic of Michael Sweet and what I thought about the evening's revelations.

"Maybe he was some kind of porn addict slacker." I looked down at the dregs of my second drink, which had been an Irish coffee minus the Irish—in other words, a lousy instant coffee with not enough whipped cream. "It doesn't really matter that he lied to his assistant and the daycare ladies about being on the golf course that day so he could get a few minutes alone to catch up on his reading."

Jessica swirled her white wine sangria, staring at the chunks of fruit as though the medley might hold clues, the way tea leaves do for fortune-tellers.

"It's so hard to believe he's gone," she said. "Are you sure he's dead?"

I nearly spit out the coffee I'd been sipping. "Don't worry," I said. "He's dead. When I was inside the funeral home yesterday, I stuck my fingers up his nostrils to make sure he wasn't breathing."

"Very funny," she said, rolling her eyes.

"I really did," I said, and then I told her about Peggy Wiggles walking in on me. I also caught her up on what I'd overheard Samantha saying in the washroom. I left out the part about Jinx being the other party present.

We both agreed that it was a sad, tragic situation.

Jessica used her straw to stab the fruit chunks in her glass so she could eat them.

"Quinn never told us the big news," she said. "Should we go to the casino tomorrow to find out?"

"We can go, but I'll need to be wearing a full disguise so Trigger doesn't spot me on the security cameras and rip my legs off."

She tilted her head and gave me a curious look. "Do you actually own any disguises?"

"What kind of self-respecting PI wouldn't have an arsenal of disguises?"

"A PI like you," she said. "You hate shopping."

She had a point. My preferred method of shopping was to pop my head into Blue Enchantment when I saw a nice mannequin in the window and buy the whole outfit without setting foot in the changing rooms.

"Guilty as charged," I said. "But I recently acquired a trunk full of my dad's old clothes. You'd be surprised how much a men's jacket and a fedora can change your appearance."

She rolled her eyes. "Tell me you don't have spirit gum and a selection of beards and goatees."

"Don't be ridiculous," I said. "I only have *one* mustache, but Jeffrey thought it was a creature to be mauled and eaten, so it's really just half a mustache."

Jessica put her face in her hands and laughed.

I laughed as well.

After the week I'd had, from turning in an old friend, to pulling apart a family and watching a decent woman go crazy, it felt good to laugh and plan a caper.

CHAPTER 33

SATURDAY

On Saturday, Jessica's mother came by to drop off some wigs so we could disguise ourselves for the visit to the casino. She stuck around for a while, visiting, and we were happy to have her join us for dinner.

We skipped a traditional main course and instead enjoyed a large antipasto platter of cheese, vegetables, and smoked meats. Jessica leaned toward a vegetarian diet but ate meat sometimes, especially when it was high-quality prosciutto wrapped around asparagus.

After the antipasto, I cleared away the dishes while Jessica scooped out gelato for dessert.

I wasn't going to have any of the Italian ice cream, but Mrs. Kelly insisted I have some, and assured me that my figure was "still perfect" even if I was showing some evidence of a diet that included gas station hot dogs.

On her way out after dessert, Mrs. Kelly gave me a warm hug and thanked me for being a "remarkable young woman" and a "true friend" to Jessica.

As she drove away and we waved to her from the living room's front window, I said to Jessica, "Your mother is the best."

"Too bad your father didn't think so," she said, laughing. Long ago, when we'd been much younger and blissfully naive, we'd schemed to get our two single parents to fall in love. We agreed it would be the greatest thing. We would be stepsisters, and she could team up with me against our other sister, Sunny. It was a great idea, or so we thought.

The first step of a typical Jessica-Stormy-matchmaking scheme was to find something at the Kelly household that was broken. This wasn't difficult, considering how boisterous Jessica's older brothers were, but we weren't above breaking something intentionally. Then, when it was time for my father to retrieve me from a sleepover, I'd ask him to bring his tools and do some handyman work for Mrs. Kelly. Being a good fellow who would go to great lengths to be of service to the community, he would always oblige.

At the time, to our immature minds, our scheming had seemed to work. Each fix-it trip brought them into closer contact. We would hear the two of them talking and laughing. Unfortunately, my father had been faking it. He interpreted Mrs. Kelly's appreciation of his talents as an indictment of men in general. It must have been the wording of her compliments. She would say things like, "Aren't you useful, for a man!" It was just her dry sense of humor.

Thinking back, I had to give credit to my younger self. I didn't yet know what wasn't possible, so I didn't put any limits on my hopes. Now that I was older, I had reservations about everything. I'd failed at so many things over the last two decades. Career. Relationships. Attempts at finding a relaxing hobby that didn't get me in trouble.

Some days it took considerable effort to reframe all my mistakes as simply steps to acquiring wisdom.

I wondered, in the future, when I was looking back on tonight, would I see going to the casino as a terrible mistake? Probably. But I was going to do it anyway. The excitement of doing something I wasn't supposed to do was an effective way for me to be present, in the here and now. I wasn't like Jessica, who was a more cautious, fearful soul. Taking risks made me feel alive. Maybe that was why we got along so well—we complemented each other.

She looked up from her bowl of ice cream. We'd had a second helping after her mother left. It was Jessica's idea, I swear.

"You've got zombie eyes," she said. "Are you sleep-eating?"

"Just thinking about how the passage of time changes things and gives you perspective."

"Still waters run deep." She lifted the small dessert bowl to her mouth and poured the melted gelato into her mouth. "Shall we go try on those wigs?"

"Sure," I said, patting my full stomach. I got up and "accidentally" set my gelato bowl on the floor for Jeffrey to lick clean. Jessica did the same.

We brought her mother's wigs into the bathroom, which had the largest mirror. She showed me how to pin back my real hair and then how to fasten the wig, which was a strawberry-blond color.

"This looks like real hair," I said. "Seriously. This must have been expensive."

"It would have been, but it was a donation. From when she was doing her chemo."

"What?" I took a step back and turned to look at Jessica. "When was that?"

She waved her hand. "It was a couple years ago. You were busy at Fairchild, and we weren't talking all that much." Her eyes started shining. She blinked rapidly and looked down at the sink. "She's clear now, so it all worked out. Please don't bring it up with her. She doesn't like talking about it." She didn't say the words, but I heard *neither do I*.

"I'm so sorry," I said. "I didn't even know."

"Actually, you did," she said softly. "I mentioned it once, but then you didn't ask again, so I thought maybe it was too painful for you to talk about, because of how you lost your mother when you were so young."

I was speechless. What she was saying sounded familiar, or at least it sounded like something I might have done. I'd been so focused on my career, and on Christopher, that I had put Misty Falls and all of its contents behind me. And then I'd been so mystified about why I had such a big hole in my heart.

"Don't sweat it," Jessica said. "Stuff happens. That's life." She picked up a wide-toothed comb from the edge of the sink and smoothed down my strawberry-blond wig. "This color looks cute on you. Not natural or anything, but totally cute."

I looked in the mirror and imagined Mrs. Kelly, bald from her chemo treatments, wearing the wig.

Grim reality definitely took away some of the fun factor.

"No wig for me tonight," I said, slipping it off.

Jessica, who could be perceptive to the point of reading my mind at times, asked, "Because it's a chemo wig?"

"No," I lied. "I just think it will be too itchy. My scalp already feels like it's crawling with ants." I gestured to the other wig, the bright blond one. "But you should wear that one. You'll look like Marilyn Monroe."

"Or my old Sunday school teacher. She had hair just like that. And her name was Marilyn, coincidentally enough."

"Stop stalling and put it on," I said.

She did, and the transformation was surprising. She applied some extra concealer over her nose to conceal her freckles, and she looked like a different person.

"Gorgeous," I said. "And Jessica, I'm not just saying this because you look like a movie star, but you mean the world to me. And I'm so sorry about not being a better friend to you in the past. If there was one thing I could change, I—"

She clamped her hand over my mouth. "That's enough, Sappy McSapperson."

I raised my eyebrows and allowed myself to be silenced.

Jessica, the blond bombshell, whispered theatrically, "You had me at 'you look like a movie star.' Now let's go have a fun Saturday night at the casino."

I nodded. She released her hand from my mouth slowly.

"I'll go make sure Jeffrey has enough food," she said. "We wouldn't want His Royal Fluffiness to starve while we're having Roomies' Night Out."

She left me alone in the bathroom.

I was ready to go, but I stalled by trying on a few shades of lipstick.

Jeffrey came in and jumped up on the vanity counter with ease, like a dark gray puff of smoke. He gave me a questioning look, his green eyes inquisitive.

"You sure do know your name," I told him. "Yes, we were talking about you a minute ago. How come you know your name, but you don't know what it means when I say *don't touch*?"

He blinked, looked down, and tentatively swatted a tube of lipstick with one gray paw. His rose-colored toe pads were a similar shade to the lipstick.

"Don't knock that over," I said. "Don't touch."

He curled his toes, claws extended, and delicately pushed the tube toward the brink.

"Okay," I said. "Go ahead. Give it another nudge and see what happens."

He gave it another delicate swat, sending the tube swirling around in the sink like a skateboarder in a skate park bowl. He tilted his head and watched it even after it had stopped rolling, as though it might suddenly reverse direction and spin out again.

"Good work, genius." I picked him up, gave him a kiss on the top of his head, and put him down. He caught the smell of the food Jessica was preparing and scampered off.

I looked at my lips in the mirror, sighed, and reached for a tissue.

"This is why I don't wear lipstick," I muttered through gray-fur-covered lips.

* * *

Before Jessica and I left, we popped over next door to see if either Logan or Jinx had changed their minds about coming with us.

Logan wasn't there. He was out picking up groceries, according to his little sister, Jinx, who was sitting on a beach towel on the living room floor, painting her toenails.

Jinx said, "We've got a full evening planned, between eating chicken wings and watching old movies. Hey, why don't you drop by after and fill us in on your bossy cheerleader friend's big announcement? We can save you some chicken wings, and I'll be happy to share the couch. It *ain't no thaing*. I'm kinda curious about the news. It'll be a nice change of pace from all the funeral stuff."

Jessica and I exchanged a look, grinning.

"We already know what it is," Jessica told her. "The newspaper says they're announcing the role of Kinley tonight, and that it's a child who lives in Misty Falls."

"It's going to be Quinn's daughter, Quinby," I said.

Jinx asked, "How can you be sure it's her kid?"

"Because Quinn's excited about it," I said. "And Quinn only gets excited about things that benefit her."

Jinx made an *ah* face. "I know people like that."

Jessica wrinkled her pale, freckles-hidden nose at me. "Quinn's going to be unbearable."

I replied, "More than before?"

All three of us laughed.

Jinx said, "Jessica, I love this blond bombshell look for you. I almost didn't recognize you when you came in." She finished applying dark red polish to her toenails, put the lid back on the bottle, and waved for Jessica to twirl around. "Let me see you spin!"

Jessica obliged, spinning out the bottom of her bright yellow dress. She had purchased the dress after seeing a similar one on a famous redhead actress in a musical movie. Because the weather had cooled recently, she'd paired it with cream-colored cable-knit tights and an orange cardigan. Paired with the bright blond wig, she looked like the personification of autumn leaves.

Jinx said, "You look like you're about to burst into song about the changing seasons."

Next, Jinx looked me up and down. "And you, Stormy, look like you're heading out to smoke cigars and play poker with the other gentlemen."

I tilted my fedora forward. "I'll take that as a compliment."

We said goodbye to Jinx and went to my car.

Jessica was moving slowly, as though distracted. She had her arms crossed.

I asked her, "Do you need a warmer jacket? I've got one in the trunk."

She dropped her arms and shook them out. "I'm fine. Just wondering if we should even go to this thing. A night in with chicken wings sounds pretty good, and I don't normally eat chicken wings."

"We don't have to go," I said.

"Actually, we do. Quinn phoned me this morning and made me swear on the sacred bond of the cheerleader squad."

"Sounds like a legally binding verbal contract." I looked up at the dark sky. The long days of summer were so far away now.

Jessica sighed. "I wish I wasn't such a worry wart, but you know how I am." She fussed with the yellow skirt of her dress, which was sticking with static electricity to her cable-knit tights. "Stupid Quinn," she said. "Stupid static electricity."

I popped open the trunk of my car and waved her over. I pulled out a dryer sheet and used it to quickly de-static her skirt.

"You're prepared for everything," she said with admiration.

"Dryer sheets are great multi-purpose items," I said. "You can clean your windshield, wipe off pet hair, sharpen scissors, de-squeak the soles of new shoes—" I stopped myself.

"Don't stop," Jessica said. "I love that my best friend is so smart and handy." She skipped over to the passenger-side door. "Now let's get to the casino and find Quinn. We wouldn't want to be late, or she'll make us run laps like the good ol' days."

CHAPTER 34

The Canuso Lake Casino and Resort was busy that Saturday night, but not as busy as it had been two weeks earlier, for the official *House of Hallows* TV series casting call. We were able to park in the main parking lot, albeit a fair hike from the front door.

We stepped out of my car and got ready to walk in.

"You forgot your hat," Jessica said.

She was right. I'd left my fedora in the backseat of the car, since a woman wearing a fedora—or really anyone, in these modern times—would have been suspicious. I explained to Jessica that I'd only left my house wearing the hat to make her laugh.

"But it looked good," she said, smirking. "That hat really brought your whole old-man look together."

I smiled down at my father's old clothes—a button-down shirt and a pair of trousers with suspenders, topped off with a vest. My outfit was drab but not too scruffy, perfect for blending with a crowd. Plus I liked how the suspenders kept my pants up without making the waist tight. It was much easier this way to keep my shirt tucked in.

"Since you like the hat so much, I'll wear it to Quinn's hootenanny next Friday."

Jessica stared at me blankly as she bit her lower lip dramatically. In her blond wig and dress, she looked exactly like the femme fatale in a gritty film noir detective movie.

"Stormy, it's a dance," she said. "Don't you want to be a pretty girl on Logan's arm?"

"It's a *dance*," I said. "Who's got two thumbs, a law degree, and doesn't dance? My boyfriend, Logan Sanderson."

"Oh, right," she said glumly. "I guess he's not perfect after all."

"He's close enough," I said. "Christopher wasn't much of a dancer, either. The first time we met at that rock concert in Paris, I thought he was doing a comedy thing—a parody of how a guy so white his last name is *Fairchild* dances." The band that night was from Japan, playing American Rockabilly music, so Christopher's jokey dancing had seemed appropriate enough. The two girls I was traveling with thought he was hilarious. It wasn't until much later that I found out Christopher really danced that way all the time.

Jessica smiled and shook her head. "I can picture it now," she said. "With those white-soled Vans sneakers of his flashing under the lights."

"I wish you could have been there," I said, and I meant it. I had wanted her to come with me at the time, but she either hadn't been able to save up the money for a trip to Europe or was too nervous—maybe both. Had I done everything I could have to convince her to come? Probably not.

But that was the past, and here we were, having a whole new adventure.

We locked the car doors and headed toward the entrance right behind a loose crowd. As we walked,

I gave Jessica some tips on how to disappear into a crowd.

Looking "normal" is a subtle art. One key is to not try too hard. Dressing in all black like a ninja would be one such example of trying too hard. You should wear normal, plain clothes, keep smiling, and continue carrying on a casual conversation with your companion. Yes, bringing a friend will make you appear less conspicuous.

"Don't look up," I said to Jessica when we entered the main atrium with the water feature.

"But shouldn't I make a mental note of the locations of the security cameras?"

"Just assume they're everywhere, and remember this: The ones on the ceiling point down and capture the tops of people's heads. When you look up at the ceiling, your face suddenly shows up in a sea of brown heads, attracting the attention of anyone monitoring the screens. Our brains are geared toward recognizing a human face. Looking up is a sure way of getting security's attention, which we could use to our advantage if we had another party operating as a decoy."

"Uh-oh," she said. "I shouldn't have worn a yellow dress with an orange sweater. Or does it matter? The screens are all in black and white, aren't they?"

"A casino this up to date will have color cameras on the floors, probably fifty with three-sixty degree views, plus more in the choke points. The lighting in here is more than bright enough to get a good picture. It's only outside, on the exterior grounds and parking lots, where they'll have cameras that are black and white, because they get a crisp image with lower light."

"But we're inside. So why did you let me dress up like a buttercup?"

I chuckled. "You might notice that nobody's looking at *me* right now."

"Is that all I am to you?" She laughed. "A decoy body?"

I gave her my best noir detective impersonation. "Sweetheart, you're so much more than a skirt to me. Why, with my brains and your looks, we could really go places."

She rolled her eyes and led the way toward the ballroom where the casting announcement was being made.

We located Quinn and her family sitting at a reserved table near the stage where the casting announcement would be made shortly. It was the first time I'd seen the trio of McCabes all together.

Chip's round cheeks flushed red with a blush that carried all the way across both ears when he made eye contact with me. We hadn't seen each other, much less spoken, since Monday of that week, when he'd dropped by my store to casually ask me about digging up "dirt" on people for blackmail. As I looked his way, he slid down in his chair, arms tucked tightly at his side, as though he was trying to disappear behind the drinks-menu card standing upright on the table. Whether or not he still suspected his wife of sneaking around with a photographer, he certainly looked embarrassed about having brought it to my attention.

Quinn, on the other hand, was standing over the table with an aggressively wide-legged stance, waving both arms wildly as she regaled the others seated at the table with a story about how much champagne they'd special-ordered for their gala on Friday.

Jessica greeted her with a hug and two cheek kisses. It seemed to take Quinn a few minutes to recognize Jessica under the wig.

Quinn scowled at her, "Is this your new look? I liked you better as a redhead."

"It's just a wig," Jessica said. "What's this about a gala? I thought your party was a hootenanny?"

"Oh, it's still at the barn," Quinn said slowly. "But this might be the last year a barn will be able to hold everyone."

"Mom," Quinby said, tugging her mother's arm. "When can I take off this coat? It's hot and itchy."

All eyes turned to the youngest McCabe, who was sporting beauty-pageant-style full makeup, and a brown trench coat.

"In a few minutes," Quinn snapped at her daughter. "We've waited this long, and we don't want to ruin the surprise."

"But I'm hot!"

"Come here, duckie," Chip said. "I'll unbutton you a bit. I know how much it sucks to be overheated."

"Don't," Quinn snapped at her husband. "Leave it."

The round-cheeked mail carrier's ears became even more red. He grumbled something I couldn't hear, and then told his daughter to be patient. "Just a few more minutes," he said. "Your mother knows best."

Jessica and I exchanged a look as we took our seats across from the McCabes. Jessica leaned over and whispered, "Quinn knows best."

I suppressed the urge to giggle. *Quinn knows best* was a phrase we used to say whenever the head cheerleader made us do extra laps or ordered our celebratory pizza with half the cheese left off. Said with enough sarcasm, it was almost enough to make up for the taste of sad, cheeseless pizza.

Jessica and I introduced ourselves to the others at the table. I recognized Quinn's parents, though the Baudelaires didn't recognize me until I said my name.

"Your hair," said Mrs. Baudelaire with a note of horror. "I do hope it will grow back. You were always such a lovely girl, Stormy. How is your father?"

"He's got a new hip and an old car and couldn't be happier with retirement."

"Is he in remission then?"

"From what?"

Mrs. Baudelaire glanced at her husband, who wasn't paying any attention to the conversation at all. She looked back at me with a thin smile. "Never mind. I'm getting my wires crossed." She smiled across the table at her daughter and granddaughter.

"We just couldn't be more excited about tonight's big announcement."

"Yes," I said. "I can't imagine what the good news will be."

She nodded and picked up her glass of wine.

A few minutes later, curiosity must have gotten the better of Mrs. Baudelaire because she started up a conversation with me again. I'd been checking messages on my phone and set it aside politely.

"I have a theory," she whispered. "Don't let my husband overhear me. Is he looking at me now?"

Mr. Baudelaire had wandered away from the table in search of the washroom.

"Nobody's listening," I assured the woman.

"And is this conversation... *off the charts*?"

"If you mean *off the record*, then yes."

She smiled dazedly, her eyes slightly unfocused. "I think the Canuso boy is going to take the blame for killing Michael Sweet to protect his little sister. She's the one who did it. I've seen her lose her temper a few times in public. She created quite the spectacle around herself, that girl. People don't talk about her much, now that Della Koenig is on everyone's lips. And the Countess when she's in town. But a year or two ago, tongues would have been wagging about that woman with the ridiculous name. Tagger. Who would name a child such a thing? I mean, there's that golfer, Tiger. I can see that, but only for a boy."

"Trigger," I said. "Her name isn't Tagger. It's Trigger. All the siblings have horse-themed names."

"But a trigger is part of a *gun*," Mrs. Baudelaire said, waving a hand dismissively, as though I hadn't been smart enough to understand a word she'd said. She glanced up as her husband returned to the table. Loudly, she said to me, "There's nothing like a summer wedding. June or July, if you ask me."

"Thanks for the tip," I said, winking. "I'll keep that in mind."

* * *

Getting planning tips for my nonexistent wedding turned out to be the highlight of the evening.

Watching Quinby go on stage dressed as Kinley following the casting announcement only made me feel sad. I kept thinking about Q's best friend, Sophie, and how she should have been there. Samantha's kids were currently with family members, so the little girl was being taken care of, but it was a shame she had to miss the party. She'd already lost so much when her father died, and this was likely the first in a long string of things she was going to miss out on. Poor kid.

For the McCabes and Baudelaires, Jessica and I pretended to be shocked and surprised when the announcement was made. We congratulated the families, stayed for one drink, and then slipped out without letting anyone know we were leaving—a classic Irish goodbye, I thought to myself with a smile.

We were halfway across the exterior parking lot when we were spotted.

Or to be more accurate, I was sniffed out.

The two heart-faced huskies, Juno and Echo, bounded toward me. They recognized me from our day together and happily licked my hands.

I tried to shoo them away, but it was too late. I'd been spotted. A dark-haired blur moved toward me.

I braced myself for a confrontation with Trigger Canuso, but it wasn't her after all. It was the smaller of the two security guards I'd bribed for information the previous time I'd been at the casino.

The young man saw right through our disguises. "If it isn't the fountain girls," he said, grinning. "Sorry about the dogs. They're good girls, but they get excited when they see someone they like."

"It's nice to be liked," I said. "You're not working tonight, are you?"

"It's my day off." He pulled the dogs closer. "Sorry, but I shouldn't be talking to you. The lawyer said not to talk to anyone."

"That's good advice," I said. "You shouldn't talk to anyone. My lawyer tells me the same thing."

"You have a lawyer?"

I glanced over at Jessica, who was fidgeting with the buttons of her sweater. She wanted to get home and enjoy the rest of the evening on a sofa, and didn't look very pleased at me for starting a conversation with one of the people we'd specifically dressed up in disguises to evade.

I gave her a wide-eyed look, trying to communicate that I knew what I was doing. Ever since Quinn's mother had drunkenly gossiped to me about Colt's little sister being involved in Michael's death, the pieces had been clicking together in my head. It didn't make sense for Colt, a pacifist and gentle soul, to have stabbed a man to death. But it did seem like something his short-fused little sister might do. And it made a certain sense that he would knowingly take the fall for something to protect his sister. He wasn't at all like the Koenig brothers, Brandon and Drake, who'd turned on each other when the chips were down.

The Sweet homicide wasn't my case, but I'd already been involved so much. Would it kill me to explore a hunch by asking just a few questions?

Jessica shrugged, as if to tell me she was fine with me doing whatever I was going to do anyway, permission or not.

I turned back to the security guard with a big smile.

"Of course I have a lawyer," I said. "I am a suspect, after all. You're too young to know this, but Michael Sweet and I go way back, all the way back to high school. We had a run-in recently, when I confronted him about some suspicious bruises I saw on his wife." I glanced over at Jessica, whose lips were pressed together in a straight line. She wasn't going to say a peep, let alone disagree with any of my bluffing.

The security guard looked me up and down as he chuckled. "Lady, I don't think you killed anyone," he said. "I bet you've never even been hunting."

"I haven't," I said. "What's your name, in case the judge doesn't believe me and I need a character witness?"

He glanced around the parking lot and then up at the security cameras that were presumably stationed at each light post.

"Nick," he finally said. "Nick Tanner. No relation to the Canuso family, but I—" He clamped his mouth shut and shook his head. "I really shouldn't be talking to you. The lawyer said not to talk to anyone."

As a good lawyer should. Most people aren't good at keeping secrets. That's a good thing for society, but it's bad if you're trying to keep the details of a legal case confidential and your client blabs to anyone who bats an eyelash or offers a kind word their way.

But I had a sneaky trick up my sleeve.

"Your lawyer is right," I said. "You shouldn't talk to anyone." I started to walk away then stopped. "But before I go, how about you? Do you have any questions about the case that I could answer for you?" I paused and smiled. "Ask away."

The ace I had up my sleeve was knowing how busy lawyers are. Not just my own boyfriend, who was sporadic about returning messages, but all lawyers, everywhere. Even the best lawyer couldn't keep his or her client up to speed on absolutely everything at all times. And clients don't like not knowing.

Nick Tanner stared at me in disbelief. "For real? No tricks?"

I held my hands out wide. "I'm an open book, if you'd like."

His mouth moved silently for a moment, like the lips of a fish considering whether or not to bite the wiggly worm on the shining hook. Finally, he spoke. "Do they have any other suspects, or do they think it's Colt for sure?"

I looked down at the two dogs and then up at the security guard. Nick was a cute guy, midtwenties, and he didn't wear a wedding ring. If he had Colt's two dogs with him, that meant he was more than just an employee. He was close to the family despite not being a relative, which could mean a few things, including that he was dating Trigger Canuso.

I asked him, "How well do you know Trigger Canuso?" I quickly waved my hand as though erasing a chalkboard. "Scratch that. I promised not to ask you any questions. Forget I said anything."

"Trigger didn't do anything wrong," Nick said, his voice thin and straining. "She was with me that day. For the whole day."

"Oh. I didn't know she was dating you, too."

His whole body tensed, and then he straightened up, puffing his chest visibly. "Who else is she seeing?"

I turned and looked at Jessica. "Didn't you see Trigger around town with that big firefighter guy, Mitch?"

She opened her mouth and made a sound like a record scratching.

I turned back to Nick. "You know how rumors are. It might not be anything. I'm sure she's totally faithful to you."

"She'd better be," he sputtered.

"You mean since you're her alibi," I said.

"Exactly," he said.

I couldn't help but smile. I had this poor young man's number. Now I was extra glad for my choice of outfits, because I tucked my thumbs into the front of the armpits for my vest and took a wide stance. I'd never felt more like a private eye.

"Nick, you should ask me about obstruction of justice," I said with a cool, steely tone. "Ask me about the minimum sentence for lying to police in a statement."

His shoulders rounded, and his chest caved inward. "What is it?" He fidgeted with the dog leashes in his hands, switching them back and forth so he could wipe his palms on his jeans.

Keeping my voice low and slow, I explained, "Here in Oregon, lying in a police report is considered a Class A misdemeanor, with a recommended one-year incarceration and a fine of over six thousand dollars."

"Wow. That's intense." He clenched his jaw and flared his nostrils. I could almost hear his teeth grinding on this new information.

"And she would know," Jessica piped in suddenly. "Stormy lies to the police all the time."

I gave my best friend and accomplice a look that was part *thank you* and part *seriously?*

Nick asked me, "Can you take it back if you made a mistake? Like a retraction or whatever?"

"An uncooperative witness can become cooperative," I said. "They do have some leeway about people making mistakes. Of course, if a person were to make a retraction, it would be better sooner than later."

He looked up at the nearest security camera again and tugged the dog leashes as he backed away. "Yeah. Good to know. Like for the future or whatever."

"Glad I could help."

* * *

We were driving back home when my phone started ringing. We had been talking about this new development in the case and how relieved we were that Colt might simply be taking the blame for his sister. Neither of us wanted to see the troubled young woman go to jail, so we weren't exactly happy, but it did make me feel less awful about turning in Colt.

The phone kept ringing, and it was the special tone I'd given my store manager.

"That's Brianna calling," I told Jessica. "Can you answer for me?"

She dug my phone from my purse and answered. "Hi, Brianna. This is Jessica. Stormy's driving."

She listened for a minute.

"Oh, no," she said with a groan. "That's got to be illegal or something."

While she talked, I had a tough time staying focused on the road ahead.

"Can we get the video taken down?" More listening. "Of course I want to see it. Send me the link." Jessica shot me a worried look. "Yes, I'll tell her." She thanked Brianna and ended the call.

"Do I even want to know?" I asked.

"Maybe you should pull over," she said.

My phone dinged with the sound of an incoming link via text message.

I pulled the car over to a rest stop and put it in park.

CHAPTER 35

SUNDAY

"Let's watch it on my big TV," my father said. "Make your phone do the thing." He waved one hand expressively from his seat on his recliner. "The thing where it sends its picture to the television."

Kyle Dempsey jumped up from the couch eagerly. "I'll do it," he said, elbowing me out of the way.

"This must be what it's like to have a bratty little brother," I muttered.

My father shot me an amused look.

It was just the three of us for dinner that night. Logan was seeing family again with his sister, and Jessica was at her mother's.

I couldn't relax. Ever since my suspicions about Trigger had been roused, I hadn't felt like sitting around. I got up from the couch and went over to supervise Kyle with the TV settings.

My father settled back in his recliner and kicked up the footrest. "Stormy, since you're up already, and so close to the kitchen, I could use a refill."

"Same here," Kyle said without looking up at me.

"Sure thing, Dimples."

My father snorted. "Don't call him that," he said.

"Everyone calls him Dimples. Even you call him that."

He gave me a very serious look. "But when I say it, it doesn't sound affectionate. You make it sound dirty."

I rolled my eyes.

He continued, "You let him take you to a movie. That's right. I know all about it. I've got eyes and ears all over this town."

"Yes, Dad," I said, channeling my inner snarky teen. "Dimples and I sat next to each other in a crowded theater. But we sat in the back row so we could kiss and grope each other the whole time."

My father frowned. This wasn't the reaction he'd been hoping for.

"He gave me so many hickies," I said. "But I gave him twice as many."

My poor father looked like he regretted bringing up the subject.

Kyle looked like he might throw up.

"Stormy, thanks again for coming with me," Kyle said. "It's more fun to watch a movie with a friend."

"And thank you for not wearing that pink V-neck shirt again tonight. I wouldn't have been able to control myself."

He self-consciously straightened his shirt, which was a bright white T-shirt from a resort in Mexico. "I didn't turn on my full *Esquire* look today."

"Well, you look very nice, honey," I said in a gravelly, chain-smoking waitress voice. "I'm sure some day a nice young lady will make an honest man of you."

He gave me two thumbs up. My father just shook his head and grumbled, "Still waiting on that beer."

I went to the kitchen and got the drinks, as requested.

Kyle was a number of years younger than me. So young, in fact, that I had been his babysitter once upon a time. I had literally changed his diapers. That detail about our shared personal history was something Captain Milano liked to mention whenever the opportunity arose. Little did he know, he and my father didn't have anything to worry about. I appreciated Kyle Dempsey's good looks the way I appreciated a fine oil painting. Besides, age difference aside, I'd decided at a very young age that I'd never date a cop. The one exception I'd made for Tony had been a huge mistake, and I wouldn't make it again.

There were over a dozen bottles of beer in the fridge. I took three out and popped off the caps. The beer was from a local microbrewery that my father's dimple-faced prodigy was a fan of. It was a bit too hoppy, and not much better than my father's cheap can of choice, but at least the label was pretty; the logo featured a stag standing majestically in front of Misty Falls.

When I returned to the living room, both the rookie cop and his retired mentor were enjoying the video on the big screen.

The video was what my employee had called me about the night before. It was security camera footage of myself and Jessica taking a dunk in the casino's water feature. It hadn't gone viral in the *global* sense. It certainly wasn't as share-worthy as a Korean pop song with an eye-popping video, or cats stealing dog beds from shame-faced dogs. But the footage had gone viral popular by Misty Falls, Oregon, standards, with over a hundred thousand views and climbing.

I'd already seen the video more than enough times on my phone, but the resolution was surprisingly good, and there was more to see now on my father's large screen.

The video started with the scuffle between Michael Sweet and the security guards. There was no audio on the security camera footage, so Michael could have been yelling about anything. I'd been there, so I knew it was hate speech toward the Canuso family and other members of their tribe.

On the left side of the screen, a dark-haired woman and her red-haired friend rose above the crowd, in front of the fountain. That was yours truly and her partner in crime.

On the right side of the screen, the crowd parted to afford a perfect shot of Colt handing his jacket to a member of staff. The shot was perfectly framed and told a clear story without a single word. Colt's face was in profile when he sucker-punched Michael Sweet in the guts.

A split second later, something spooked a few people in the crowd. And then others panicked in a chain reaction, bumping into more people who then realized they were hemmed in by other kids and families and subsequently panicked themselves. Individual people moved chaotically. But to the bird's-eye view of the camera, the movements became part of a larger pattern, not unlike dominoes toppling. It was a good lesson in crowd dynamics. The dance was almost beautiful in how natural it was, like a herd of animals responding to a predator in their midst. The crowd swirled, crushed, and rebounded.

Meanwhile, on the left-hand side of the screen, where I could barely stand to look, the two women standing on the rock wall surrounding the fountain flew into motion. One at a time, they threw their arms in the air as though this was a choreographed flash mob. And down Jessica and I both went, into the swirling water.

We flailed in the water for an eternity.

"That's funny," I said. "I don't remember being in the water for so long."

"They've slowed down the video," Kyle said. "And added hippo noises."

"That seems a bit cruel," I said.

He turned up the volume on the TV. There was no sound from the event itself, but some clever person had added an audio track of what sounded like a wild animal watering hole in Africa.

"That's an elephant," my father said. "Hippos don't bellow like that."

"I don't think it's an elephant," Kyle said. "It might be creature sounds from a King Kong movie."

"I know," my father said triumphantly. "I'd recognize that horrific noise anywhere. When Stormy was a little girl, that was the same sound she'd make when she had to take a bath with her sister."

Playing along, Kyle said, "This must be the actual sound from the event that day. Of course. Look how perfectly the sounds match up to Stormy's mouth!"

I knew when I was beat, so I took a seat on the couch and let them make fun of me.

After a few plays of the video and more mockery, my father suddenly tilted his reclining chair upright.

"Back it up," my father said. "Hit rewind."

"There's no rewind," Kyle said.

"You know exactly what I mean, Kyle. Don't make me swat your smart butt with a rolled up *TV Guide*."

I grinned at Kyle. "That's not an empty threat."

"I know," Kyle said as he used the controls on his phone to scroll the video back again.

"Look at Colt's face," my father said, pointing his finger excitedly. "You can see this very specific look come over him, even as he's mid-punch. I know that expression. It's regret. He's not happy about what he's doing, even at the moment he's doing it."

"You're right," I said. "He regrets punching Michael immediately."

Kyle said, "A brief flicker of regret doesn't prove he's innocent."

"But don't you see? That's not the face of a man who stabs a guy repeatedly," I said. "Colt lost control on Saturday, yes. He threw a single punch, but that was it. One punch was all the anger he had in him."

"Until he stabbed the guy."

"Michael Sweet was stabbed between twenty-three and twenty-five times. Plus some slashes. How long would that take?"

Kyle blinked at me. "Is that a serious question?"

I picked up the remote control and pretended to stab him, counting out the stabs. At twenty, I switched hands because my arm was getting tired. When I was done, I said, "That's a lot of stabs. When I'm making baked potatoes in the microwave, I stab them with a fork first, and it's a fair amount of work if you have to do more than one potato."

"Baked potatoes," my father said, rocking his chair forward and getting up. He headed toward the kitchen, muttering about preparing baked potatoes to pair with our meatballs.

Alone with Kyle, I said simply, "You guys can't charge Colt with the murder. He didn't do it."

"That's not my decision." He took a long pull off his bottle of beer and wiped his mouth with the back of his hand. "If you're so sure about your friend's innocence, you shouldn't have called in the report about the blood stains on his shirt."

We both looked at the screen again. The video being projected from Kyle's phone had frozen on a single frame. It was seconds after the punch, when Michael had rolled forward, his chin over Colt's shoulder.

I jumped up and ran to the TV. I pointed to the spot on the big screen, pressing through the soft buzz of static electricity floating on the surface. "What's that on Michael's chin? Is his lip bleeding?"

Kyle adjusted the image, zooming in on the frozen frame. The image became pixellated, but it was clear to us that Michael Sweet's lip had been split during the altercation, and blood was present.

"That's how Michael's blood got on Colt's shirt," I said. "It happened days before the homicide."

Kyle took another long pull on his beer. His dimples had disappeared. "Wasn't it his other shoulder?"

I pulled up a mental image of Colt Canuso leaning over to pet his dogs that day in Central Park. I could see the stain, but not which shoulder it was on.

However, trying to remember what I saw gave me an idea. My employee had taken a photo of Colt early on Monday morning.

On my way to the couch to get my phone from my purse, I bumped the coffee table with my leg. I didn't even feel the pain in my shin, though I nearly knocked Kyle's beer on the floor. He cursed and caught the bottle midair.

While I pulled up Brianna's contact information, I quickly explained to Kyle what I was doing.

We both waited in quiet excitement for Brianna to reply. Would she send me the evidence to exonerate my friend? I hoped she would.

CHAPTER 36

While we waited for Brianna to message me back, Kyle and I went over the basic facts of the case.

Since it was Sunday, tomorrow would make the homicide two weeks old. Each day the case went unsolved, the chances of an arrest diminished. We reviewed what we knew, hoping to see new connections. Kyle had gotten a few more details out of Samantha to fill in the picture.

Michael Sweet had woken up Monday morning at the usual time. His ribs were still bruised from his altercation with Colt Canuso two days prior, but it was only enough bruising to make him grumble and not enough for him to take a painkiller.

Samantha got dressed and ready for her day. It was a regular Monday, so she would be meeting with buyer and seller clients, and checking on paperwork at the office downtown, which was owned by the real estate franchise. Before leaving the house, they bickered briefly over Michael taking the day off to play golf. It would cost them for the course fees as well as daycare for the baby, but Michael assured Samantha they were about to come into a windfall, and money wouldn't be an issue for long.

They left their house at the same time, with Samantha heading to the office to meet their part-time assistant, Harper. Michael picked up Sophie's friend Quinby from the McCabes' house and then drove the best friends to their school. Next, he dropped the baby off at daycare, bragged about spending the day on the green, and then disappeared. He didn't have a tee time at the course, so whatever he did that day, it had been planned.

"Was he in communication with Trigger Canuso?"

Kyle took a while to answer. "He didn't have plans to meet her that day. At least not any that were through his phone or social media accounts."

"But there was something going on with her."

Kyle winced, as though fighting an internal battle over divulging the information to me.

"Oh, hell," he said. "It's all public anyway. Michael spent a lot of time on Sunday posting comments on some of Trigger Canuso's internet accounts. Telling her how cute she was, and what a fine young woman she'd grown up into."

"He was trolling her," I said. "Trying to provoke a reaction."

"That's what I thought. She's got that crooked face thing, where one side of her head is smaller than the other. Poor girl."

"It's called hemifacial microsomia, and it's probably what made her tough."

"Getting beaten by her stepfather daily was what made her tough."

I was temporarily speechless. "What?"

"The only reason Colt stuck around after high school was to protect his little sister. He's a good man, Stormy. He and his uncles opened the casino to help their entire community, not for their personal gain. If he goes to prison, I don't know what's going to happen. They took on a lot of debt for the expansion, and if Colt's not around to manage the enterprise, well..." He looked down at the label he was peeling from his beer bottle. "Things could go downhill out there at the lake."

"We need to figure out what happened that day," I said.

"Maybe the best-case scenario is this one goes unsolved."

I hissed, "Don't you dare let my father hear you saying that."

He yanked the label off the beer bottle, ripping it messily.

We sat in silence for a minute. My father called out from the kitchen that dinner would be ready in seven minutes. I could hear the microwave whirring.

No response yet on my phone. I sent Brianna another message.

Kyle picked up one of the old magazines from the side table and leafed through it.

Something occurred to me, so I asked Kyle, "Did you guys find any dirty magazines at the crime scene?"

"Not that I recall. Why?"

I told him about how the Sweets' part-time assistant had covered for Michael with some clients, after they found some materials he'd left behind.

Kyle seemed puzzled by this, setting the *Reader's Digest* aside and rubbing his smooth chin for a long time.

Finally, he said, "Why would someone buy a magazine when they have the internet? I mean, it's all there, and it's free, and you can—"

"Gross." I held up a hand, begging him to stop sharing. "Dimples, I don't want to know."

"Michael Sweet was your age, though, so I guess he'd do it the old-school way." He shifted his chin-rubbing hand down to his Adam's apple and scratched it thoughtfully. He had some razor burn and raised red bumps that looked itchy. I remembered what I'd said to my father about hickies, and pondered how soft Kyle's skin looked.

Then I found myself looking at his lips and wondering how soft they were.

I cleared my throat and forced my thoughts away. *Picture his bare baby butt*, I told myself. It didn't work, and I pictured his adult butt instead.

I grabbed a throw pillow from behind me and hugged it to my stomach. I grabbed my bottle of beer and chugged the remainder.

Kyle was watching me.

I wiped my mouth with the back of my hand and let out a good burp. *That'll reset the tone*, I thought.

"That was well brought up," he said. "Too bad you weren't."

I looked down at my phone. "Come on, Brianna. What kind of millennial are you, letting your phone go unchecked for seven minutes?"

Kyle snorted. "Not all millennials are the same."

"You're all the same when it comes to your phones," I teased. "All of you wacky, tech-obsessed youngsters."

Just then, Brianna came through. She even apologized for taking so long. She'd sent the photo she'd taken of Colt Canuso on Monday morning, just hours before the homicide.

My fingers trembled as I opened the attachment and zoomed.

My heart immediately sunk. The room spun around me, closing in.

Colt was wearing a shirt that was indistinguishable from the one on the video.

I handed the phone to Kyle and cursed. I cursed loud enough to get my father's attention in the kitchen.

He came out, and we explained to him what I'd hoped to get, only to be disappointed.

"Same shirt," Finnegan Day said. "He's probably got a half-dozen in the identical style, to go with his suits." He took the phone from Kyle and stared at it. "I've always admired the bolo tie, but I couldn't pull one off." He glanced up at Kyle. "Were there any ligature marks? If I wanted to kill someone and I had a bolo tie on me, I'd use what I had on hand."

"No ligature marks," Kyle said.

The microwave beeped repeatedly in the kitchen. "Potatoes are done," my father said. "Let's eat before it gets cold."

* * *

After dinner, I was outnumbered by boys when it came to TV channels, so we watched the NFL game.

We watched football for nearly an hour without speaking. I tried not to think about the Sweet homicide. It wasn't my case, and it wasn't my business.

Finally, my father muted the television during commercials and turned to me with a sympathetic expression. "Stormy, it was worth a shot," he said. "I'm just as disappointed as you are that your friend wasn't wearing a different shirt that Monday morning."

"I doubt that," I said grumpily.

"I've been where you are right now," he said. "It's not a good place to be. But you can't give up just because one idea didn't work out."

"What's to give up? This isn't my case."

Kyle patted me on the shoulder. "I won't give up," he said.

I pulled my shoulder away and shifted over to the edge of the couch.

After a few minutes, I asked Kyle, "What have you got on Trigger and where she was all day Monday? I know she wasn't with her dumb boyfriend."

He glanced over at my father. Neither of them said anything.

"Off the record," I said.

Kyle pulled his head back, giving himself a small double chin. "What do you mean, *off the record*? You're not a reporter." He narrowed his sky-blue eyes at me. "Is this one of your dirty private eye tricks?"

I shrugged. "Would you prefer a pinkie swear?" I held up my pinkie finger.

My father chuckled.

Kyle said, "Colt Canuso doesn't have a great alibi for the time of the murder. He was supposed to attend a men's group meeting. His two security guard friends were at the meeting, but Colt never showed up. When he met up with them later, he said the dogs had been acting up, so he took them for a walk."

"I asked you about Trigger," I said. "Where was she that day?"

"She was not with Rick Tanner all day," Kyle said. "He did change his statement, thanks to your helpful suggestion. He met up with her later at about four o'clock in the afternoon, and she was agitated." He quickly added, "More agitated than usual."

"Why are you sitting around drinking beer and watching football with my dad when you should be out solving this case?"

"Cops don't work twenty-four seven. We're allowed time off."

"You need to figure out where Trigger was all day."

Kyle gave me a grumpy look. "Don't tell me how to do my job. I worked a lot of high-profile cases before I moved back here to Oregon."

I took out my phone and called someone.

Kyle demanded, "Who are you calling now?"

"Harper. She's the part-time assistant for the Sweets. It's okay. I'm friends with her."

"That doesn't make it okay." He gave me a serious look, which was downright adorable thanks to his dimples.

"Harper," I said brightly when she answered the call. "Hey, how have you been? You sure bolted out of there on Friday night."

Harper was hesitant to answer. "Uh... Your friend Quinn gave me a ride home. She's kind of intense."

"Sorry about that," I said. "Did she demand to know your waist measurement? That's her way of bonding with a new girl."

"Actually, she did," Harper said, bemused.

"That means you're in," I said.

We talked a bit more, and Harper shared her perspective on Quinn's terrifying driving skills in the Land Rover. I laughed and smiled broadly at Kyle, who was looking more confused by the minute.

I tilted the mouthpiece away from my mouth and whispered to him, "Subtlety is an art."

Harper was saying something about a party. "Will you be there? Quinn said we'd be celebrating her daughter getting that big TV role."

"Of course I'll be at Quinn's hootenanny. Why not?" I turned to my father and made a gagging face. He barely took his eyes off the television.

"Thanks for checking in on me," Harper said. "These last two weeks have been the absolute worst."

"I can imagine."

Brightly, she said, "At least you and Jessica have been so nice to me. And your dad, too. I think he might have paid me too much for the car."

"Nonsense," I said vehemently. "My father has never paid too much for anything in his life."

Finnegan Day's eyes lit up. He grinned at me from his recliner, Hobo Pride evident.

"My battery's running low," Harper said. "But I'll see you Friday night, right?"

"I'll be there with bells on."

I ended the call and filled Kyle in on what I'd learned, which was nothing yet. "But I'll be socializing with her Friday night," I said. "You can't get more subtle than that."

"And you think she knows more about Michael's side hobbies than she's been telling us?"

"She didn't tell you about the magazines, did she?"

Kyle was speechless. I glanced over to catch my father giving me an approving wink.

Kyle said, "I'm coming as your date to this hootenanny."

This again? I thought we'd gotten past Kyle's puppy crush on me.

"Good idea," my father said. "Bring Kyle with you. Work as a team to find out what people know about Trigger. Plus, if Samantha's there, he can protect you from her."

"I doubt she'll be at a hootenanny."

"Be safe," he warned. "If you see that woman, make sure you know where the big kitchen knives are at all times."

"Dad! Samantha wouldn't hurt a fly."

"Never be hasty to rule out the spouse," he said.

I looked over at Kyle. "Samantha continues to be of interest," he said.

I let the information sink in, and I considered my options. Logan and his sister might be interested in the party, but that didn't mean we couldn't go as a big group. My car would hold five people, albeit things would get cuddly in the backseat.

“Dimples, can you dance?”

“I can,” he said with a twinkle in his sky-blue eyes. “That doesn't mean I should.”

CHAPTER 37

When I got home Sunday night, the lights next door at Logan's were off. His vehicle was in the driveway, which meant both Sanderson siblings had hit the hay early.

I walked in my own door to find Jessica asleep on the couch with Jeffrey curled up beside her. Neither of them stirred. I switched off the TV, which was showing the end of the nature documentary marathon that I'd wanted to watch at my father's.

The kitchen counter was clean, which made the recent addition of a flower bouquet jump out at me. Was it for Jessica or for yours truly? The flowers were all cat-friendly, with no dangerous lilies that could harm my curious Russian Blue cat. And it was a good thing, because by the look of the yellow petals strewn about, he'd taken a sample nibble.

Next to the vase were a card and a small blue box.

The interior of the card read: *Sorry I haven't been much fun lately. I'll make it up to you soon. I hope you enjoy the gift in the box. Love, Logan.*

For me! I also hoped I would enjoy the gift in the box. I opened it breathlessly. I wasn't much for wearing jewelry on a daily basis, but that didn't mean I wasn't a fan of receiving it. Back when I'd been growing up, my father used to take me to Ruby's Treasure Trove every single birthday so I could pick out something special. I still had every single piece, even though their monetary value was low and the style was more suited to a pre-teen girl.

The box didn't contain jewelry; it held a small, gray, dark-whiskered mouse.

I picked up the mouse and was so shocked by the feel of it in my hand that I immediately dropped it on my foot. *What on earth?* I picked it up gingerly, by the tail. It was eerily realistic for a cat toy, seemingly covered in real fur.

I looked in the box, at a small paper tag that proclaimed the furry thing to be of premium construction and 100% natural materials. The label went on to explain that the company's products were all recycled, made from unwanted leather and fur coats that had been donated to charities but were unsalable. The label also specified that it was an *object d'art*, not a toy. So that was how they got around the regulations against making toys out of anything but new materials. You can't just sell consumers any ol' thing made out of random bits and bobs. I knew a lot about these rules, thanks to my experiences ordering for Glorious Gifts.

Jeffrey, who had silently jumped up on the counter without me noticing, snaked one gray paw over and effortlessly grabbed the mouse from me. He sank his teeth into the fur body with an excited growl and took off with it, bounding down the hallway.

I crossed my arms and looked at the wall dividing my side of the duplex from Logan's. He meant well, but he wasn't so great at selecting gifts. For my birthday, he'd taken me to dinner and then given me a computer mouse pad with his law firm's logo on it. "Everyone likes useful things," he'd said. "And your other mouse pad is all worn out and tattered." His gift had been entirely office supplies, including a matching Tyger & Behr mug and a set of pens.

I picked up the card and read the neatly printed interior text again. *Sorry I haven't been much fun lately. I'll make it up to you soon. I hope you enjoy the gift in the box. Love, Logan.*

Was the card meant for Jeffrey? It didn't have my name on it. If this was Logan's idea of a funny prank, it was way too subtle for me.

I sniffed the flowers, which had no scent at all, and then headed off to prepare for bed.

I found Jeffrey in the bathroom, where he was making the excited SNARF SNARF sound he usually reserved for dirty wool socks. He had successfully eviscerated the recycled-fur mouse and was conducting an autopsy on its white cotton innards. I reached down to take away the stuffing before he choked on it. He made a sound that was part growl and part SNARF, grabbed the inside-out mouse hide, and ran off.

At least he was enjoying the gift, albeit not as intended.

When I was done brushing my teeth, I went to the living room to check on Jessica. She was already sitting up, yawning. She asked, "Done in the bathroom?"

"Yes," I said. "And I think I'm done with Logan."

"I told him it was a bad idea," she said.

"You think?" I sputtered. "A cat toy? Made out of germy old fur that's been god-knows-where? What was he thinking?"

"You didn't find the robe, did you?" She got up and folded the sofa blanket. "I told him he was being an idiot. He doesn't know you like I do, does he? Go look on your bed before you say something you'll regret."

I went down the hall. There on my bed was another box, larger than the first one I'd found on the counter. Inside was a beautiful silk robe, dark red. It didn't look as warm and cozy as the multicolored robe I'd snagged from my father's former girlfriend, Pam Bochenek, but it was beautiful. It looked expensive.

"Your secret is safe with me," Jessica said from the doorway. "I won't tell Logan his surprise was so bad you were on the brink of ending things with him."

"I hadn't meant it," I said. "You know me. I say dumb things when I get mad."

"What's that expression your father has, about Freudian slips?"

"Where the tongue slips, it speaks the truth."

She made a mouth-smacking sound and a sour face. "I need to brush these teeth or throw them away." She shuffled off to the washroom.

Jeffrey jumped up on my bed and hunkered down in the middle of my pillow with his flattened mouse hide, which had a disturbingly accurate shape; it truly did resemble the carefully skinned and tanned pelt of a mouse. He began licking the fur side lovingly. I could hear the raspiness of his tongue on the long-dead material. *To each their own*, I thought.

I pulled off my clothes and slipped on the dark-red silk robe. The fabric was cool and made me shiver. I slipped it off, put it on a hanger in my closet, and pulled on a favorite threadbare sleeping shirt. I rubbed the goose bumps on my arms and stared at Logan's gift. While I was admiring the robe, it slithered off the hanger and pooled on the floor.

I wondered, *why red?* Why not a color that looked less like a puddle of blood?

I dug through my closet, found one of my padded fabric hangers, and hung it up again.

As I switched off the lights and crawled into bed, I hoped Jessica wouldn't remember our conversation in the morning.

* * *

The week passed quickly and without any major disasters, unless you count all the times I found Jeffrey's chewed and mangled mouse pelt in various places a person doesn't want to find a mangled mouse pelt, such as inside my shoe and tucked in my bed. Once, I looked down to find it on my lap, and I had no recollection of Jeffrey even being in the room with me. Had the revolting thing gained consciousness and started moving freely about the house? Surely it had, for self-ambulation was the only logical explanation.

Jessica didn't bring up our Sunday night conversation, and for that I was grateful. We all say dumb things when we're tired or agitated.

I had some investigation cases that became my focus on Monday and kept me busy straight through to Friday. Logan was busy as well, with work at

Tyger & Behr, and also with his sister, who'd decided to stick around Misty Falls a bit longer. Jinx had gotten a few meetings about getting on the hair and makeup team for the upcoming *Hallows* filming that would be taking place in our corner of Oregon soon. I hadn't considered the local economic impact of a large HBO production until Jinx and Jessica had a discussion about rising rent prices in the apartments around town. There was even talk of our town plus two nearby towns working together to create a new "Hollywood Northwest."

Rumor had it people were getting excited about speculating on local real estate. Jessica told me that the tiny house Samantha had been trying to sell, which now had the dubious distinction of being a violent crime scene, had received several competing offers.

"That's good news for Samantha," I said to Jessica on Friday. "She could use the sales commission."

"Until the insurance money comes in," Jessica said.

We were eating a quick dinner of grilled cheese sandwiches and canned soup before we headed off to Quinn's family's farm for the evening's hootenanny.

Jessica tapped the crumbs off her grilled sandwich and casually asked, "Do you have life insurance on yourself?"

"I don't have any dependents," I said.

"Poor Jeffrey," she said. "Left to fend for himself without his mommy."

"Stop," I said, laughing through the sudden heartbreak. "You're going to make me cry. I know you're joking, but it's a horrible thought." I looked over at the cat, who was curled up with his mouse pelt on the sofa.

"What about the bank? Don't they have insurance to cover the mortgage?"

"Sure, but it's only for their benefit." I looked down at my red tomato soup. "But you make a good point. I should make sure my will is up to date, and that you'll be looked after."

She snorted and ate her sandwich without further comment.

* * *

After dinner, Jessica sprung a whole new surprise on me.

"Come on, it'll be fun," Jessica said.

I shook my head. "Nothing fun has ever started with the phrase *Come on, it'll be fun.*"

Jessica stuck out her lower lip, pouting. "Last Sunday, I had to dig around in my mother's storage unit for hours."

I picked up the cheerleader uniform delicately, as though it might turn to dust, like a mummy in an old horror movie.

"It looks smaller than I remember. Are you sure this one is mine?"

"Your name's on the label," she said. "I'm sure it still fits. Maybe it'll look even better, now that you have more curves to fill it out."

"I'm worried my curves are in all the wrong places."

"Maybe you should lay off on the gas station hot dogs."

I gasped in mock horror. "Is this about how my jeans keep shrinking in the laundry?"

She gave me a motherly look. "Funny how we used the same detergent and washing machine, yet *my* jeans haven't been afflicted."

I dropped the uniform back on the bed and clutched my chest as though fatally wounded. I fell onto the bed next to Jeffrey, who opened one sleepy green eye.

"What do you think?" I poked his tummy. "Should we go on a diet together?"

He closed his eyes, yawned, and stretched into a croissant shape.

"You don't need to diet," Jessica said. "Just stop eating carbs after dark and your jeans will fit again."

"Everyone knows carbs taste twice as nice after the sun goes down."

She sat on the bed on the other side of Jeffrey. "Or don't worry about it. You're beautiful, and you have a perfect figure."

"You're a bad liar."

"But I'm not lying. You do look great, and I love how you're not neurotic about your appearance. I'm trying to be more like you. I'm trying not to project my issues onto you. Please forget everything I said about the gas station hot dogs."

"No, you do have a point." I patted my waistline self-consciously. According to the scale, I had gained a number of pounds in a short amount of time. At first, I'd assumed something had happened to the scale while I was using it to weigh garbage, but the fit of my clothes certainly corroborated the theory that some of my parts were getting fluffier. I'd had a single day of panic in which I thought I might be pregnant, but that theory was quickly ruled out.

"You're perfect how you are," Jessica said.

"I could try to cut back. But if I don't eat the gas station hot dogs, that leaves the nachos with the melted cheese."

"Can they even legally call it"—she made air quotes with her fingers—"*cheese*?"

"You're making me hungry, and we just ate."

She held up both hands. "Not my intention at all."

I leaned over and grabbed Jeffrey's rear paw, caressing his dark-rose-hued toe pads. "What's this? It looks delicious. I could eat these little jelly beans."

His ears twitched but he didn't react, not even when I pretended to put his paw in my mouth.

Jessica and I played with Jeffrey for a few minutes, until he suddenly jumped up and ran off as though he'd just remembered he had an important business meeting.

"No more stalling," Jessica said. "Put on the cheerleader uniform or don't. Your choice. Either way, we should get going so Quinn doesn't make us do laps for being late."

I checked the time. "Dimples should be here any minute." The doorbell rang.

"Timely," I said.

Jessica arched one eyebrow. "I love it when that happens."

CHAPTER 38

The three of us piled into Kyle Dempsey's car. He'd volunteered to be our designated driver so that Jessica and I could partake in adult beverages. Jessica sat in the passenger seat, and I took the back. Kyle kept glancing in the rearview mirror and then looking away.

I told him, "Take a picture, it'll last longer."

"You just look so different," he said. "You've got legs."

I tugged at the hem of my pleated cheerleader skirt. "So does Jessica," I said. "Why don't you look at *her* legs for a while?"

"She wears dresses all the time," he said. "I've seen her legs plenty."

"Thanks a lot," Jessica said, laughing. "You and Mitch must have gone to the same charm school."

Kyle brought the car to a complete stop at the first major intersection. I usually treated that corner as a *yield*, not a *stop*, but the young man was a cop, through and through. A cop in a deep V-neck T-shirt. Tonight's selection was an azure blue that brought out his dreamy eyes. Not that I had noticed.

Kyle glanced over at Jessica before turning right. "What's going on there, anyway? Mitch has been walking around with a long face for the last week. He thinks he screwed things up with you. What exactly did he do?"

"It's more like what he didn't do," Jessica said.

My ears perked up. I'd been trying to get Jessica to open up about her stalled romance with the firefighter, but Kyle had gotten further in two minute than I had in two weeks.

Kyle gave her a dazzling grin. "What didn't he do?"

She twirled one of her red pigtails. "The whole thing seems so stupid now. We went out for pizza and drinks, and I paid for the meal, and then he didn't thank me."

"That's all?"

"I don't know how to explain it, but he sort of acted like he'd paid for it. When he dropped me off at home, he said I could treat him next time."

"Did you pay for the pizza right in front of him?"

"No." She twirled her pigtail again. "I went up to the waitress station while he was in the washroom. It was supposed to be a surprise."

"Mm hmm." Kyle checked over his shoulder, turned on the signal blinker, and carefully changed lanes. "Did you happen to notice Mitch dropping a pile of cash on the table as you were leaving?"

Jessica was quiet for a full minute.

Kyle explained, "It's just that Mitch usually pays cash. At least he does at the Loose Moose, when he's picking up a round. And he never has to wait for the bill because he's really good at adding up drinks, food, and tip in his head. I've never met a guy who's so good with numbers."

"Oh," she said quietly.

"There's a surprising amount of math firefighters do in the field. There's calculating friction loss based on the hose length and diameter to adjust pump pressure, and then all the geometry. Do you know what a chain is?"

"Yes," she said slowly. "It's a metal rope made of links."

"A chain is the basic unit for measuring distances in fire-control work. It's equal to sixty-six feet. There are eighty chains to a mile."

Jessica was quiet.

I piped up from the backseat. "Now you're just showing off," I said.

Kyle flashed me a grin in the rearview mirror.

"Mitch thought he paid for dinner," Jessica said. "Because he did. We both did. That lucky waitress got a huge tip."

"You probably made her night," Kyle said.

"I'm so stupid," Jessica said.

In unison, Kyle and I both said, "No, you're not!"

I reached forward between the seats and squeezed her shoulder. "Tell Mitch what happened. He'll probably laugh."

"He probably will," she said grimly, as though having him laugh at their misunderstanding would be unbearable, because it would feel like him laughing at her.

"Tell him anyway," I said.

"I'll think about it," Jessica said.

Her answer seemed to satisfy Kyle, because for the rest of the drive he didn't bug her about it. But I knew that Jessica's *I'll think about it* meant that she had no intention of doing so. The thing about her insecurities was she would paint herself into a corner, and rather than admitting her mistake and walking out, she'd stand there until the paint dried and everyone else's attention moved on to something else. She'd stand there forever if she had to.

The other thing was, I couldn't say for sure that she was wrong to do so. Her older brothers loved her, but they'd been merciless in their teasing. Any weakness she admitted to—any vulnerability—would be exploited by them. Many of her boyfriends had been the same way, mocking her inability to handle money and joking about taking her paychecks and putting her on an allowance, for her own good.

Jessica often played dumb because then people weren't so quick to jump on her when she did make a mistake. She was careful about who she let into her heart, who she trusted enough to be herself around. She took rejection so personally, more so than other people. Sometimes I wished I could go on the internet and order her an extra-thick suit of skin to wear as protection. But I couldn't. So I tried to be a positive person in her life by doing other things, such as wearing my old high school cheerleader uniform despite feeling utterly ridiculous in it.

The sweater was awfully tight, and worst of all, it was made of a polyester blend that didn't breathe. I reached for my purse to get some tissues to use for mopping up some of the sweat, but my purse wasn't next to me. I'd left it at home, along with my phone and everything else I regularly carried. Suddenly, I felt naked and exposed. Jessica had locked up the house, and then since Kyle was driving, I hadn't needed my keys so I forgot the whole kit and caboodle. And now we were halfway to the Baudelaire farm.

I settled back on the seat and fanned air through the sweater as best I could.

* * *

We weren't late, but the hootenanny was already in full swing by the time we arrived at the Baudelaires' old farm. The family hadn't lived on the premises for a long time. For the last decade, the family had been renting out the surrounding farm fields to an adjacent farmer, a Russian man who'd been trying to get them to sell the land to him for years.

Kyle filled us in on the gossip while he drove along the bumpy road, following the chain of lit tiki torches and signs directing us where to park. The Russian, whom everyone simply called "the Russian" rather than using his actual name, had been either the object of or the source of several nuisance calls to the local police department. It sounded rather juicy. Kyle promised he would fill us in on more details some other time, when we had an entire evening to kill.

Jessica asked him, "Is it safe to be here on this land like this?"

"The old farmhouse and the barn are not part of what the Russian is renting. After some recent disputes between the Baudelaires and the Russian, it has been clarified." Kyle chuckled. "Without a single shot fired."

"You're not filling me with confidence," Jessica said.

"Don't you worry, ma'am," he said with an authoritative tone. "I'm here to preserve the peace, to enforce law and order over this fine land." He glanced in the rearview mirror at me. "And dance."

We climbed out of the car and headed into the party.

Kyle Dempsey wasn't joking about the dancing. As soon as we walked into the barn, he hit the dance floor with Jessica on his arm. They kicked up bits of hay as they twirled around to the folk music.

The music was of the folk variety, and it was as loud as it was live, played by a band of at least seven members, including one person with an enormous stand-up bass.

The folk band's fiddle player stepped forward to play a solo piece. It took me a minute to recognize the star fiddle player as Chip McCabe.

Once again, I was completely surprised to witness another facet of the man I knew mainly as my father's mail carrier.

Chip was wearing, as usual, a pair of shorts, but instead of walking shoes he wore pointed-toed western boots. With his chubby knees, the outfit gave him the look of a little boy. His shirt was also a western style in a dark burgundy, studded with rhinestones. The other six band mates wore matching shirts.

On the drummer's bass drum was the name of the band: Rain Nor Heat.

I had to smile at their cleverness. Surely the band was comprised entirely of mail carriers, and the name was taken from the unofficial creed of the

USPS: *Neither snow nor rain nor heat nor gloom of night stays these couriers from the swift completion of their appointed rounds.*

Rain Nor Heat was upbeat and cheerful, perfect for a hootenanny, and from what I knew of folk music, professional quality.

Since my two companions were on the dance floor, I headed over to the punch bowl, scanning faces and waving hello as I walked.

There were many familiar folks in the crowd, but I kept peering around. I was looking for one person in particular: Harper. Sunday night on the phone, she'd assured me she would be here tonight. Should I have offered her a ride? I wished I'd thought of it sooner. I had been looking forward to picking her brain about her bosses, the Sweets. Harper might have let it slip to someone that Michael hung out at their empty house listings to spend quality time with himself. If she was friends with someone who was also friends with Trigger Canuso, that would explain how Trigger might have discovered Michael's whereabouts the day he was killed.

Talking to Harper was a long shot, but experience had taught me that long shots paid off on occasion.

I spotted two young women who also worked at the Olive Grove and went over to talk to them.

"Do you know if Harper's coming tonight?"

They were both so distracted by my cheerleader uniform that it took them a minute to answer. One looked at the other and asked, "Doesn't she have that bad sinus cold that's going around?"

"She'd better have it," the friend replied. "She was going to take a few of my shifts for cash, but then she backed out at the last minute and I had to miss my sister's shower." She looked at me with a pained expression. "Baby shower, not wedding shower. Much to our parents' horror."

"Congratulations," I said anyway. "It seems like so much fun to be an auntie." I glanced around, trying to come up with more small talk. I had nothing, so I cut to the chase. "Are either of you friends with Trigger Canuso?"

They gave each other a look, and then the first one wrinkled her nose. "Not really. I mean, we know who she is, and we don't have a problem with her, but..." They looked at each other again.

"Never mind," I said. "Thanks for letting me know about Harper. Maybe I'll stop by her apartment tomorrow with some chicken soup."

As I walked away from the girls, I could hear them whispering my name and giggling. My body felt heavy, and I suddenly wished I was at home, or anywhere but a barn dance. I wouldn't normally have cared about people talking about me behind my back, but wearing my high school cheerleader uniform must have put me in touch with some of my youthful insecurities.

I headed toward the refreshments table. Another familiar face popped out of the crowd: my trusty employee, Brianna. Was I ever happy to see her. I scooped myself a cup of pink juice from the punch bowl and went to join her.

Brianna looked like a stylish farm girl, in denim shorts and a plaid shirt tied above her navel. She'd styled her hair differently for the occasion—two pigtails. Before she saw me, she'd been twisting the pigtails around to cover her ears, which she felt stuck out too much even though they were perfectly adorable.

"Hey, Brianna," I said. "Are you getting lots of new source material for your web comic?"

She stared at my cheerleader sweater and then my skirt. "Stormy? Is that you?" She lifted her red plastic cup of punch to her nose and sniffed it. "Don't drink the punch," she said. "There must be magic mushrooms in here because I'm trippin' balls. I swear you're wearing a cheerleader uniform."

"Ha ha," I said. "It was all Jessica's idea, but something tells me Quinn put her up to it."

"Sounds like Quinn." She patted the sleeve of my sweater. "Where did you get this sweater? It looks so real."

"It's real. This is mine. From high school." I could tell she didn't believe me. "Brianna, once upon a time, I was a cheerleader."

"Sure you were," she said with wide eyes. "Tell me another one." She followed up her sarcasm with a hiccup.

"Go easy on the punch," I said.

With exaggerated slowness, she replied, "Oooookay, boss."

Rain Nor Sleet finished their song, and the crowd of about two hundred people applauded. Brianna and

I didn't have anywhere to set our red cups, so we shouted *Whoo* sounds, as one does.

The next song started up, at an even more upbeat tempo than the last one.

"Your cousin Chip is quite the fiddle player," I said to Brianna. "Is the rest of your family as musically talented?"

"Sort of. My mother and the other white McCabes are into folk and country. My father's side is more about classical piano and violin." She grinned. "Stereotypical Chinese Americans, I know."

"What do you play?"

"Video games." She hiccuped again and waved to someone across the way.

I followed her gaze across the crowded barn to her parents and her grandma, Lily, on her mobility scooter. They saw me and waved excitedly, so I waved back. Brianna's mother was blond, like many of the other McCabes. All three Changs were laughing and clapping along with the music.

"This isn't their first hootenanny," I observed.

We watched the band and the action on the dance floor as we finished our drinks. I offered to refill Brianna's red cup. I gave myself another serving of punch and filled hers with half punch and half ginger ale.

When I brought her the cup, she said, "Do one of your famous Irish toasts!"

"Just for the two of us? Sure." I rattled off the first one that came to mind. "May the hinges of our friendship never grow rusty."

Brianna grinned with delight, and we clinked red plastic cups.

We watched the band play a few more songs. They took a break and switched over to DJ music, with the volume turned down so people could socialize more easily.

The cavernous barn filled with the sounds of conversation, seeming even fuller than it had been moments before. The soft lighting from strings of white lanterns crisscrossing overhead was universally flattering. I looked down at my bare legs, pleased to see that the little bruises and imperfections didn't show at all.

The din of conversation rose up around us. Snippets floated over to my ears. Several people were talking about the upcoming filming of the *Hallows* series, and young Quinby's role. There would be many opportunities for locals to play extras; it would be an economic boon for the town. Even my gift shop would benefit. All of this news certainly added to the festivity of the annual event.

Brianna said to me, "I heard from a friend that the role of Kinley was actually cast *months ago*, and the open casting call here was just a publicity stunt to sell a carefully crafted narrative."

"I never knew you were such a conspiracy nut."

She waggled her eyebrows. "How much do you know about microwaves and government monitoring?"

I rolled my eyes. We had a few known conspiracy theorists in town. They came into the gift shop sometimes to talk to Brianna when the library turfed them out. She humored them and took notes for her web comic. Her art was a great way for her to take life's lemons and turn them into lemonade.

A few people came over to chat with me.

Ruby Sparkes came over to give Brianna one of her warm, matronly hugs. They chatted for a few minutes about Brianna's comic, and how things were going at the store. She smirked as she asked my employee if her boss was being good to her, or if she was looking for a career change.

"Don't you dare poach my best employee," I told Ruby.

She tilted her head back and roared laughter before giving me a hug as well.

"Aren't you adorable," she said. "What's Logan Sanderson dressed up as? A scarecrow? Or the Tin Man?"

"Probably his regular business-casual look," I said. "He's not here with me. He was tired, and his sister claims to be dangerously allergic to both hay and folk music."

Ruby swayed as her eyes flitted around without focus. She'd been enjoying the punch, by the look of her.

After a moment, she patted me lovingly on the shoulder. "Stormy Day, never mind what people say. Logan's a good fella."

I asked, "What do you mean?"

She flopped her head from side to side, her purple-red curls bouncing softly. "You two suit each other," she said. "You're a real power couple. If one of you runs for mayor someday, you can whip this whole town into shape!"

"Ah, the power," I joked. "Imagine me as mayor. I would appoint Jeffrey as one of my chief advisers, of course. Do you think I can get people to call me Her Royal Highness?"

"Sure," she said with a hand wave, barely listening to me. "If you'll excuse me, I see a gentleman I'd like to ply with more punch." With a girlish giggle, she was off.

I turned to say something to Brianna, but she was gone, off talking to some guys her age. Rather than cramp her style, I wandered off in search of my companions.

The alcohol in the punch was tickling at my brain in a pleasant way.

Tonight was going to be fun.

I couldn't say what it was, exactly, but I had a strong premonition the hootenanny was going to end with a bang.

CHAPTER 39

When Rain Nor Heat started up again, Kyle insisted I dance with him.

"Hang on a minute," I said.

Our hosts had dropped a sheet from a hay loft, forming a makeshift projection screen. Quinn was setting up her laptop with a projector, and displaying recent photographs of her daughter dressed up for her starring role. After a dozen photos, the screen abruptly turned a bright, blinding white. It was a business card, an advertisement for the photographer.

"That guy's name looks familiar," I said to Kyle.

He looked up just as the advertisement dissolved into an image of Quinby's angelic face as she posed with a sword she could barely hold up.

"Let's dance," he said. "No more stalling. You know that expression, *dance with the one who brought you?* Come on already. I promise I'll keep one eye on the screen and only one eye on those legs of yours."

"Dimples, I'm only going to dance with you if you promise not to look at my legs at all."

"I can only promise to try," he said, giving me a double eyebrow raise as he steered me onto the hay-strewn wooden dance floor.

The song stopped before we'd taken even one dance step. Everyone clapped, and a few people called out requests. The band immediately started up a new tune, this one a much slower tempo. All around us, couples got closer, the women wrapping their arms around their dates' necks.

"When in Rome," Kyle said, placing his hand on my waist.

I put my hands loosely on his shoulders and tried to relax. I hadn't danced this way in years, but it came back to me. They say the body has a memory of its own.

After a minute, I said, "Stop it."

His arms stiffened, and he increased the space between us. "Stop what? I'm not too close, am I?"

"That's fine. But you keep gazing at me. I can feel your eyes on me. Look at the screen up there and tell me what's strange about the name of that photographer."

"I'm not *gazing* at you." He blew air up his face, fluffing his fair hair away from his sweaty forehead. "You're basically a big sister to me."

"Good," I said.

"What would you think if I started calling Finnegan Dad?"

"I would think you had acquired some sort of brain parasite."

"He could be my dad, sort of. There are two ways I could make it legitimate."

I frowned up at him. "Is one of those ways getting adopted by him? You seem a bit old for adoption."

"Or I could marry your sister," he said. "Sunny."

My feet stopped moving. "That will be difficult, since she doesn't live here."

He raised one eyebrow. "Hasn't Dad—I mean Finnegan—told you? She's coming back."

I snorted and started dancing again. "I'll believe it when I see it."

"Sooner or later, everyone comes home again. When I moved away, I thought it was for good, but look at me now."

"Maybe I will." I leaned back and looked him up and down. If he was going to gaze at me and my legs, I could do the same. "You've got a trim figure, Dimples. How do you keep all those bottles of beer and donuts from settling around your waistline?"

"By hitting the gym five days a week. You should come with me some time. I can introduce you to my personal trainer, but I must warn you. My trainer *will* make you cry."

"I don't cry," I said. Even as I uttered the lie, I didn't know why. I'd cried more than once over Colt facing a homicide charge, and about Samantha Sweet's family being torn apart. I'd cried more in the last week than I had through my entire breakup with Christopher.

The song finished, and Quinn took to the stage. She and her daughter, Quinby, were dressed in matching trench coats.

"Thank you all for coming," Quinn gushed.

Everyone applauded, and the louder it got, the taller she stood.

"On behalf of my parents and the other Baudelaires, as well as the McCabes, I'm so glad you could make it. This might be our last Autumn Hootenanny for a while, because we'll be super busy soon." She patted her stomach. A ripple ran through the crowd. Was she announcing they were having a second child?

She yanked her hand away from her stomach and clutched the microphone.

"Because of Quinby's starring role," she said quickly. "Some of the filming will be on location right here, at the farm! Isn't that wonderful news?"

The crowd cheered. Quinn raised both hands in the air forming a V for Victory.

She scanned the crowd, stopping on me as she brought the microphone to her mouth again. "And now I'd like to invite two of my oldest and dearest friends up on stage to join me in a cheer."

I stiffened and glanced around like a cornered rodent, but there was no escape. Jessica had gotten me into my cheerleader uniform for a reason, and this was it. As she dragged me onto the stage, Quinn unbuttoned her trench coat and tossed it aside. Her daughter did the same. Quinn was wearing her old head cheerleader uniform, and her daughter was wearing a smaller replica.

The next several minutes were both familiar and strange. We did some cheers, and my body remembered most of the moves. The crowd roared. They seemed to enjoy it almost as much when we messed up as when we got the routines right. I was sweating like crazy from the exertion, but I didn't care. I lost myself in the group effervescence. I was, for the first time in what felt like forever, having a great time.

* * *

For the second-to-last song of the evening, Rain Nor Heat gave me a chill down my spine with their original song about a vengeful ghost in Colorado who lured a killer off a mountain cliff.

Kyle Dempsey, who'd gone outside to take a phone call, came to tell me some good news. "I've got Trigger Canuso waiting at the station. She asked for me specifically."

I gave him a high five. "You're going to crack this case wide open!"

"Thanks to you," he said. "I don't think we'd have broken her if you hadn't leaned on me to work a little harder."

"Dimples, I can't take credit for this one. I feel like I've been more hindrance than help."

He glanced down at my pleated cheerleader skirt. "At least we didn't wreck a cruiser."

"Not yet."

"Speaking of cruisers, I need to get back to the station pronto, and I'm your chauffeur."

"Go ahead. Jessica and I will hitch a ride back into town with someone else."

Right then, Jessica appeared beside us. "Are you talking about me?"

"You're just like Jeffrey," I said. "I say your name and you appear."

She yawned as she looked at the keys in Kyle's hand. "Oh, good. We're leaving," she said. "I'm so tired."

"It's up to you," Kyle said, and he explained how he was leaving now and heading to the station.

Jessica yawned again. "Would it be an obstruction of justice to get dropped off at my house?"

Kyle grinned, dimples deepening. "It's no problem to add five minutes to my trip."

I asked Kyle, "Will you let me know how it goes at the station?"

"If it goes well, I'm sure you'll find out soon enough." He paused, frowning as though fighting an internal battle. "Can you keep something to yourself?"

"Better than you," I said.

"Trigger didn't do it." He glanced around, making sure no one was paying much attention to our conversation. "The last time I talked to Trigger, she swore she drove past the house because she was interested in buying it as a rental property, and she saw Samantha going inside at eleven o'clock on the day of."

I snorted. "How convenient that Trigger just *happened* to be driving by at that time."

Kyle shrugged. "Stranger things have happened. Sometimes people end up in the wrong place at the worst time."

"Good luck getting the truth out of her."

"It's going to be a late night," he said.

"Maybe when I'm done helping Quinn clean up here, I'll catch a ride to the station. Can I sit in the observation room if I bring you something to eat?"

"It's Misty Falls. Everything's closed by now."

"I happen to have a place," I said knowingly. "The best hot dogs in town."

"You're on." He gave me a wink before turning to leave with Jessica.

As I watched them walk away, I noticed how Kyle Dempsey took Jessica's hand and led her through the crowd so she didn't get knocked down by enthusiastic dancers.

I tilted my head and wondered, *Kyle and Jessica?* Maybe. If she didn't come clean with Mitch about the misunderstanding, she had other options.

* * *

The band played one more original tune and then, when everyone begged for an encore, two more classics.

After they unplugged the music equipment and turned on a few industrial flood lamps, the crowd quickly thinned and dispersed.

I'd gotten in such a good mood doing the cheers, that I'd happily agreed to help Quinn clean up the barn and stack up the rental chairs. She and Chip had arrived in separate vehicles, so he gave his blond wife a kiss goodbye and left carrying their sleeping daughter.

An hour later, the novelty of stacking chairs had worn off, plus my body was starting to send me subtle signals that I should have stretched before doing so many enthusiastic high kicks up on the stage.

Quinn thanked me for being such a supportive team member.

"You're welcome," I said. I would have followed up with something sarcastic about no longer being a member of her personal entourage, but I was too tired to hassle the woman. *Let her enjoy her glory*, I thought. Being a stage mother was going to be difficult, and she had no idea what was in store for her. Then again, if anyone was suited to the role, it was Quinn.

"Grab my laptop and we can get out of here," she said.

"Sure thing."

The laptop had been disconnected from the projector, which had left already with the AV rental company, along with the large speakers. As I leaned over to close the screen, I paused to watch the slideshow that was still running.

When the image showing the name and website for the photographer flashed up, I hit the spacebar to pause the slideshow.

The name of the photographer was Dwayne Greer.

As in Dwayne Effrain Greer.

His name was one of the ones on the sign-in sheet for Samantha's last open house before the murder. The police had looked into his whereabouts on the following Monday simply because he had a criminal record with some priors for public indecency and intoxication.

He'd checked out, with an alibi for the whole day. He'd been in Seattle.

The knowledge of this key fact shifted around everything I knew about the Michael Sweet homicide. Plus there was tonight's bombshell from Kyle about Trigger allegedly seeing Samantha at the house.

"Stormy, you're not going to barf, are you?"

I snapped the laptop shut and smiled at Quinn. "That punch was powerful stuff," I said. "Do you mind if I take one last trip to the outhouse before we drive back to town?"

"Be my guest," she said. "But the exterior lights are all taken down."

"Can I take your phone and use the flashlight function? I'd take mine, but I forgot my purse at home."

She narrowed her eyes at me. "My phone?"

"Just to light the way."

She walked over to the wall of the barn, grabbed a lantern from a hook on the wall, and handed it to me. "Watch out for bears," she said.

I took the lantern and left the barn with a nervous laugh.

I walked toward the row of portable outhouses that had been rented for the annual hootenanny. The property had a genuine outhouse as well, with a genuine wooden seat that gave genuine slivers— hence the rentals.

Once I was sure Quinn wasn't watching me, I doubled back toward the barn and hung the lantern on a tree branch so I could investigate the burn barrel.

As teenagers, we'd gathered around this old metal barrel countless times, warming our hands and toasting marshmallows over the open flames.

I sniffed the inside of the barrel. Something had been burned there recently.

My heart felt like it might burst out of me from excitement.

I searched around for a stick from the ground and used it to poke around in the barrel's ashes. It turned up a chunk of something that hadn't burned. I leaned over, not caring that the edge of the burn barrel was getting soot on my sweater, and dug through the ashes with both hands. I pulled out a skinny, metal plate.

I'd seen something like this once before, on a reality TV show, when an angry housewife had driven over another housewife's expensive collection of designer shoes. It was the support for a stiletto shoe.

I plunged my hand into the bucket of ashes, digging eagerly for a second matching metal plate, even while part of me hoped my hunch was wrong.

Jackpot.

I pulled up a second piece. It was a perfect match. Either these were the shanks of a pair of women's stiletto heels, or I'd ruined a vintage cheerleader sweater for nothing. The thin sheet of metal would have run under the arch of the foot, connecting the heel to the ball, providing a counterbalance to stop the heel from caving in.

My hunch was right.

"Put that down," came a voice from behind me.

I whirled around to face Michael Sweet's killer.

CHAPTER 40

Quinn McCabe, still dressed in her old cheerleader uniform, stared down at my sooty hands. She made the disgusted face I'd seen her make so many times when I and the other cheerleaders weren't performing up to her high standards.

"Stormy," she said with disdain. "Your sweater is ruined. What are you doing digging around in that dirty old burn barrel?"

"Just helping you clean up. I thought someone dropped some silverware in here." I held the two pieces of metal limply. "Are these salad tongs?"

"Maybe." She stuck her chest out, but she didn't move her arms. Her hands were behind her back, hiding something.

I dropped the pieces of metal back into the barrel. They landed with a clang, and a thick puff of ashes enveloped me. The cloud was enough to tickle my nose but not enough for me to use as a magician-style cover and disappear.

"Whatever it was, they're burned up," I said, dusting off my hands. "No point in fishing them out now."

Quinn's eyes narrowed to the smallest slits. Her face was lit by the lantern I'd hung on the tree behind me, but I knew my face was in the shadows.

"Just leave it," she said. "It's probably just scrap that was in a bag of garbage someone used for kindling a fire. Probably some old junk the Russian was trying to get rid of."

I brushed my fingertips over the black streak across the waistline of my sweater. "I guess we're about done, right? What else do you need tidied up before we leave?"

She didn't move her arms or reveal what was in her hands.

"Stormy, I don't need your help any more. You can just take off."

I forced a laugh out. "Quinn, you're my ride back into town. Remember? I don't have my car here."

She swished her mouth from side to side.

"No," she said. "You're up to something. Tell me what's going on."

"What's going on? Well, you're the one who's acting super weird and hiding something behind your back. Why don't you tell *me* what's going on?"

"I didn't do anything," Quinn said.

I glanced down and shifted the toe of my shoe so it was under the stick I'd used to stir the ashes. I didn't have my purse with me, so I didn't have any of my EDC goodies, but I could use whatever was nearby. With a simple kick, I could have the stick in my hand without needing to bend over.

"Tell me what you know," Quinn said. "Why are you snooping around?"

"Chip knows," I said. "He asked me to follow you around town and find out who you're having an affair with."

"No, he didn't. Chip would never do that."

"He did. Ask his cousin, Brianna. She was at my shop when he came by to meet with me."

She swore under her breath and said his name.

"Quinn, you two can work it out," I said. "It's the photographer, right? Dwayne Greer?"

She blinked. "What?"

"That's who you were having an affair with. You were on your way to meet the photographer on Monday, the day you saw me at my store. The day Michael Sweet was killed. You were with the photographer that day. It's why you were dressed up in that short dress with the high heels."

Her gaze shifted from me to the burn barrel. If I'd had any uncertainties about the burned metal having come from Quinn's spike heels, they were gone now. She hadn't been with the photographer that day. The police had questioned Dwayne Greer because he'd visited the open house two days before the murder, and his name had been in the visitor log. He was not a suspect, because he'd been in another city all day Monday. Which meant he hadn't been meeting with Quinn.

"That's right," Quinn said, taking my bait. "I was meeting Dwayne that day. But it meant nothing to me. It was purely physical. That's all. You can't tell my husband."

"I won't tell Chip." But I will tell the police that you're a killer.

She seemed to pick up on my thoughts. "Liar!" She finally moved her arms, revealing what she'd been holding behind her back.

It wasn't a knife, or a gun. But it was also much more terrifying than the stick I had by my foot. It was an ax, probably taken from the wall of the barn.

How the hell was I supposed to protect myself from attack by ax?

"You're a tattletale," she growled. "You probably already told him. Is that why he's been acting strange lately?"

I kicked up the stick and caught it in my hand. It wasn't much of a weapon compared to the ax, and would splinter in half with one whack, but it was longer than her weapon. I could use it as a lance, poke her in the eye before she could get close enough to hit me with the ax. Unless, of course, she threw the ax at me.

I carefully stepped to the side, putting the burn barrel between us for protection.

She screamed, "Stop moving!"

Calmly, I said, "Quinn, if you'll just put the ax down, we can talk this over. I won't tell Chip about your affair. I'm not even working for him. I told him to find someone else, because I wouldn't take his money."

"You're lying," she growled. "You're trying to trick me."

She lowered her shoulder and hefted the ax with the authority of someone who knew how to hit a target. Suddenly, I remembered a demonstration she'd done for us at a party. Right here, next to the barn. We'd been teasing her about being a farm girl, and she'd shut us up by throwing an ax at a target and hitting it dead center. Could I duck down in time to avoid getting an ax dead center in my chest? My confidence in my evasive maneuvers was evaporating by the second.

With a cold voice, she said, "You know everything. You know about me and Michael."

"Is he Quinby's father? She's got his angelic smile."

"He was blackmailing me," she said. "When he found out she had the role, he wanted me to make him the manager. And he wanted half her earnings."

"Sounds like good ol' Mikey," I said.

"He was already bragging about the money to his stupid wife," Quinn said, spitting the words with contempt. "He was going to ruin everything." The fingers on her free hand twitched, as though she was pointing at her stomach, trying to tell me something. "Everything."

I took a wild guess. "Are you pregnant?"

The ax slipped down. She didn't drop it, but her grip loosened enough with shock that the handle slipped down. Was it enough to ruin her aim? I had an urge to rush forward, to charge at her now and tackle her. But I had a stronger urge to stay behind the barrel and keep trying to talk my way out of danger.

"I don't know," she said. "It's too soon to say, but maybe."

"Quinn," I said softly. "You can start a new life. Take this opportunity right now to get into your car and leave town."

Her voice trembling, she said, "You're bluffing. You don't know anything. And even if you did, you can't prove it."

I turned my head very slowly and deliberately, as though glancing down the road toward the property's entrance. But I only moved my head. I didn't take my eyes off the petite blond murderess. I hoped the shadows would conceal where I had my focus.

With a casual air, I said, "Actually, I'm surprised Officer Dempsey isn't back here yet. He asked me to stay behind and stall you while he got some paperwork done at the station. An emergency search warrant."

"It's not true," she growled, adjusting her stance and readying her ax-throwing arm.

I unlocked my knees and prepared to drop for cover.

"He had to get a statement from Trigger Canuso," I said. "She drove by the house and saw you going in that day to meet Michael. She mistook you for Samantha, because you're both blond, but she figured it out. Now everyone knows. It's just a question of time."

She didn't say anything. An owl hooted somewhere in the woods.

I told her, "I've got a thousand-dollar withdrawal limit on my bank card. We can stop by the bank machine. I'll give you the cash so you can get the hell out of here. Change your hair and start a new life. Have the baby or don't. It's your choice, Quinn. Right now. You can stay and face the consequences, or you can run. I'll help you out and give you a head start."

"Why?"

"Because you're my friend," I said. "You made a mistake, but I know, deep down, you're a good person." Her eyes relaxed slightly. She was buying it? My lying skills had really improved lately.

"I loved him," she said.

"I know," I said. "It was just an accident? You were talking to Michael and things took a turn. He can be so infuriating. And then you couldn't help yourself, because you had to protect your family. It was all Michael's fault."

She rotated the ax. In the thin light of the sole lantern, the blade glinted menacingly.

"They won't believe me," Quinn said.

"We need to get rid of these metal supports from your shoes. That's the only physical evidence connecting you to the crime scene."

Her free hand went to her stomach. The metal supports weren't the only connection. If she'd conceived a child that day, and it was Michael's, that would seal her fate. The horrifying realization now hung in the air between us.

Her voice lowered to a spooky, robotic tone. "A mother does what needs doing to protect her family."

"Don't kill me," I said. And then, because it was worth a shot, I said, "Please."

And that was when she threw the ax.

I dropped to the ground. I could hear the helicopter-like sound of the ax whipping through the air just above my head.

I'd avoided an ax to the chest, but now I was on the ground. Quinn had been on her feet, and that gave her the edge. She launched herself at me.

I fought to keep the stick between us, but it was like being attacked by a wildcat.

I heard the clang of my own skull being hit against the side of the burn barrel. Then the clang of what I hoped was Quinn's head and not mine again.

The light of the lantern dimmed and shut off. We were in total darkness.

Her hands were around my throat, crushing my windpipe. I couldn't breathe, and I couldn't see. My stick was broken, but I clutched the thicker piece and struck at her, again and again.

Why wasn't she letting go? My eyes stung, and not just from the lack of oxygen. Was Quinn's head bleeding and dripping onto my face? I could taste blood. Hers or mine, I didn't know.

Just when I thought things couldn't get blacker, they did. What little I could see of the stars in the sky blinked out. I was losing consciousness.

I gripped my battered stick, which was now slick with something, and kept flailing.

Quinn was heavy on top of me.

And then she was lighter.

She was rolling off me.

No. She was being pulled off me.

A flashlight blinded me.

"Stormy," came a male voice.

"Dad?" My voice was hoarse.

"It's me, Kyle," he said.

The flashlight blinded me again.

My head was swimming. My eyes were watering so bad from pain I couldn't see what was happening.

Kyle said, "Hold still and stay there. I've got to catch the other cheerleader, then I'll be back for you." I felt him adjust my position on the ground, tilt me slightly to the side. "Keep breathing," he said, and he was off.

I could see the bright light flashing against the bare autumn trees.

I started coughing and didn't stop until everything went black.

CHAPTER 41

A hand appeared between the green curtains of my examination room at the hospital's emergency room.

"Knock knock."

"Nobody home," I said groggily.

"Are you decent?"

"I'm wearing a cheerleader uniform that, at the rate I'm currently swelling up, I'll probably have to cut myself out of."

The curtains parted, and Kyle Dempsey entered the semiprivate space.

"Fancy meeting you here," he said.

"*Deja vu*," I said. "We've been here before."

"I suppose we have." His sky-blue eyes twinkled.

"On the plus side, at least we didn't wreck a police cruiser." I coughed. My throat felt raw and bruised.

Kyle took a seat on the chair next to my bed. "When is someone coming to get you? I thought Finn would be here already." He looked around, frowning. "And maybe Logan?"

"They're wheeling me into a corner and keeping me overnight," I said. "They promised me eggs Benedict with crispy bacon for breakfast, but I'm starting to think that was a lie." I coughed a little more. "Some of these nurses have a very dark sense of humor."

"They sure do." Kyle shook his head. "There won't be any eggs Benedict. You'll be lucky if you get a few raisins and some brown sugar with your oatmeal."

I groaned. "Oatmeal? You should have let Quinn kill me." I coughed feebly.

Kyle got up and poured me some water from the pitcher at the side of my hospital bed. He tried to hold the cup to my mouth for me, but I took it from him. My arm shook, and I dribbled half of the drink on my cheerleader sweater, which was covered in a mix of soot, grass stains, dirt, and no small amount of blood.

"They tried to cut that filthy sweater off, but you wouldn't let them," Kyle said.

"Did I threaten a lawsuit?" I dimly recalled yelling something to that effect.

"That's the rumor," he said.

Grimly, I said, "Logan will be so proud of me."

Kyle chuckled. "You must be feeling pretty rough. How bad does the concussion feel?"

"Uh..." I was tempted to complain, but I tried to view my current discomfort in a more positive light. "It could be worse," I said honestly. "Earlier tonight, a woman upstairs gave birth to a twelve-pound baby. No epidural. I'm probably having an easier night than she is."

He grinned. "But she gets to bring home a baby."

I frowned. "Now you're making me miss Jeffrey. Can you run over to the house and pick him up for me?" I patted the bed next to me. "Plenty of room."

Kyle laughed. "You must be on a lot of painkillers. I can't tell if you're joking."

"Me, neither." I patted the bed again. The room was hazy. "Where's Jeffrey? He should be here. I'm stinky, and he likes to smell my clothes when I'm stinky."

I wondered, am I in a hospital? Did Kyle and I wreck another police cruiser?

"You're welcome, by the way," Kyle said.

The room came into focus again. The medication they'd given me for the pain was coming and going in waves. For a few seconds, I felt completely lucid.

"Thank for showing up in the nick of time and saving my life," I said. "How did you know to come back? Was it your interview with Trigger?" I struggled to sit upright. I had to warn Kyle! "Dimplessss," I said, slurring. "The blond woman that Trigger saw at the house was Quinn! You've got to look out. She could be anywhere." I could feel my eyes bugging out of my head, all the better to see my enemy. "Is she behind that curtain?"

"Quinn?" He looked at me like I was crazy. "You're pretty drugged up. We can talk about this later."

"There's no time to explain," I said. "Come here. I'm going to steal your gun." I beckoned him toward me with my finger. "Here kitty, kitty."

"You're not getting my gun," he said with an amused, patronizing tone I did not care for. "I've learned to be a lot more careful around you wily women."

"Hah!" I coughed some more and then sighed. My throat felt pretty nice. The pain medication was kicking in.

"Stormy, I think I had a premonition or something," Kyle said. "Instead of waiting and bringing Quinn in tomorrow, I had this gut feeling I had to drive out to the barn immediately."

I giggled. "You wanted to see me one more time in my cheerleader uniform."

He shook his head, grinning. "Yeah, that must have been it."

I fluffed up my pillows. Whatever they'd given me wasn't making me sleepy. I felt like I could stay up for hours and hours, just talking and catching up with Kyle.

I asked him, "How's Quinn?"

"Not happy. We arrested her."

"Good," I said. "That was a good choice. You're a very good cop."

My compliment made Kyle laugh.

He said, "Milano is working with her now, getting the whole confession."

"Good," I said. "She always liked him. She had a crush on Tony Baloney. Did you know that? The first time Quinn ever threatened to kill me, it was after she found out about us." I whispered, since it was supposed to be a secret, "Kissy kissy. Me and Tony Baloney." I stuck my tongue out. "Gross."

Kyle gave me a sidelong look. "Are you messing with me?"

"Of course not," I said. "It's a secret. Nobody knows. Nobody." I waved a hand drunkenly. "Ha ha. Just kidding. It's not true. I'm a big liar."

"You're pulling my leg?"

"Blblb," I said. I meant to say something else, but I couldn't recall what it was, and my tongue wasn't cooperating. I did know, on some level, that it was time for me to stop talking.

"You must have a thing for men in uniform," Kyle teased.

"Dimplesssssss," I said, back to my slurring. "Can you get me some coffee with chocolate in it but no coffee?

"You want a hot chocolate?"

"Ooh. That sounds good. Get it with chocolate."

He left to find the coffee machine.

I gave myself a stern talking-to about keeping my mouth shut. I couldn't quite put my finger on what it was I'd said that I shouldn't have, but I knew I'd better stay quiet. Starting now.

When Kyle returned, I got him to keep me entertained with videos on his phone. I managed to stop talking, stop spilling secrets. After a while, I forgot all about what it was that I was trying not to bring up again.

Kyle Dempsey stayed by my side and kept me awake for the next few hours, constantly annoying me with his periodic inspections of my pupils, which felt a lot like him attempting to kiss me.

* * *

The hospital room was brightening with natural light when I heard the unmistakable sound of an irritated lawyer in the hallway.

"But I *am* her family," Logan Sanderson said with vehemence.

Kyle, who'd nodded off in his chair, jerked upright. "Your boyfriend's here," he whispered.

"Why are you acting surprised? I didn't call him, and I told the nurses not to, so that means you called him."

Kyle held up both hands as he got to his feet with cat-like agility. "Stormy, I swear I didn't call anyone, not even Finn." He went to the doorway and peered out. "Logan's looking the other way, so I'm going to sneak out while sneaking out is an option."

I didn't want him to go. I didn't want to be alone. "My pupils. I think they're funny."

Kyle flashed me his dimples. "Get your boyfriend to check your eyes. See you around. Maybe at family dinner." And then he was off.

He moved so stealthily; his shoes didn't make a sound on the hospital floor. The pain medication was still affecting my senses and imagination. Suddenly, I got the strangest idea Kyle Dempsey was actually a ghost, and that was why he didn't make noises. The thought sent a chill up my spine. Then I heard Logan yelling for him. "Dimples! Hey! Officer Dempsey! Where is she?"

Kyle must have pointed to my room because Logan appeared in the doorway immediately, red-faced and breathing hard. He grabbed the sides of the doorway with both hands and stayed there, leaning in but not entering.

"You found me," I said.

His jaw worked, and his cheeks reddened, but no sound came from his mouth. His knuckles were white.

I adjusted myself to be more upright. "What's wrong? Is everything okay back at the house?"

He nodded, shook his head, then nodded again.

Finally, he spoke. "You ding-dong," he said.

"Me?" I pointed to my chest. "I don't know what Tony Baloney said when he called you, but I didn't do anything wrong. I was simply in the wrong place at the wrong time."

He stayed in the doorway, still breathing heavily. "Tony didn't call me. Nobody called me."

"Then why are you here?"

"Because I heard sirens, and I checked with Jessica, and she said you never came home. We've both been driving around for the last two hours looking for you. We drove out to the barn, and the police had it taped off and wouldn't tell us anything. And your father—" He leaned forward, wheezing to catch his breath.

"My father had his phone turned off." I crossed my arms. "I left him a message. He would have called you right back in the morning."

He looked up at me, his expression still difficult to read. He looked angry. I'd never seen Logan like this, but if I saw a man I didn't know making that face, I'd say he was angry.

I asked, "Are you mad at me?"

"No," he said, practically growling. "I'm not mad at you."

I tapped my fingers on my forearm. "That's not terribly convincing."

He looked away, out into the hallway as someone in blue scrubs rolled by with a cart of cleaning supplies.

"Come in here and sit down before you get us both kicked out." I jerked my head toward the chair, which was a mistake. Stars danced around the room. It was too soon after my incident for head jerking.

Suddenly, Logan was at my side, holding my hand.

"Hey," he said softly. "I didn't want to find you inside this hospital, but I had to check."

"Cheer up," I said, my voice even scratchier than it had been a few hours earlier. "At least I'm not in the morgue."

"Don't joke," he said.

"Don't joke? You might as well ask me to refrain from breathing."

"Your voice..." His eyes widened. "Your neck..."

I squeezed his fingers. "I promise I'll get better right away if you could stop being mad at me right now."

He frowned. "I told you, I'm not mad."

I licked my lips. "Could you get me some chocolate?" I batted my eyelashes. "I think it would help my throat."

"No," he said, and he pulled out his phone, set it on the edge of my bed, and started sending a message using one hand. "I'm letting Jessica know which floor we're on. She can get chocolate for you. I'm not leaving your side. I'm not leaving you for one minute."

"Okay," I said softly, still not sure if I was in trouble or not. He seemed really upset with me.

After a moment, I said, "Logan, I feel like I haven't seen you in a long time."

He squeezed my hand. "It's my fault. This is all my fault. I let you down." He clenched his jaw and looked away from me.

"You are mad."

"I'm angry," he said. "Dogs get mad. Humans get angry."

"Don't be." I pulled my hand away. "I told you the truth. I didn't do anything wrong."

"No, Stormy. I'm angry with myself. I shouldn't have let you down like this."

"You couldn't have known that a cheerleader was going to use my head to make gong sounds on a burn barrel."

He blinked at me. "I have no idea what that means."

I took a deep breath. "As soon as Jessica gets here, I'll start from the beginning."

Right on cue, Jessica appeared in the doorway. She didn't even pause before running in at full-tilt and throwing herself at me on the bed.

CHAPTER 42

TWENTY-TWO DAYS LATER

A SNOWY SATURDAY MORNING IN NOVEMBER

I was awoken by sweet little kisses. From Jeffrey.

Apparently, something I'd eaten the night before was of interest to him. Unlike my other roommate, Jeffrey was fully in support of gas station hot dogs.

I gave him a hug, which he tolerated for a whole ten seconds before wriggling out of my arms and securing a safer spot on my pillow. He flung out his hind foot and started licking his tummy in an elegant cat-ballet pose.

I shifted my head over, which gave me a twinge of pain. I waited for it to get worse, but thankfully it was a mere twinge that was caffeine-related, my morning reminder that I would need my first cup of coffee shortly.

Over the last three weeks, I'd recovered from my battle injuries. The rusty old burn barrel out at the Baudelaire farm probably had a few nasty dents on it, thanks to my skull. I tried not to spend much time thinking about that night, and fighting Quinn off in the darkness. Even without the ax in her hands, she'd been a terrifying foe, like a wolverine. The memories brought back the feeling of her hands around my throat, choking me, and the heavy thud of pain at the back of my head.

Someone knocked gently on my bedroom door.

I relaxed my clenched fists and took a deep breath. It was just my roommate. I was safe at home.

"Coffee," I called out with a croak.

"Ready and waiting," Jessica replied. "Stormy, you've slept in long enough. I've already eaten my first breakfast, and I'm thinking about making a second breakfast. Would you *please* tear yourself away from the arms of your lover and get your butt out here?"

Jeffrey extended his ballerina hind leg and braced his toe pads against the tip of my nose.

"I'm trapped," I called back. "He's using my face to rest his foot while he cleans his unmentionables."

Jessica pushed open the door and gave us a bemused look. "You two are revolting."

"At least one of us has had a bath today."

"Go jump in the shower," Jessica said. "I'll bring your coffee in and put it on the shampoo ledge."

"Marry me."

She laughed. "Go shower first."

I carefully extracted my face from underneath Jeffrey's elegant paw and slid out of bed to get ready for Roomies' Day Out.

* * *

We'd had another fresh snowfall, and the world outside the door was a winter wonderland.

Before Jessica and I left the house, we let Jeffrey check out the backyard. He ran out onto the snow and stopped. He lifted one front paw from the snow and turned his head to give me a dirty look, as if to say, *why did you let the snow delivery person put all this snow here?*

"It's going to be around for a few months," I said. "Jeffrey, this isn't your first winter. And you *love* the snow. It's just a bit of a shock at first."

He hopped over to a new spot, found it was just as cold on his toes as the last spot, gave me another dirty look, and then shot past me back into the house.

"You'll get used to it," I said. "A person can get used to anything." I gave him a kiss goodbye, pulled on some warm mittens and a knitted cap, and left with Jessica.

* * *

Our plan for Roomies' Day Out was a cheap date. We took our toboggans to a nearby park, where the creek valley had formed a perfect sledding hill. It was where all the kids in town met to go sledding, and both Jessica and I had been there countless times as kids.

The park looked like a scene from a postcard that day, with fresh snow on the hill and dozens of children in bright-hued snow clothes laughing and playing on the hill.

I was reluctant to get on the wooden sled Jessica had brought.

"Isn't there an age limit? Or a weight rating?"

She adjusted her pink knitted cap and narrowed her bright blue eyes at me. "Fine. I'll go first, chicken butt."

"You're the chicken butt."

"You are." She climbed onto the sled, secured her boots under the curved front, and started jerking her body forward and back to tip the sled over the berm. "Give me a push, chicken butt."

"As you wish, chicken butt." I gave her a push and off she went, leaning left and right like a pro to stay on the packed snow trail. I cheered for her all the way down. I really wasn't that fearful of taking a sled ride down the hill, but the concussion recovery had made me cautious.

"Hey, lady," came a male voice behind me. I knew that voice.

I turned around to see Quinn's husband, Chip McCabe, approaching me.

"There you are," he said as a greeting.

"Hi, Chip." I gave him a wave with my red mitten.

He got to within ten feet of me and stopped. He glanced around before asking, "Do you wanna build a snowman?"

I was relieved he hadn't said anything about his wife, who'd killed Michael Sweet and then tried to murder me with an ax to cover up her crime.

"A snowman," he repeated, smiling. He was wearing shorts with a winter jacket and a scarf.

"A snowman," I said slowly. He and I had met in my father's neighbor's front yard, thanks to a snowman. "Chip, you don't think that's a little macabre? Me, you, and a snowman?"

He used the end of his scarf to wipe some sweat from his wide forehead. "As long as you don't put another dead body inside the snowman, I think it will be very tasteful."

I let out a low laugh. "Chip, I didn't put the body into the snowman. I just ripped off his head."

"Hard to believe that was almost a year ago."

"Almost," I said.

He looked down the hill and scanned until he stopped on a little girl, his daughter Quinby. She was talking to Jessica. By their body language, Quinby was trying to get Jessica's assistance in rolling a large snowball through the fresh snow.

Chip said solemnly, "And now everything has changed."

"I heard they cast another little girl in the role of Kinley," I said. "How's little Q taking the news?"

Chip turned back toward me, his expression blank. "Her mother killed her genetic father," he said. "My wife was so worried about losing control over her child's career that she stabbed someone to death."

I felt my breath catch in my throat. I was glad for the ten feet of distance between us.

Chip said, "So, I think that an acting job is the *least* of her concerns."

I looked down at my boots. "I'm sorry," I said.

I heard Chip sigh. "No, I'm sorry. I shouldn't have snapped at you like that. You didn't do anything wrong except care about people."

"Caring about people is the most common predetermining factor in having your heart broken."

He tilted his head to the side. "Who said that?"

"I did. Just now."

He rubbed his smooth chin. "It's a good line. You've got the heart of a poet. I might use that in a song for Rain Nor Heat." He raised his eyebrows. "If that's okay with you?"

"Be my guest."

Quinby was calling for her father from the bottom of the hill.

He turned and waved at her and Jessica. "What is it, Q?"

She called back, "Look, Dad! It's the bottom of a snowman!"

"Good job, Q! I'll be down there to help you in a minute!"

He slowly turned back to me and gave me a shy look.

I didn't say anything.

Chip said, "I don't imagine things will ever feel normal between us, but I hope we can put the past behind us for the sake of the children."

"Of course," I said. "For the children."

He raised his eyebrows and gave me an intense look. "We are all on the same side, right?"

I swallowed. Were we? I knew which side I was on.

"Let's hope you don't have to testify," he said.

"But I will have to testify if they ask, if it goes to trial."

"She'll take the plea." A dark expression came over his face. "I told her to take the plea and save us all from more pain."

"Okay." I kept my expression neutral.

The corners of Chips mouth tilted up cruelly. "The Queen Bee will have her gossamer wings yanked off."

I said nothing.

His daughter called out again from the bottom of the hill, more insistently. Chip waved at her before giving the thumbs-up gesture. Jessica and Quinby were being joined by Quinby's best friend, Sophie Sweet. Not far behind Sophie was her mother, Samantha Sweet. She had Michael Junior bundled up and in her arms. Samantha looked up the hill, spotted us, and waved with her free gloved hand.

I returned the wave. We still hadn't spoken since the day I'd come to her house, the day she'd had her kids taken into temporary custody. I'd heard through Jessica that she was doing much better now and didn't hold anything against me, but nobody had encouraged me to call her. Jessica had specifically told me to give the woman some space.

Samantha Sweet turned her back to me and put Michael Junior down to play in the snow. He took two small steps and immediately face-planted in the snow.

"Samantha's feeling much better now," Chip said.

"Good to hear," I said neutrally.

"They changed her medication, and the delusions are gone. Hard to say if it was the pills, the case being closed, or just time passing. Maybe all three."

"It's good that she has a clear head," I said. "That's all that matters."

Chip took a few steps toward me. I fought the urge to flinch or roll away down the hill.

He stopped in front of me and carefully patted me on the shoulder. "A wise person told me that caring about people is the most common predetermining factor in having your heart broken." He grinned. "Did I get that right?"

I smiled back at him. "More than you'll ever know."

He cleared his throat and turned away. "I'd better go make that snowman," he said.

"Someone's gotta do it," I said.

Without looking at me, he said, "We're the ones left behind with the broken pieces. But we're going to make it. You keep putting one foot in front of the other. You just keep living, because it beats the alternative."

* * *

The air was crisp but the sky was bright and cheerful as Jessica and I walked home after sledding.

Jessica's boots crunched through the snow as she once again wobbled away from the shoveled sidewalk. Her legs were so shaky from multiple dashes back up the sledding hill that she didn't have the best sense of balance. She kept clinging to my arm and laughing, nearly knocking me down as well.

I was teasing her and not looking where I was going when I tripped over my own boot and knocked us both onto someone's lawn. When I tried to get up, I bumped a shrub and it retaliated by sending a stream of snow straight down the back of my jacket.

"Talk about irony," I said as I got upright and started shaking snow and water out of my clothes. "I didn't fall off the toboggan or get snowy at all, until I was three blocks from my house."

"Statistically, that's where accidents happen," Jessica said.

I made a face as the melted snow trickled down my spine and straight into the back of my jeans.

"Refreshing," I said with a grimace.

We got back on the sidewalk and continued on our way home. Jessica asked what I'd been talking to Chip about, so I filled her in, and we talked about the Sweets and the McCabes.

"I predict a future merger of the Sweet-McCabe clan," Jessica said.

"Chip and Samantha? Together?" It seemed strange, but then again it always seemed strange when two adults you already know start dating each other.

"They're already somewhat together," Jessica said.

I gasped. "Scandalous." It had barely been three weeks since one of their spouses had been arrested for killing the other one's spouse.

"Neither of them wanted to stay in their old houses, with all the old memories."

"Can't say I blame 'em," I said.

"They both moved, and they're sharing a new house."

I stumbled and broke rhythm in my walking pace. "Not the murder house!"

"Not at all. Somebody else bought that. They're actually renting a McMansion in a new subdivision. It's one of the Canuso family's investments in town. Colt gave them free rent for a few months. I guess this is what people mean when they say tragedy brings people together in strange ways."

Quietly, I said, "That was nice of Colt."

"Have you talked to him?"

"No." But not for lack of trying. I'd sent him some messages, but he hadn't responded. He'd taken down all of his public social media profiles as well. I had no idea what was going on in his life. I'd talked it over with my father and Kyle, and our best guess was that Colt had suspected his sister was involved with the homicide, which was why he'd not been fighting too hard against the charges. He must have known the blood on his shirt came from the scuffle at the casino, but he hadn't even said as much to his own lawyer. What a guy. Willing to take a murder charge to protect his sister.

"Things will settle down," Jessica said. "Life was pretty crazy after the whole thing at the Flying Squirrel Lodge, but people's attentions shifted."

"Thanks to the death at the Koenig mansion."

She punched me on the shoulder playfully. "Cheer up. There'll be another weird crime soon enough."

I laughed hollowly.

We got back to the house, and Jessica immediately got out the cocoa powder and a saucepan to make hot chocolate.

I paused by the coat hooks, watching the melted snow dripping off her jacket and all over our shoe rack.

"Maybe I'll give these soggy things a tumble in the dryer," I said.

"Ooh, that sounds fun," Jessica said. "Just the way you phrased it," she explained.

"I'm a fun girl," I said, grinning.

I gathered up the soggy coats, hats, and mittens, and headed through the door leading to the basement that ran across the full width of the house. I checked the pockets for tissues, receipts, and hard candies before tossing the jackets into the dryer. Tissues weren't too bad, but I'd learned the hard way to check for hard candies or gum before sending damp jackets for a tumble.

My load was short by one mitten, a red one. I'd dropped it on the stairs. I headed back up and stopped when I heard voices.

The same staircase led up to two doors—one for my side and one for the side Logan Sanderson had been renting for the last year. The two units had good side-to-side sound privacy, but anyone down in the basement could easily hear conversations through the hollow-core basement access doors.

By the sound of it, Logan's sister Jinx had returned from her week-long trip to visit their grandmother. I was about to knock on their door and ask if they wanted some hot chocolate when I heard my name being spoken.

Oops. Walk away, I told myself. People who listen in on conversations get what they deserve!

But the mitten I'd been reaching for had snagged on a protruding nail on the wood steps. It took me several seconds in the dim light to unsnag the yarn loop, and by then I'd already heard enough to hook me.

"Of course Stormy likes jewelry," Jinx was saying to her brother. "Just because she doesn't wear a ton of it doesn't mean she doesn't want a ring."

A ring? I couldn't have pried myself away from that hollow-core door if it had been crawling with black widow spiders.

"I don't know," Logan said. "She values her independence, and that's one of the things I love about her."

"All the more reason to get married," Jinx said. "Two strong people can make a strong bond. That's what Grandma told me to tell you. Also, she says most people treat money like it's limited and time like it's not, and that's what wrong with the world."

"Huh? But time *is* money."

"Says the lawyer," Jinx said with a giggle. "But seriously. Sorry I don't have a box for it, but here you go. It's official. We Sandersons don't have much in the way of family jewels, but what we do have, you're now in charge of. Grandma can't wear it anymore, and it would make her so happy to see Stormy wearing it when you go visit her."

"But we don't even have a date set for me to bring her out to see the family."

"You'd better get busy planning," Jinx said. "Grandma's not going to be around forever. She says the angels have been visiting her bedside."

"Grandma's been saying that for years."

There were footfalls and then banging in the kitchen. Their voices got softer as they moved further away from the hall, but I could still hear them if I pressed my ear against the door.

Logan asked his sister, "You don't think it's too soon? We haven't even been dating a year."

"What do you want? I mean deep down, sky's the limit, what do you want from Stormy?"

"Everything," he answered without hesitation.

Everything. My heart felt like it was skipping jump rope.

"Then give her the ring and propose, you big dummy." There was a break in the conversation as they moved things around in the kitchen. "What's the hold up? Why are you making that face?"

"I'm worried that I'm going to let her down."

"Then don't let her down."

"Jinx, she almost died. I should have been there. I'm such an idiot, making her go to a barn dance without me just because I don't dance."

"You couldn't have known," she said soothingly. "You can't protect her from everything."

"Then what's the point in trying to be her husband?"

"What are you talking about?"

"She doesn't need me," Logan said. "Not even half as much as I need her."

"So?"

There was a long pause. The television came on, and I heard the ditzy local weather girl talking about the snowfall warning in effect for that night.

Logan answered his sister's question, but I couldn't make out the words over the television. Maybe it was for the best. I already felt like a dirty private eye for listening in on their private conversation.

It took considerable effort for me to walk back down the stairs, toss the mitten in the dryer, and turn it on. With the machine running, I definitely wouldn't be able to hear any more of the talk.

I walked back upstairs and into our side of the house feeling like I was floating on a cloud.

I couldn't stop smiling.

Jessica thought my good mood was from a day of sledding and fresh air followed by hot cocoa. And that was definitely part of it.

But I was also smiling because Jinx, who I barely knew, had all but welcomed me into the family. And now Logan had a ring with which to plan a proposal.

And soon I would be able to tell him he was wrong.

Smart as he was, he was wrong.

I *wanted* to be with him every bit as much as he needed me. My last engagement hadn't ended well, but my life had changed a lot in the last year. This time it would be different.